D0374895

BRIAR AND ROSE AND JACK

BRIAR AND ROSE AND JACK

A Novel by

Katherine Coville

CLARION BOOKS
Houghton Mifflin Harcourt
BOSTON   NEW YORK

Clarion Books
3 Park Avenue
New York, New York 10016

Clarion Books is an imprint of Houghton Mifflin Harcourt Publishing Company.

hmhbooks.com

The text was set in Garamond.

Library of Congress Cataloging-in-Publication Data
Names: Coville, Katherine, author.
Title: Briar and Rose and Jack / Katherine Coville.
Description: Boston ; New York : Clarion Books, 2019. | Summary: Ugly Lady Briar, beautiful Princess
Rose, and Jack plot the downfall of the evil giant who plagues their kingdom while the girls face a curse
that only true love can break.
Identifiers: LCCN 2018051214 (print) | LCCN 2018055668 (ebook) | ISBN 9781328632555 |
ISBN 9781328950055 (hardback) | ISBN 9781328632555 (ebook)
Subjects: | CYAC: Fairy tales. | Characters in literature—Fiction. |
Princesses—Fiction. | Giants—Fiction. | Blessing and cursing—Fiction. |
BISAC: JUVENILE FICTION / Fairy Tales & Folklore / Adaptations. |
JUVENILE FICTION / Family / Siblings. | JUVENILE FICTION / Social Issues /
Prejudice & Racism. | JUVENILE FICTION / Fantasy & Magic.
Classification: LCC PZ8.C834413 (ebook) | LCC PZ8.C834413 Bri 2019 (print) |
DDC [Fic]—dc23
LC record available at https://lccn.loc.gov/2018051214

Printed in the United States of America
DOC 10 9 8 7 6 5 4 3 2 1
4500755922

To Anne Hoppe

PROLOGUE

SOMETHING COMES. High above the great forest, a full moon spills its lambent light on an ocean of treetops. Some premonition borne on the wind inspires the sea of leafy limbs to dance and sway, murmuring softly to one another of signs and portents. Massive oaks and chestnuts, a thousand years old, catch the whispers on the wind and feel their sap rise. They sigh to their neighbors, passing on the sibilant message: *Something comes.* Small silver birches, glowing white in the moonlight, slap their round leaves together in excitement while the towering beech trees, the sentinels, watch and wait.

Something comes. Something in the arc of blue-black sky, in the array of stars, in the music of the celestial spheres. It plays at the edges of consciousness. It is there, in the hoot of the tawny owl and the churring trill of the nightjar. It disturbs the hunt of the wild creatures prowling far below the forest canopy — the wolf, the fox, and the pine marten. They pause and listen. It cools the savage temperament of the badger and the wild boar. It rouses the diminutive roe deer from their sleep, tantalizes the moths, and bestirs the crickets. Even the mice and the moles, tunneling away beneath the earth, feel it: *Something comes.*

Looming in the west above the Enchanted Forest, a great mountain ascends to a permanent ring of clouds, but none of the birds or beasts go near it.

Far to the east of the mountain, rising from a glittering moat, the dark silhouette of a castle stands out against a flash of summer lightning. In the sudden light one can barely see where the outer wall has been repaired after being knocked down by a marauding giant. Now a plucky red pennant flies from its topmost spire. Narrow window slots glow with yellow candlelight, for all the castle is awake, waiting and listening in an expectant hush. There is only the sound of the wind in the trees, the occasional birdcall, and, though only a few can hear it, an inexpressible harmony in the air.

Until a scream splits the night.

High in the keep, a king paces impatiently. His seven counselors stand clustered together, as if to consolidate their power. Chief among them is the bishop, for he is the head of the church, and in this land and time the church wields nearly as much power as the king himself. But even the bishop has no answers on this night. The counselors all consult among themselves with charts and diagrams, trying to conceal their puzzlement, for the signs are contradictory. King Warrick has ordered his counselors out and called them back a dozen times. He relies on their predictions but has no patience with their present confusion. He is accustomed to having his wishes granted with speed and deference. Nature,

2

however, is impervious to kings. It defers to no one, and it keeps its own time.

Within the lord's chamber, Queen Merewyn lies abed, great with child. Unlike the king, she is infinitely patient. She has spent her life discharging, with a practiced smile, such tedious royal duties as are given her, but her heart is not in it. All she has ever wanted is to create something truly beautiful, and her wise woman has seen that it will come to pass in the birth of this long-awaited child. It is Queen Merewyn who screams, for it is the time of her travail, but between her pains, her lovely, tired face is serene; her most cherished dream is about to come true.

Only one woman is allowed to attend the queen, an unsightly crone named Hilde. She is part wise woman, part midwife, and some say part fairy, though she wields only a few pedestrian magic tricks. She has been with the queen through many a barren year and has used all her skills and wisdom to bring Queen Merewyn to this moment.

The time is at hand. Outside the chamber, King Warrick hears a lusty little cry announcing the presence of a new life. He stops his pacing and listens, triumph in his face.

"At last!" cries the king. "An heir!"

His counselors gather round and congratulate him on his virility and good fortune, foretelling a bright future for what must surely be the perfect child. But within the chamber, Hilde trembles as she bathes the newborn and wraps it in an embroidered blanket, feeling a surging sympathy for the infant even as her heart sinks within her. She places the baby in Queen Merewyn's arms, and the queen looks down upon it with all the love she has saved for this moment.

"A girl, Your Highness," Hilde says, her voice quavering.

The queen draws back the blanket, and she gasps. The infant has a heavy, protruding brow, a sagging eyelid, and coarse, asymmetrical features. The queen is speechless. This is not the beautiful creation she was promised. But something happens. Though it is said that a newborn cannot really see and cannot really smile, the baby's eyes seem to look directly into hers, and the ugly little face breaks into a smile. The queen is charmed. "Ahh," she croons, "the sweet little thing!" and she holds the baby closer.

Hilde draws a deep breath, relieved that the queen has accepted the child. But the moment is cut short. The queen is racked by another pain.

A second baby is coming.

Outside the chamber door, King Warrick waits irritably for news of his offspring. Is it a boy or a girl? Why does the woman Hilde not come to give him news? Is there some calamity with his lady wife? Only a deep fear of women's mysteries keeps him from barging through the door. That and a will to avoid the displeasure of Hilde, for whom he holds a grudging respect. An exhausted scream from within the chamber reassures him that the queen is alive, but as time drags by, the king and his seven counselors brace themselves for some misfortune. At last there is silence within, and after what seems like an eternity, the door opens. The king is invited in. A baby is placed in his arms.

"Your daughter, Your Highness," says Hilde.

The king looks down on an infant's face so perfect it might have been sculpted by a master miniaturist, with a fuzz of silky golden hair, skin like fine porcelain, long, curly lashes, and lips as red as cherries.

"Is she not beautiful," demands the king, "even for a baby?" He holds out one finger for the infant to grasp in her little fist.

"She is, Your Highness, surely the most beautiful baby in the Kingdom of Wildwick, or beyond. And your lady wife has given you twins."

"Twins!"

"Yes," Hilde answers nervously. "You have another daughter. Your firstborn."

"Where is the other? Let me see!"

Hilde moves her short, squat frame from where she stands in front of the cradle, which she has been blocking. The king hands her the beautiful baby and bends over the cradle, pulling back the blanket from the other infant's face.

"What?" he exclaims, straightening suddenly. "What's this?" Turning to his weary wife, he cries, "We can't have this! What have you done?"

Calmly the queen replies, "I have done nothing amiss. If I had, surely both babies would be affected! She is our daughter!"

In a panic, King Warrick calls in the seven counselors. He says nothing while the bishop, who is the chief counselor, views the babies. The king only waits for his reaction, hoping it is not as bad as he fears. But then the bishop pronounces his judgment. Bishop Simon has dedicated his life to seeking after perfection, but his own wicked heart has twisted his quest into something terrible: he has come to hate and fear all imperfections as evil — except his own blatant imperfections, which he readily excuses. And so, shocked by the baby's malformed face, he blurts out in fear and loathing, "It is a demon! A changeling! Surely no royal infant could be so hideous! Its outward appearance can only be a reflection of the evil within. This child shall never be fit to rule, and your subjects will never tolerate it. You must hide it before the populace catches wind of the occurrence and loses all faith in the royal line!"

Then, one by one, the other six counselors bend over the cradle where the two infants lie; they gasp, then straighten, muttering and shaking their heads. One of them, the king's steward, says, "This child will never be accepted!"

Another, his best knight, says, "The people will never fight for her!"

Several others, the king's wise men and scholars, tell him, "The bishop is right. It's hopeless."

The king, his worst fears confirmed, dismisses all his counselors with a curt gesture.

"What are you going to do?" asks the queen, her panic rising.

"We shall see!" King Warrick replies, and follows after them.

Queen Merewyn's head falls back onto the pillows. She realizes that, exhausted as she is, she cannot rest yet. There is still a battle to be fought, for her firstborn daughter. She begins to think.

The moon is setting when the king returns. With some hesitation, trying to put on his best kingly manner, he announces to Queen Merewyn that it simply won't do to acknowledge such an imperfect baby as their daughter and heir. "You heard what Bishop Simon said! The people will believe she is a changeling, or worse—a sign of heaven's judgment, or even that she brings some kind of curse. She must go!" he spouts. "We'll send her away, to be raised quietly in obscurity, and no one will be the wiser. The other child will be the heir!"

This was as the queen anticipated. "Of course you know best, dear," she answers with her sweetest smile. "I'm sure you wouldn't have taken it lightly to disown your own child."

The king is nonplussed, having expected strong resistance. "Yes—well," he blusters, "it was a very difficult decision to make."

"Of course it was. And I'm sure you had a struggle to keep your counselors in their place. They're so clever and ambitious, and probably jealous besides. Not every man can sire twins, you know."

King Warrick harrumphs. "I can handle my counselors," he says, though this is not strictly true. The bishop in particular exercises a strong hold over the king by making him fear for the welfare of his kingdom, and for his immortal soul. But after half an hour of the queen's gentle flattery, casual leading comments, and skillful sowing of doubts, the king has reached the conclusion, all on his own, that despite what his scheming counselors have said, it is really wisest to keep the firstborn at court, where they can watch over her. They will raise and educate her as they would the orphan of some far-off noble family, and her identity will remain secret, even from her.

"And what of your counselors? Can you trust them?"

"They will keep silent on pain of death!"

Queen Merewyn, knowing she has done the best she can for her firstborn daughter, praises the king for his wise plan. Then she lays her heavy head down to rest.

"You can't sleep yet," the king says. "We must give them names!"

"Yes, of course," the queen agrees. "I had thought of only one name for a girl: Briar Rose."

"Perfect. Then we shall name the first one Briar, and the lovely one Rose."

The queen would like to object, but having already won her most important point, she thinks better of it.

King Warrick walks over to peer down once again at the two

babies, now snuggled together, almost clinging to each other. He grins and muses aloud as to whether King Edgar's baby daughter can hold a candle to his perfect Rose. He decides to put on a great feast and invite all the nobility, and all the fairies in the kingdom, and everybody who is anybody, and show her off. The queen does not object, for she is already sleeping.

Sitting forgotten in a dark corner, the crone Hilde has heard it all. She knows, without being told, that to reveal the identity of the firstborn princess after this would be to forfeit her own life, but she feels a great sympathy for the child, who is as ugly as she is herself. As she sits there watching over the tiny figure in the cradle, a lifetime of injustice and cruelty rises unbidden in her memory. She can see the child's future as no one else can. When dawn sends its first pale rays through the window, a resolve forms in her battle-scarred heart; she will be the nurturer and protector of this child as far as it is within her limited power. And she begins to think.

It is the day of the king's feast. Jugglers practice in the great hall. Acrobats rehearse their tumbling. The minstrels tune their lutes and lyres. Fresh rushes and fragrant herbs have been strewn about the floor, white linen spread on the trestle tables. Servants rush hither and yon in confusion, hustling to obey the orders of the temperamental cook and his assistants, who rule the day. Three whole oxen are roasting in the castle's kitchen as food is prepared for two hundred guests: trays of succulent venison, fish, quail, turtledoves, and a whole roasted peacock decorated with its own resplendent tail; vegetables, picked fresh from the garden; baked apples, peaches, and pears; nuts and cheeses; and the cook's masterpiece, a cake sculpted to look like a full-size unicorn. King Warrick has decreed that this will be a day to remember, though the predations of the local giant have left him in straitened circumstances and the royal coffers can barely withstand the expense. This beautiful daughter, he tells his wife, is a sign of a turnabout in their fortunes. His counselors, in fact, have already consulted the stars and calculated the beautiful child's ultimate value to the kingdom down to the last silver penny.

As the sun grows closer to the horizon, the guests begin to arrive. Wine, mead, and ale being plentiful, no one goes thirsty. The people commence their drinking, which will be prodigious, and promenade about the hall, showing off their finery. The king's counselors, noblemen, and knights escort bejeweled ladies. Merchants and craftsmen, even the peasants, will all be served, though the pickings will be thinner farther down the table from the king.

Suddenly the hall buzzes with tiny winged creatures that look like hummingbirds. The fairies have arrived, eight of them, though they will each change into their full human size for the festivities. Their places are set on either side of the king and queen, to honor them, for the fairies' goodwill is greatly esteemed. Alas, there is still one more fairy in the kingdom, the gray fairy, but she is demented and universally disliked for her ferocious temper. On this blessed occasion, with everyone of consequence invited, no one wants to risk her disrupting the festivities with her hateful behavior. The king and queen have solved the problem by the simple expedient of neglecting to invite her. And so she, alone of all the fairies, has been excluded from this glorious event, an understandable but potentially disastrous decision.

The evening is perfect. Six courses are served, each more elaborate than the last, and between the courses the jugglers and the jester and minstrels perform. Then the king orders that the magical singing harp be brought forth, its enchanting music filling the guests' hearts with wonder and good cheer.

In a small antechamber behind the hall, Hilde has brought the infant Briar to be near baby Rose, who is tended by her own nursemaid, Lady Beatrice. It was the work of less than a minute for Hilde to obtain from Queen Merewyn the office of Briar's godmother, and then to volunteer to be her nursemaid. True to the king's instructions, no one knows the real identity of the child. Fortuitously, the reclusive Duke of Wentmoor, having recently died of some rheumatic complaint, had been followed by his widow in less than six months. The story given out about Briar is that she is the orphaned daughter and only child of the late Duke and Duchess of Wentmoor, and no one questions it.

The babies have just been fed and are sated and sleepy. Hilde waits nervously for the king to summon Lady Beatrice forth with little Rose, to display the beautiful baby in her gilded cradle, which has been placed on the dais between the royal thrones.

Only a short while now until the gift-giving will commence. Hilde's hands tremble at the thought of what she will attempt to do. When the eight fairies begin to bestow their blessings, she must work fast and well if little Briar is to have any share of them. Hilde is desperate enough to take the chance, even if her ruse might be discovered. The minutes pass with agonizing slowness. She feels cold sweat on her forehead and down her back. But she does not waver in her purpose.

The king's summons comes. Hilde prods Lady Beatrice to wrap baby Rose securely in her blanket and sends her out into the great hall. Then, stabbed by a sudden fear of her own ineptness, she feels that she must practice her magic trick one more time. She has rehearsed it at length, but it seldom goes the same way twice. Hastily she looks about her and chooses two objects on opposite sides of the room, a carved box and a pitcher. With a muttered incantation and a deft movement of her hand, she calls upon the power of all the saints to switch the objects. Both objects vanish into thin air, leaving a slight smell of smoke. "God's thumb!" she mutters. Beginning to question her ability to pull this trick off, she shakes her hand as if to loosen its powers and tries again.

Something goes awry. The objects are back, but each has

taken on some characteristics of the other. The pitcher has square corners now, and the box has a spout!

This has never happened before. What if the baby princesses are affected in this way? She has never tried this trick with actual people, only with dogs and cats. What if they were stuck so, half of one princess and half the other? She quickly decides that it would not be so bad. Making a determined effort, she closes her eyes and draws inward to a still, quiet place within herself. Casting the spell again, she manages to return both objects to their original states and to switch their places as she had intended. As she stands wondering what she did differently this time, she listens closely to the goings-on out in the great hall. The gift-giving has started! She hears a fairy's tinkling voice reciting an insipid little poem, as they always do when presenting their gifts. Quickly now! She must switch the babies! Standing over little Briar, she rolls up her sleeves and pronounces the spell along with making the hand movements.

Nothing happens. Hilde can hear the fairy out in the great hall saying, "I bestow the gift of beauty!"

"No!" Hilde cries. That was the gift she most wished to secure for little Briar, and now it is too late! "Why is that always the first gift?" she moans, banging her head against the wall. "Baby Rose is already beautiful! What a waste! What a waste!" Lost in bitter regret, she has developed a sizable lump on her forehead, but then she remembers herself. Now another fairy's voice can be heard in the hall. Quickly Hilde casts the switching spell again, watching the baby anxiously for the result, but again, there is none. Now she can hear the second fairy bestow the gift of riches on baby Rose. Another gift lost!

Hilde resists the urge to bang her head again. She tries the spell once more, adding an elaborate motion, this time with both hands. Nothing. Frantically, she goes to the door to see what is happening without. There is vicious jostling among the group of fairies, for they are excitable creatures and sometimes waspish, and each is anxious to give the best gift. Finally, a determined fairy clad in pink elbows her way to the fore, spitting savage epithets. She bends over the royal cradle, wand in hand, rhyming trite nonsense in perfect meter while mayhem goes on behind her. "I give you sweetness!" she finally cries with a flourish of her wand, but one of the other fairies jolts her arm, and she drops the wand. Gasps are heard all around, and she gives the offending fairy a kick. Everyone watches as sparks spurt out of the end of the wand, then sputter and die, and the wand turns a cold gray color, like ash. The pink fairy picks up her wand and waves it at the baby again for good measure, but the tip falls off, and she storms away.

"Bah! Sweetness!" mutters Hilde. "She's better off without it!"

Gratified that at least she did not secure the gift of sweetness for Briar, she calms herself, closes her eyes, and draws herself inward, performing the spell yet again. This time, when she opens her eyes, there is baby Rose, exactly where Briar had been a moment before. Restraining her glee, Hilde hastily goes to the door and flicks her wrist, casting a spell of confusion over the gilded cradle in the hall. Of all the spells, confusion is the easiest to cast, and she knows from experience that a little confusion is all it will require for people to see whatever they expect to see. She feels a surge of excitement as the fourth fairy winds up her mawkish poem with a giving of the gift of wit. Wit! A lovely gift! A perfect gift! Trembling with excitement now, Hilde waits to see what will happen.

One by one, the fairies come to the cradle and recite their little poems, always ending with a gift. The fifth fairy, an ethereal sprite dressed all in green, curtsies to the king and queen and approaches the cradle.

> *"She'll move with beauty, like the swan*
> *With elegance and grace, anon.*
> *Light of foot and born to dance,*
> *All who see, she will entrance."*

Hilde growls her disapproval and whispers bitterly to herself, "Dance! When will she ever get to dance? Still, every gift is a boon. One mustn't be hasty."

The sixth fairy, clothed in white sparkles, says in a high soprano voice,

"I give the music of the spheres;
May heavenly harmony fill her ears,
Inspiring her voice to lovely song,
And giving her pleasure all life long."

"Very well. Very well," Hilde mutters. "Give something of practical use!"

A regular melee breaks out among the fairies, with several turning the others into various farm animals, but such is their power that no one dares chastise them. Some revert to their hummingbird size and harry one another with their buzzing and their needle-thin wands. One flies over the others, making her way to the fore, saying, "Me! I'm next!" She changes to human size, swatting the tiny ones away. Altering her demeanor to one of grave dignity, she proceeds to give the princess the gift of strength. Hilde is gratified. This is not a gift she had anticipated, but it could come in handy. She mentally counts the number of fairies who have given their gifts and counts how many are left. Three gave their gifts to baby Rose: beauty, riches, and perhaps sweetness—only time will tell. Four have given gifts to Briar: wit, dancing, song, and strength. One more remains. Anxiously, Hilde argues with herself as to when to switch the babies back. To be fair, she should let Rose have the last gift; then they would each have four. But what is fair about the hand Briar has been dealt? Rose has already been made the heir and will inherit the entire kingdom. Hilde thinks she will see that Briar gets everything she can.

As she ponders this, there is a lightning strike and the ear-splitting boom of thunder in the hall. People are screaming and stampeding, and there is the sound of furniture crashing to the floor. Hilde peers cautiously out the doorway and beholds another fairy. She is dressed in dark, muddy gray and has a face full of iniquity. Hilde knows immediately who she is: the other one, the ninth fairy, the one who was left out. She notices a fluttering below the dark fairy's sleeves and, looking closer, sees that the fairy has tied together the feet of small sparrows and hung them upside down from her wrists to flap and worry themselves to death. The fairy wears them like jewelry. She steps toward the cradle and looks down on the baby princess with an expression of overflowing malice. Quickly, Hilde makes a choice. She will switch the babies back and keep Briar safe. She is about to try when another possibility occurs to her. If she can make the two babies disappear, as she did the bowl and the pitcher, and do it at the crucial moment, she may be able to save them both from the dark fairy's wrath. She racks her brain. Exactly what were her words, and what order did she say them in? And her hands, did she use one or two?

Out in the hall, the evil one spews her contempt on the king and queen, who have jumped to their feet. She freezes them in their places. Everyone else is held in thrall by their fear of her.

"So you hate me, do you?" she cries. "Why else would you exclude me when you've invited everyone of any importance whatsoever? Why else would you spurn me when you've invited every other fairy in the kingdom—gold, red, purple, yellow, blue, pink, white, green—to come and give their gifts to this mewling infant? *But you don't want mine?*

"Well . . . I can be generous too. I'll give my gift anyway! I'll return hate with *more* hate! I'll make sure you will feel my hatred for the rest of your lives. I have only to take away that which you love most. I'll stretch it out, so you'll know every day as she grows that you will lose her, lose her just as she comes into full flower!"

"No! Please!" begs the queen. "Not the princess! She's innocent!"

"I care not for her innocence! She is merely the means to an end—my revenge upon you all!"

Standing in the doorway of the little room, Hilde has made herself ready. She listens for the exact moment to act.

"On the princess's sixteenth birthday—"

Hilde pronounces her spell.

"—she will prick her finger on the spindle of a spinning wheel—"

Hilde makes the motions with her trembling hands as well as she can.

"—*and die!*"

There is a soft pop. Hilde looks down and beholds a baby

with porcelain skin and lips as red as cherries—and a heavy brow and a sagging eyelid. Which baby is it? And which baby has been cursed? Briar or Rose? Both? Neither? She hears the insane laughter of the gray fairy as the entire assembly screams in horror at her pronouncement. Hilde looks out into the hall just in time to see the fairy vanish in a miasma of sickly yellow smoke. Frantic now to switch the babies back to themselves, she is about to pronounce the magic words when Lady Beatrice comes barreling in the door, throwing herself on Hilde and crying hysterically. Hilde puts her arm around Beatrice and comforts her, holding the young woman's head down on her shoulder so that she can't see what's in the cradle as Hilde quickly casts the confusion spell over it. She forces herself to pat Lady Beatrice's back, telling her that the worst is over and urging her to collect her wits and return to her post.

Meanwhile, out in the hall, the pink fairy shouts out, "Bertana! Bertana has not given her gift yet! Maybe she can help!" and the last few fairies begin rounding up the frightened farm animals, turning them back into fairies, searching for Bertana. Finally, a donkey is turned back into an elderly fairy dressed in gold. Standing erect, she smooths white wisps of hair that have come loose from her tidy bun. Her dignity has been severely wounded, but she steps forward and offers herself to the distraught king and queen.

"Your Majesties, my power is not equal to that of the gray fairy, but perhaps I can soften her spell." She goes to the cradle and pauses a moment, aware that this is the supreme challenge, the apogee of her career, the moment she has been building toward for all her two hundred years. She paces back and forth and whispers, "Hmm. Ahh. Yes."

Hilde drags Lady Beatrice to the door, desperate to know what is going on without, and sees the gold fairy approach the gilded cradle. Is there another gift to be given? Is there hope, then? She covers Lady Beatrice's mouth tightly with one hand. "Shh!" she hisses, and startled, the girl stops her noise. Hilde hears the strong chanting of the gold fairy, condemning hatred, defying death with the quiet power of love, and softening the curse with a promise of peaceful slumber, to be awakened by true love's kiss. It brings tears to Hilde's eyes, and she prays that whichever princess was touched by the curse, this gift will touch her too. Only a moment does she ponder these things, and then she sees the face of the gold fairy looking down at the baby in the gilded cradle with shock and puzzlement. The fairy must be seeing glimpses of the baby's mixed-up face! The confusion spell is fading! She must switch the babies back immediately, before the gold fairy sees too clearly.

Fighting panic, Hilde shoves Lady Beatrice out the door and leans back against the wall. She takes a deep breath, forcing herself to close her eyes and search for that inner stillness, the way she did before. That must be the key. Fear threatens to overcome her until, with an effort requiring all the strength and wisdom she can summon, calm at last wins out. She exhales slowly, casts the spell, and opens her eyes. There is no baby in the cradle. Where is she? Are they both gone? She looks out at the fairy's face and sees her shake her head, as if seeing double. Agonizing moments pass, and then, with a little pop, Briar appears in the cradle in front of Hilde, completely herself, and Hilde sees the gold fairy bend over the gilded cradle in the hall, crooning affectionate nonsense to little Rose.

The king and queen rush to the cradle's side, and the queen grasps baby Rose to her, as if by holding her close she can undo what has been done. She turns to King Warrick. "The child can't grow up with everyone telling her she's been cursed. Do something!" The king looks about the great hall, and he signals the buglers to call for attention. Soon every eye in the room is upon him.

"This day," he announces, "a terrible conjuration has come upon us. I proclaim that *every spinning wheel in the kingdom* shall be burned! Furthermore, the princess Rose shall remain innocent and unaware of this curse until after her sixteenth birthday. Therefore I pronounce that on pain of death, no word shall be spoken, sung, or written concerning the gray fairy's curse. It must be as if it *never happened*. All of you who have witnessed this day, mark my words well. Remember! On pain of death!"

All around the hall, people look at one another with raised eyebrows—and closed mouths. But such is their sympathy for the poor wee baby that the king's proclamation is unnecessary.

No one present would add to the harm done to the child for the world.

Hilde, meanwhile, who has held herself in limbo, feels the blood rushing in her veins again with relief. She picks up baby Briar and embraces her lovingly, the sleepy little one seemingly unaffected by what has taken place. Still trembling, Hilde contemplates the future with a mixture of hope and dread unequaled by anyone present, for none knows how she has tempted and cheated the fates this day. Only time will tell whether her machinations were for good or for ill. She pats baby Briar's back and softly croons a little lullaby.

PART ONE
NINE YEARS LATER

Chapter One

IT IS A HOT SUMMER MORNING in the kingdom of Wildwick. In the distance, the sun hovers over the cloud-covered mountain. Sunlight shimmers in the hazy air, kisses the sleepy earth, and sparkles on the surface of the castle moat. Even the stony walls of the stronghold grow warm in the sultry dawn. Yet despite the glowing sun and pastoral setting, the years have not been kind to the little kingdom. The village outside the castle walls has grown shabby. The villagers themselves wearily tend the fields; the crops are plentiful, but there is not much to eat. The village baker has barely enough flour to make his bread.

Why should this be, one wonders, when their crops are so abundant? It is because of this: every year at harvest time, for many years now, a greedy giant has come stomping down from the cloud-covered mountain, demanding gold and cattle and most of their crops. Then, with one blow of his mighty cudgel, he knocks a hole in the castle wall just to show that he can. What can King Warrick do? His counselors compel him to go forth and negotiate with the great bully. So he tries, with his voice as steady as he can make it, to remind the giant that if the villagers all starve, there will be no one to raise the crops. But the giant is immune to logic, and the king always ends by giving up more of his kingdom's wealth and harvests, looking on as the giant stomps away with his plunder, back to the cloud-topped mountain. When it is over, the people are left destitute, some injured, even some dead. The castle, really a fortress, is left defenseless, its wall ruptured. By order of the king, all the able-bodied men gather at the broken wall and painstakingly rebuild it while the king levies the Giant Tax to replenish the treasury. Then he sells off more land to the filthy goblins, who pay him in gold from their underground lairs. This is a terrible choice, as goblins despoil any land they inhabit as well as everything for miles around. But despite the kingdom's poverty, the king makes sure that he and his nobles still have the best of everything for themselves, and he keeps his own secret cache of food and treasure. The poor peasants, ignorant of the king's thievery, simply sigh and make do with what is left to them.

In the light of this summer morning, however, the repaired wall looks strong and solid, almost indistinguishable from the older parts of the structure. Within the wall, the castle keep rises up, towering over the courtyard, and the early morning sun tints the masonry a ruddy gold. It filters through the window of an attic room high in the keep, where two girls lie sleeping, one dark head and one light. Lady Briar, the dark-haired one, opens her drowsy eyes, still emerging from her dreams. She rolls over into Princess Rose and gives her a poke on the shoulder. "Wake up, lazybones!" she says, and Rose's eyes flutter open. They proceed to greet the dawn with all the buoyancy and optimism natural to healthy young humans. The morning routine becomes a giggling competition to see who can get dressed and downstairs first. They perform their minimal ablutions — a few ill-aimed splashes from the water basin — and dress quickly in their linen shifts and full-length tunics, tying long belts below their waists and attaching small leather pouches for carrying odds and ends.

Briar is first out the door, but they race down the stairs to the castle chapel as the bell rings Prime. Rose skips to a halt as she sees Bishop Simon standing in the doorway of the chapel, looking accusatory and grim. His large belly takes up so much space that they must pass single file through the doorway. Rose hastily folds her hands in front of her, straightening her spine and lifting her chin in a practiced imitation of her mother's royal bearing, while Briar, who fears the clergyman's sharp tongue, does her best to remain invisible in Rose's shadow. "I win!" whispers Rose over her shoulder to Briar.

The girls enter the chapel for morning mass soberly, for they have known it all their lives as a place of power and mysteries. As the family gathers, the girls take in the carved altar, the rich paintings, and the statuary. They listen to the service silently, but their solemnity does not last. Rose signals Briar with a set of complex hand gestures, subtle nods, and eye rolls that serve as a private language between them, especially during daily services. She draws Briar's attention to young Bosley, the altar boy, whose voice cracks and changes whenever he sings the responses in the service. The bishop gives the lad a scathing look, as if the boy is deliberately ruining what is supposed to be a perfect ritual. Bosley turns crimson with shame. Rose affects a cough to hide her smirk, but Briar blushes in sympathy with him and circumspectly casts down her eyes, pretending not to have witnessed his embarrassment.

Their attention next turns to Bishop Simon. Pompous and aloof, he holds himself exempt from the most basic tenet of his religion. That is, he fails to love others as he loves himself. Indeed, his hatred of others' imperfections makes him look down on every imperfect being around him. Even the king and queen are not exempt from his judgments, though he takes care that they don't know it. The girls make fine sport of him in their private language. They look haughtily down their noses at each other while sticking their stomachs out and stifling their giggles.

They are halfway through the doxology when, standing directly behind them, Lord Henry, the king's twelve-year-old nephew, yanks Briar's hair to get her attention. She turns to find him making a gruesome face, pulling down one eyelid in imitation of her sagging eye. Briar instantly responds with an even more grotesque face, pulling both her eyes down and sticking out her tongue. The nearest adult cuffs her for her trouble, and her only satisfaction is in seeing Henry receive the same treatment. She is comforted by Rose, who links an arm with hers and turns to give Henry a look poisonous enough to wither him into oblivion. The liturgy goes on, Briar measuring the passing time by the candles on the altar burning slowly down. Yet despite the bishop's boring monotone as he reads the long scripture lesson, a few moments of curiosity, confusion, and even wonder flicker over Briar's thoughtful face as she listens to the ancient words of wisdom. She goes leaping after meanings like a young otter, pondering the imponderables. This lasts until her stomach starts growling for breakfast, and then her thoughts become more earthbound. In due time, the service is over, and only then does the family sit down for a breakfast of white bread sopped in wine.

After the morning meal, the girls report to the anteroom, which serves as the schoolroom for the small gathering of nobles' children who are being educated at great expense. At Hilde's inducement, Queen Merewyn has insisted that Princess Rose and Lady Briar be educated as well, though this is unusual for girls. Along with the handful of nobles' and knights' sons and altar boys, the queen has decreed that three other girls should be included in the class, so that Princess Rose and Lady Briar will not be the only females in the group.

Lady Arabella, the oldest of the three girls, is a distant relative of the princess's, and the assumed leader of the three. Quite conscious of her dignity, she strives for correctness and insists on being addressed as *Lady* Arabella at all times. Elizabeth, the steward's daughter, is less confident, but generally advances herself by tattling on the infractions of others. Jane, the head knight's daughter, goes along. Whatever the other girls do, whatever the situation, Jane follows like a lost puppy. Though all the girls in the class sit on one side of the room, Briar and Rose seldom pay the others much mind, being happily preoccupied with each other.

Meanwhile, Hilde and the queen watch over Rose's and Briar's progress closely. Reports of Rose are full of praise, but Briar's quick wit makes her a constant challenge for the uninspired bishop, who doubles as their tutor. Bishop Simon's reports of Briar are full of condemnation, for he has abhorred her since her birth. He sees in Briar's face a profound evil in the royal line and therefore a curse on the entire kingdom. It only makes matters worse that she associates herself with the otherwise perfect princess Rose. In his fanatic pursuit of perfection, the bishop has lost sight of his religion's teachings about love and compassion. He even preaches from the pulpit his mistaken belief that any deformity is a judgment passed on the wicked. Some gentlefolk realize how wrong he is, but he is a powerful man and they are afraid to contradict him.

Many suffer his condemnation, but it is actually Briar's innocent tendency to correct the cleric's Latin that has spawned the foulest hatred in his hypocritical soul. Such presumption from one so far below him is simply not to be borne! He looks for opportunities for petty cruelty to her, and where there are none, he creates them.

"Lady Briar," he suddenly thunders, hoping to startle her into a mistake, "what is the sum of thirty-two, forty-six, and fifty-three?" He speaks loudly and slowly to her, as if she were dimwitted.

Briar pauses for a moment and, without using her abacus, totals the figures in her head and answers. "One hundred thirty-one?"

The old bully closes in and barks, "Stand up when you speak to me! Look at me! Are you sure? Think again. Are you asking me or telling me?" He thrusts his face almost nose to nose with Briar's, and his eyes bore into hers. "Hurry now!"

As so often happens, Briar begins to suffer agonies of self-doubt and decides she must be in the wrong. She is only nine, after all, and the bishop seems all-knowing. She tries again. "One hundred *forty*-one?" she squeaks.

Bishop Simon turns his back on her while he subtly works with his abacus, then whirls to face her. "Aha!" the cleric cries, all but pouncing on the frightened child. "You are wrong! You will stand in the corner with the donkey ears on." The appearance of this leather headdress in the likeness of a donkey on Briar's head excites a general laugh and an especial sneer from Lord Henry. The other boys in the class follow his lead in calling her names, and the bishop allows them to exercise their full creativity in this before bringing them to order and continuing with the lesson. Rose sits silently helpless, but signs her comradeship to Briar in their private language. She signals with two fingers up to indicate donkey ears and rolls her eyes toward Henry. Briar signs with her thumb up in the affirmative, somewhat comforted, though she dares not alter her outward expression of woe. She stands in her corner wearing the ignominious ears as the bishop calls upon Jane. Though she is plodding, she is always an obedient girl, and because of this the bishop favors her. "Jane, the total of thirty-two, forty-six, and fifty-three?"

Jane slowly counts the beads of her abacus, starting over again several times as the bishop beams benignly at her. At last she comes up with the answer, "One hundred thirty-one!"

"That is correct!" cries the bishop, giving Jane a sweetmeat from his private supply and patting her on the head.

Briar stares at the ceiling, burning with the injustice. That was her own first answer. She pretends indifference, but she feels her eyes well up. Despite the bishop's beastly treatment of her, her sharp wit and love of learning are immutable. So as she listens to the problems the bishop poses to his other students, she does the sums in her head, and she has the satisfaction of hearing that she is correct every time.

When the students are finally released for the midday meal, Briar and Rose meet by habit on the circular stairway and wait until they are sure no one is near to hear their plans. These by no means include attendance at the afternoon-long session of instruction in manners and needlepoint that the women of the court regularly attempt to impose on them. The girls go on to the great hall, where they confer over their shared trencher, but they soon realize that Lady Arabella, Elizabeth, and Jane are listening in from across the table. Caught in the act, Lady Arabella tosses her head and says, "I declare, if you two keep skipping out on your afternoon lessons, you'll never learn courtly manners, and my mother says that in a few years, Princess, it won't matter how pretty you are if you don't know how to behave!"

This fails to have the desired effect, and in fact results in Rose and Briar meeting each other's gaze, laughing, then continuing their conversation by means of whispering into each other's ears.

"How rude!" Jane says.

"I'm telling!" Elizabeth says.

"Go ahead and tell! We're not doing anything without permission," Rose says slyly.

She and Briar excuse themselves before the nuts and cheese are served, and as a diversion to mislead the other girls, they head in the opposite direction from where they want to go. Once out of sight, they double back by another route and so avoid being forced to join the adults in the solar, the embroidery and weaving room. They have decided to go see Hilde, whose wry observations and herbs and potions are ever so much more interesting than manners and needlepoint. Hilde does not do needlepoint, so they make their way to the topmost room of the north tower, where she resides apart from the other women.

"*You* knock," urges Rose.

"Why don't *you* knock?" Briar asks.

"I'm never quite sure what to expect."

"Well, she's my godmother. I'll knock." Briar raises her hand and gives a sharp rap on the door.

From behind the door they hear, "Rats! Spoiled again!" and footsteps stomping toward them. It opens to reveal Hilde wielding a large, drippy spoon and looking none too happy. "Oh, it's you two. Well, come in at your own peril. I'm busy right now with a new spell. It could save the kingdom—if it works!"

The girls eagerly approach her worktable to see what she's doing. Everywhere is the debris of countless experiments gone wrong. The table is covered with glass jars and containers of every shape and kind, some spouting foul-colored steam, some bubbling and fizzing ominously. Some are lined up on racks and are filled with various hues of liquids and powders and dried herbs. They spill over onto the tabletop amid little piles of ashes and assorted animal droppings. And in the center of the table, in a large stone bowl, lies a handful of straw in a puddle of melted butter.

"It's missing something, but I'm not sure what. Maybe something sweet," Hilde ponders, grabbing a sweetmeat from a small container and plunking it into the center of the bowl. "Now more yellow—ah! Marigolds! Perfect!" From a potted plant at her window she picks a fistful of marigolds, whereupon she crushes them with a mortar and pestle and scrapes the result into her mix of yellow goo. "Now! Maybe one more thing. Something liquid. Liquid gold. Ah! I have it."

Behind her is a complicated cupboard with many small compartments and drawers. Among other things in it are a number of eggs of all different sizes, some white, some brown, some speckled.

"Now which is which?" she wonders aloud. She picks up a smallish brown egg and puts it up to her ear. "Hello? Hello in there. Anybody home?" She listens carefully for a minute, then says, "Oh, this will do nicely." Tapping the egg sharply on the edge of the bowl, she opens the shell and lets the thick yellow yolk drop into the brew.

"Now, for the proper conjuration. Let's see . . . We must mix it and change it and make *lots* of it.

>*"Abracadabra and behold:*
>*Turn this mishmash into gold*
>*And multiply it sevenfold!"*

Hilde watches carefully for any signs of a transformation, but other than the egg yolk spreading thick and yellow in the disgusting mess, nothing happens. Hilde's face falls.

"It needs something else!" she cries. "Something to give it a little oomph! A handful of pepper ought to do it." She pours a healthy helping of the spice out of a jar into her palm, while the girls back away. Then, throwing it into the middle of the mixture, Hilde opens her mouth to repeat the incantation just as the mess rises up in a small mountain of goo and erupts in an enormous exploding bubble. Yellow slime flies everywhere, but mostly onto Hilde, who is now spotted from the waist up with bits of straw and marigold stuck to her here and there. Briar and Rose are only lightly speckled.

Hilde shakes herself like a wet dog, then says, "Drat. I guess the pepper was a bad idea. You two had best get along. I have quite a cleaning job here."

"Can't we help? We want something to do."

"No. You mustn't touch anything. I might be able to scrape up enough of the brew to try again. Here," says Hilde, picking a few spilled sweetmeats up from the floor and rubbing the dirt off them with her sleeve, "have a little treat, and be off with you."

The girls thank her for the sweetmeats and store them carefully away in their leather pouches. "But it's too hot to sit in a stuffy solar and stitch all afternoon," Rose complains, pouting slightly in disappointment.

Hilde, who is sweaty and tired and really intends to take a nap, says, "Get along with you now, dearies. I've got a lot of work ahead of me, and I must stay focused. If you're wanting some new activity, you'll have to think of it yourselves, and if you can't think for yourselves, then you had better go and do your stitching."

Briar and Rose take this as permission to do as they like, which was exactly what they came for. They hastily retreat down the stairs, conferring as they go. Is it to be the bell tower or the kitchen first? They decide on the bell tower, and despite the mid-day heat, they bolt back down the stairs two at a time. At the bottom they slow to a walk and move with studied casualness through the scattering of people in the great hall, hoping to make it to the courtyard without being noticed.

"What ho, my saucy wenchlets!" a voice calls out behind them. They turn and see Zane, the court jester, with his parti-colored hat and garb, sticking his thumbs in his ears while he wiggles his fingers and grins wickedly. "Where are you going this fine day? Can I interest you in a song, a story, a bit of juggling, a magic trick perhaps?"

Rose puts her finger to her lips and says, "Shhh, Zane! We are on a secret mission."

"Ahh. A secret mission. Educational, no doubt."

"Yes, it's going to be very educational," Briar assures him.

"Ah, yes. The kind of education you obtain without the im-pediment of schooling."

"Exactly," Briar assents.

"Well, far be it from me to stand in the way of enlightenment.

Go ye forth, my dainty little elves, and string wreaths of flowers for your heads, the better to stimulate great thoughts. Go! Be off with you!" Zane raps each of them on the head with his baton, saying, "Poof! Poof! Disappear!"

And so they make their way through the great hall and out the door. If they dimly hear Rose's nurse calling their names somewhere behind them, she is easily ignored. They break into a run and escape into the courtyard. Then they circle around to the opposite side of the keep and dash in through the doorway at the foot of the bell tower, the highest tower in the castle.

"Beat you to the top!" they cry together, though the contest is always the same. They begin to climb the two hundred steps of the circular staircase, two steps at a time. This lasts for only twenty-six steps, by which time Rose is falling behind. At one hundred steps, Briar is well ahead, her strong legs climbing easily, while Rose is breathing heavily and holding her aching side. At one hundred fifty steps, Rose calls a time-out, to which Briar considerately agrees, and they both sit down on the stairs, resting, until Briar suddenly calls, "Time in!" and clambers up the remaining stairs, well ahead of Rose, whose legs are trembling and threatening to give out. Both girls are laughing raggedly as they near the top, and Briar thrusts herself up one last step to win the race, then goes back down and takes Rose by the hand to pull her up the remaining stairs.

The roof of the tower is an open area surrounded by crenelations, with four solid pillars supporting the housing for a great bell. A solitary soldier stands watch on the rooftop, sweltering in his chain mail, and his face lights up at the sight of the two girls, who have collapsed, panting, at the top of the stairs. "Well, as I live an' breathe!" he exclaims. "A fine pair of birds have lit on my treetop!"

"We've brought you a present, Jerold!" says Rose, drawing a sticky lump of sweetmeats from her pouch. Briar holds hers out as well.

Jerold, who is not particular, thanks them with real delight. He makes a little ceremony out of removing his metal helmet and leather gloves, then makes short work of the sweet morsels, licking his fingers when he is done.

"I suppose that was a bribe?" he demands now, though he would have taken it anyway. "I'm not supposed to tell anyone you're skippin' lessons?"

The girls just giggle, then totter over to peek out from the crenelations at the magnificent view of the countryside and the great mountain, its lofty peak disappearing in a permanent ring of clouds. "Have you seen any sign of the giant?" Rose asks, for that is Jerold's sole occupation.

"If I had, you'd a heard this here bell ringing for all the castle and the village to hear, as well you know. Never fear. I have the keenest eyes in the King's Guard, my fine ladies, an' if I see that old blackguard comin' down from the mountain, ye'll know about it."

For some time the girls stand gazing out on the beautiful landscape and down at the ant-people in the courtyard below, while a brisk breeze cools their damp brows and Jerold regales them with stories of the giant's past forays. They are deliciously frightened, and they beg for more, but Jerold finally tells them they had better be gone before the changing of the guard. Swearing him to secrecy, they head slowly back down the tower stairs, making plans for the future. Feeling increasingly adventuresome, they dare each other to climb the tower again and see the giant for themselves the next time he comes. They have recently discovered how easy it is to lose themselves in a crowd and go off on their own. It would be a simple matter to evade the adults while everyone else was stampeding into the basements for shelter. Their plan is decided and sealed with a spit promise, touching spitty palm to spitty palm. Then they go on to plan their next move of the day.

Back in the courtyard, they try to remain unobtrusive. Slipping quietly into the busy kitchen, they seek out Allard, the head cook.

"So there you are, my pretty little princess," he says to Rose. He ignores Briar as he slides loaves of fragrant bread out of the oven with a baker's peel, a flat shovel on a long pole. "And what have ye come to pilfer today?"

Rose flashes him her most charming smile, her head tilted

engagingly, her blue eyes sparkling. This has never failed her. "I need an apple," she asks of him. "No, *two!* Pleeese, Allard?"

"An apple? Now what do ye want with an apple? They won't be in season for another two months. Make it a nice dish o' berries and I'll consider it. Ye'd like a nice dish o' berries, now wouldn't ye?"

A quick conference goes on between the girls; then Rose assents.

"All right then, Princess. Here you go," he acquiesces, preparing a bowl of blueberries for Rose as Briar comes out from behind her and tries to look appealing.

"One for Briar, too!" Rose demands.

"As you like, my pretty," he says, and dutifully complies. The girls promptly transfer their plunder into the leather pouches attached to their belts. Then they make haste out of the kitchen, past the scullery, and through the kitchen garden. They slip past the stables and the mews without their usual stops to socialize with the inmates. When they come to the kennels, Briar insists that they pause for a short visit. They are quickly surrounded by the castle's hunting dogs: basset hounds, Alaunts, beagles, bloodhounds, spaniels, and terriers. Briar's favorite is a greyhound named Toby, a black-and-white brindle who adores tummy rubs. Toby licks Briar's face affectionately and wiggles all over. Rose, however, is actually afraid of dogs, though she would never admit to something so cowardly. When the dogs jump up on her, she

41

wants to run, but she forces herself to pat their heads and say, "Good dog. Nice dog."

They stay only a few minutes, then hurry on their way. They are eager to get past the gatehouse before they are caught, for most everyone in the castle knows that they should be at their lessons in the afternoon, with the other girls and the women. Yet temptation propels them onward.

They are not as unobserved as they think. From a window above them, two jaded eyes follow their progress toward the gatehouse. Bishop Simon observes them sneaking. He chooses not to interfere. He smiles to himself and settles down to wait. It is not a pleasant smile.

At last the children reach the barbican. The drawbridge is down, the portcullis up, and a steady stream of sweating peasants, artisans, and craftsmen travel in and out of the gatehouse along with horses, carts, and the occasional knight or holy man. It is easy for two small girls to blend into the bustle of humanity and avoid the notice of Durwin, the porter.

Ha! Once again they have escaped the confines and constant supervision of the castle proper and are making their way with exquisite subtlety and stealth along the streets of the impoverished little village. If anyone does observe the two fugitives, they pretend ignorance and do not meddle, but they keep a careful watch over their young princess, for such they know her to be. The girls venture forth unopposed, on past the last thatched hut at the edge of town, making their way to a sweet spot beyond the bend where a thicket grows down to the edge of a wide stream.

It is a scrubby collection of twisted trees, underbrush, and tangled vines, with a few rabbit trails the children have worn into narrow pathways. To the young adventurers it is the forest primeval. Beneath the branches, their rebellious hearts leap like deer, and every green, hazy shadow is fertile with supernatural possibilities. "Quiet!" hisses Briar as a twig snaps under Rose's elegantly shod foot.

"I am!" Rose says loudly.

"Shhhh!"

"I am!" Rose whispers.

The girls look around with eagle eyes to see if they have been followed, but there is no sign of any human presence. Today they have decided to catch a unicorn, or maybe two. It is common knowledge among the womenfolk that unicorns will come to a pure maiden sitting under a tree. Briar, having thought the matter out, remembers how much the horses in the stable appreciate the occasional stolen apple, but as none were available, the blueberries will have to do. "Do you really think a unicorn will come for blueberries?" she asks doubtfully, while Rose, whose dimpled smile has won so many hearts, never questions that the unicorn will come to her. She is already imagining the surprise and joy on everyone's faces when she and Briar cross the drawbridge bringing a real unicorn docilely home. Now, alight with excitement, the two girls spend considerable time and care choosing the sort of tree that a unicorn might find appealing.

"Over there!" Briar points to a twisted oak spreading its branches in the midst of the little woodland. They examine it from all sides and judge it fitting. They seat themselves side by side, spreading their mashed-up blueberries on their laps and warning each other to be quiet. Only the sounds of the woods can be heard now: the lazy rustling of myriad swaying leaves, bursts of birdsong, the tiny flutter and buzz of insects. It is hot, even in this shady place, and the sweet, pungent scents of the forest are simmering into a heady perfume. Briar and Rose relax in the dappled light, and they begin to talk, very softly, so as not to frighten any unicorns. They speak of everything, from grand thoughts of how the world should be run to simple-minded humor.

The afternoon passes with the slow progress of a fern uncurling, with still no sign of a unicorn, and after a while the girls begin to eat the blueberries themselves.

Finally, Briar says, "Oh, let's do something else. Something fun. Let's pretend something." Rose agrees, and they get up and wander through the underbrush, swinging on the occasional vine in search of inspiration.

"Let's pretend we are sisters!" Briar says, for this is her favorite fantasy.

"But we always play that!" Rose responds. "We need something new."

Perhaps it is inevitable on such a day that they are drawn to the water's edge. A narrow log rests on the shore, half of it floating in the water. Briar looks at it thoughtfully. "If only we could make a raft. Now *that* would be fun! We need another—help me look—we need another log."

Rose immediately falls in with the plan, and the two search in the underbrush for a fallen log of just the right size: large enough to support some weight but small enough for them to maneuver into the water. They scour the area until Briar nearly trips over the very sort of log they are looking for, a bit longer than the girls are tall and only a little bit rotted on one end. Breaking off a few extraneous branches, Briar, much the stronger of the two girls, picks up one grimy end and drags it to the water to lie next to the other log. The two logs combined look as if they might conceivably keep a child of nine afloat.

"But what do we tie them together with?" Rose asks.

"Maybe vines?" Briar poses. They manage to pull down some small vines but quickly see that they are not supple enough. Only then, observing Rose's efforts, does Briar come up with the idea of using their long tie belts, one at each end, to fasten the two logs together. The belts quickly come off, and with relative ease, they get the logs' ends on land tied up. Then, careless of their clothes and shoes, they step off into the water to tie up the other ends. Standing back to survey their work, Briar has another inspiration.

"A barge! It is like the Lily Maid of Astolat! One of us can be Lady Elaine and lie on the raft with a lily in her hand and be dead."

"Oh, I should be Lady Elaine, on account of being a princess."

"But Lady Elaine was not a princess!"

"Then we will take turns being Lady Elaine, and first you can be Lancelot, and when you see me floating dead on the barge, you beat your chest with grief and gnash your teeth and such."

Briar, who can see great scope in this role, quickly joins in the spirit of the thing, and they look for a sprig of something to use for a lily. Meadowsweet being plentiful along the bank, they deem it a suitable substitute and proceed into the water, dragging the Lily Maid's barge. Rose gingerly tries to sit herself on it as a prelude to lying down. The barge is not so easily tamed, bobbing up, down, and around as Briar attempts to hold it still. With a few failed tries and no small amount of luck, Rose sits, saturated to the waist, and, with help from Briar, actually lies down on the poetic vessel, soaking the rest of herself in the process.

Glancing up and down the edge of the stream, Briar is satisfied that they are out of view of the last cottage and that no one is around to tell on them or interfere. "Ready?" she asks.

"Shove me off!" Rose answers as she concentrates on keeping her precarious balance on the barge while maintaining the look of a dramatically dead Lily Maid, clutching her lily with one hand and holding herself on the wobbling raft with the other. Briar sees that the moment is right and pushes her out into the deep water.

For a few romantically charged moments Rose teeters atop the raft, and then the poorly tied belts separate, the logs split apart, rolling and splashing, and Rose manages one very lifelike scream before plunging into the water.

Chapter Two

FOR SEVERAL SUSPENDED HEARTBEATS Briar looks on in horror while Rose flails in the water, grabbing wildly for one of the logs.

"Oh! Oh no!" Briar cries. She runs into the water up to her waist, but the logs have drifted just out of reach, and neither girl knows how to swim. As Rose clings, coughing and spluttering, to the end of the log, Briar staggers back out of the water, her skirts sopping wet and dripping. They drag about her in the mud as she frantically looks for a long, sturdy stick.

"Hold on!" she yells to Lady Elaine. "Lancelot will save you!"

Rose chokes and finally manages to shout, "Hurry!"

In desperation, Briar uses all her strength to break a low branch off a tree, and she drags it to the streambed. She wades in again, poking the branch out in an attempt to reach Rose, who has drifted somewhat downstream.

"Grab on!" she calls out. "Grab on and I'll pull you in! Just hold your breath and grab on and don't let go no matter what! And kick!"

Rose reaches out with one hand and manages to grab the branch, but she refuses to let go of the log with her other hand. "I can't!"

"Yes, you can! Quick, before you're out of reach!"

Rose takes a deep breath and grabs the extended branch with both hands. Her head immediately sinks underwater; nonetheless, she holds on for dear life and kicks as Briar quickly hauls her in to where she can stand on her own. Rose surfaces, choking and gasping, throws her arms around Briar, and cries, "Oh, Lancelot! You saved me!" Suddenly they hear something crashing through the woods. For a moment Briar thinks it might be the long-awaited unicorn, but turning, she sees that it is a ragged, skinny boy, slightly smaller than herself, pushing his way through the underbrush toward them. A few yards from shore, he comes to a stop, observing that neither of the girls looks to be in danger, and says, "Oh! I thought you was in for it proper! Are you all right, then?"

Briar battles with warring emotions. As she and Rose stand waist-deep in the water, they exchange a wordless look. They can see that the boy intended to help them in their dire straits, but both are incensed that someone has invaded their secret haven. Rose adopts her most commanding royal manner and says, "Get you gone, boy. This is our private place!"

The boy stares first at one girl and then the other, and the girls stare back, taking in the shock of yellow hair sticking straight up from his head in a fantastic cowlick and his big, sincere eyes. He looks behind him to see whom she is talking to, for none of the village children have ever spoken to him this way. He stares harder at them, sure now that they are not from the village. Briar blushes and turns her face away, always conscious of the reactions of strangers seeing her for the first time, but the boy says only, "You sure you're all right? You look all done in. Here, I better help you."

He wades into the water and, taking Rose by one arm, leads her firmly toward shore. Briar takes her other arm, and soon Rose is collapsing on the muddy bank, making her own pool of water in the mud. She pants and shivers while the water runs off her clumped hair in little rivulets.

"Thank you, loyal squire," Briar says to the boy.

"Wait," Rose objects. "He's your squire?"

"Lancelot has to have a squire, doesn't he? Don't you want to be my squire, boy?"

"What's a squire do?" he asks warily.

"Why, everybody knows that! He waits on his knight and has to learn all about chivalry and heraldry and jousting and everything. It is very unbecoming of you to ask."

"I can't help it if I don't know nothing. No one ever taught me nothing. I'm just a poor peasant anyhow, but I'll be your squire."

"What is your name, boy?" says Rose.

"I'm just Jack, is all."

"I think we ought to grant him a boon," Briar says in Rose's ear, "on account of his coming to save us, even if we didn't need saving."

"Hmm," Rose says. "Yes. You have earned a boon, boy. What

would you like? You get to ask for something, and if I want to, I'll give it to you."

"Ask for something? Could I have some of them blueberries I saw you eating?"

"You were spying on us?" demands Rose.

"Well, I was, but I didn't mean no harm. My ma saw you headin' this way, and she told me to keep an eye out in case you should run into trouble. I didn't mean to bother you none."

The girls confer privately, taking note of his scrawny arms and legs and his dirty rags and bare feet, and they promise to bring him a whole bag of food next time they come.

The matter settled, they continue their play, first with Lancelot marrying Lady Elaine, even though he really didn't—it was just pretend. Then they have a go with Lady Elaine dramatically dying (again), then a long pause as Briar and Rose talk out the finer points of how she must be buried. They set the squire to digging with his bare hands, but his progress being too slow, they get down on their knees and help him. Their finely woven tunics are by now totally encrusted with mud, not to mention blueberry stains. When their efforts prove unsatisfying, they decide that Elaine's ghost would most likely remain aboveground, haunting Lancelot anyway, a concept that affords even more enthusiastic play, with the squire trailing along behind. The squire soon grows weary of this and complains that there is nothing good for him to do. He says that he is going home, and Briar and Rose, getting hungry, decide that they had better go home too. They bid Jack goodbye and trudge back through the village, their muddy skirts dragging. When they finally reach the drawbridge, the traffic has slowed, and as they enter the gatehouse, Durwin spots them easily.

"Princess Rose!" he shouts. "Where have you been? Half the castle is looking for you, and if they find out you slipped by me, my pay will be docked again!"

Rose has the good grace to look abashed, calling out, "I'm sorry, Durwin!" but the girls hurry past him and on into the courtyard. They try to stay in the shadows, knowing they have reached the area of greatest peril. From here to their attic bedroom, the way is fraught with the danger of discovery, and they are both fearful of being caught in their present frightful state. They go as quietly as thieves, sticking close to the walls, listening for sounds of approach. They can hear Rose's name being called from several different directions but are finally forced to take their chances going up the central stairway of the keep. On the second level, they must pass near the archway that leads to the chapel. They are tiptoeing along in their sodden shoes, making slight squishing sounds, when Bishop Simon emerges from the chapel door and blocks their way.

"Princess Rose! Oh, my dear princess! What has happened to you? Why, you're half drowned!" He looks at Briar with hellfire in his eyes, and pulling himself up to his full height, he rages, *What have you done?*"

Briar stands, speechless, staring stupidly as she tries to think of an answer that will deflect Bishop Simon's wrath. The girls have not prepared a story, placing all their hopes on returning undetected as they have often done before. As the clergyman grabs Briar by the collar and shakes her, she realizes that he is not waiting for an answer. Rose looks on, her hands to her mouth, terrified and helpless. The clergyman calls out, "Here! They're here! I've found them!" several times, and people come running to see. Bishop Simon had spread the alarm early in the afternoon that the girls were missing and had done his best to upset everyone as much as possible about their disappearance. Then he had watched from his window for their return, intending to blame the whole affair on Briar. Though the girls' absence all through the afternoon may not be too terrible an infraction, to find them soaking wet is a stroke of luck he had not anticipated. Brimming with malice, he intends to make the most of it.

A small crowd has gathered about them, and Lady Beatrice, Rose's nursemaid, bursts in upon them. "There you are, Princess!" she says. "And look at you! Why, you're soaked from head to toe! And muddy! And your dress and shoes are ruined! You certainly don't look like the most beautiful princess in the land now!" She glares accusingly at Briar, whose friendship with Princess Rose has always rankled her. Having absorbed Bishop Simon's teachings, she has long believed that Briar's character is as malformed as her face, and she considers both to be an affront to Rose's beauty and sweetness. It is perfectly clear to her that any misbe-havior of Rose's has *always* been the result of Briar's bad influence. As she surveys the evidence of Rose's near drowning, she an-nounces that she has known all along that the association would lead to trouble.

"She's been dunked right in!" she exclaims. "And look at *this* one," she adds, pointing a finger into Briar's face. "Why she's only wet up to the waist! What did you do, push her in?"

"Well . . ." Briar objects weakly, remembering that she did push the makeshift barge, with Rose on it, out into deeper water. With everyone accusing her, she begins to doubt herself and won-ders if she has indeed done something unforgivable.

"No!" Rose objects.

But her nurse takes her by the arm and says, "Don't try to protect her! She pushed you in, *didn't* she?"

"I asked her to!" Rose has the temerity to say.

"Oh, certainly you did!"

"A likely story!" is repeated all around.

The bishop picks up the accusation and shouts as if it were established fact, "She pushed her in! She must have pushed the princess right into the deep water!"

There are gasps of horror, and someone cries, "The little ver-min! Give her a good sound beating and see what that teaches her!"

Other voices chime in until there is a general cry, "Beat her!"

Now, beatings are not such an uncommon way to discipline children in the Kingdom of Wildwick, where it is mistakenly believed to be a healthy means of building character. But, though Briar has known the occasional switch on her knuckles, she has never in her life been beaten, and the very words fill her with a bottomless dread.

The nurse, not wanting her delicate Rose to witness the spectacle, pulls her away, saying, "Hurry! We must get you cleaned up before anyone else sees you like this!"

Rose wants to object, though she is frightened by the rage of the adults. "No!" she cries helplessly, but the grownups are all-powerful, and they are not listening to her. She meets Briar's agonized glance with mute misery as Lady Beatrice hustles her away, leaving Briar to the tender mercies of the eager bishop and his crowd of onlookers.

Bishop Simon often feels himself called upon to improve the characters of his young charges, and he will not shirk his duty now. In fact, such cruelty has become a source of deep satisfaction for him. It is a chance to vent his rage against all the imperfections. He calls for his cane, which is quickly fetched. Several volunteers, not wanting to seem remiss in the care of the young, hold the terrified Briar as the clergyman raises his arm. Then he rains down blows upon her tender young back, sowing seeds of a bitterness that will never entirely leave her. She cries out again and again, and the blows continue all the harder, while the impassioned bishop shouts, "Take *that*, you demonic thing!" and the onlookers nod with satisfaction. At last it is over, and she is freed.

She has only one thought, and that is to get away, far away, from them all, and though she feels near collapse, she forces herself to move her legs and run. As she is overcome with shame and humiliation, it does not occur to her that anyone might take her part. She runs down the stairs, back the way she has come. Past the kitchen. Past the stables and the mews. As she runs past the kennels, Master Twytty, the kennel master, calls out, "Lady Briar! What's the matter? Won't you come in and pet the dogs?" But she only shakes her head and runs onward, past the armory and away across the courtyard. Though she is observed by a few, no one thinks to stop her or comfort her. A crying child is none of their business, and her face, off-putting in the best of times, is unfortunately repellent in her grimace of pain and grief. Briar makes for the gatehouse unopposed and darts past the watchful Durwin despite his objection.

Out in the village, she barrels blindly into a crowd and nearly upsets a peddler's cart. The peddler shoves her roughly out of his way, and a woman points at her face and screams. Everyone around her is looking at her with horror, crossing themselves to ward off evil. Though some have observed her sneaking through town with the princess, none have seen her up close until now, and they have not grown used to her as have those who dwell inside the castle. They see her through eyes of fear and superstition.

"Monster!"

"Goblin!"

"Changeling!" they cry as they make the sign against evil, and Briar realizes they are talking about her. She covers her face with her hands and dives in through the crowd to escape. They back away as if her touch is poison, and she bolts down the street, intent on getting past all the staring people, past the village, and finding her way back to the peaceful haven of the woods. Her body hurts with every move, with every jolt from the pumping of her legs, and she feels dizzy and weak. Before she can make it to the edge of town, she collapses by the side of the road to catch her breath and clear her head. A woman in a nearby cottage sees her there and gasps in loathing. She waves her broom at Briar and cries, "Shoo! Shoo! Get away with you!" So Briar picks up her suffering body and compels it to move.

Finally, she passes the very last cottage. She lopes on doggedly to the place where the woods begin, and looking to be sure she is not observed, she slips silently in among the trees and ferns. She finds the great oak tree near the stream, where she and Rose sat innocently waiting for unicorns, and she crumples beneath it, crying for a loss she cannot put a name to. The tears come faster and harder, and her whole body heaves with sobs. She will never go back. Not if she has to starve alone in the woods. Not if wild beasts come and rend her to pieces. She hopes they will. She hopes her mangled corpse is found and everyone who has been cruel to her will be racked with remorse.

For a long time she pours out her pain on the patient earth, while the treetops rustle soothingly in the sweet breeze, whispering to her of timeless peace. As her sobs grow quieter, she begins to hear another sound, faint and ethereal, something like chimes or panpipes or a multitude of harps, but even more exquisite — something so tantalizing that it makes Briar sit up and cease her crying so that she can listen. She pushes herself painfully to her feet and looks around through tear-bleary eyes, trying to discern where the music comes from. Taking one faltering step, then another, she finally sets off in the direction of the waning sun, making her way through the scrubby little thicket of woods. Staying close to the streambed, she goes farther from home than she has ever gone. Still she continues on, the way through the thickening trees and underbrush seeming to open before her, and slowly but surely, she enters the deep forest.

Here the light is dim and tinted with green. Above her, in the canopy, she hears the leaves rustling and whispering to one another in sweet harmony with the music. She hears birds chirp excitedly as she passes. A red fox appears ahead of her, opening a narrow path, and she follows it over fallen logs, ducking under low branches. She can no longer see the stream, but she pushes on after the fox. Her feet sink slightly into the carpet of moss and dead leaves while the smell of damp humus fills her nostrils.

Sometimes the music seems to come from one direction, sometimes another. She hums to herself, trying to imitate the melody. It is high and sweet and has a complex, repeating rhythm, like a round. Briar is so absorbed with it that for a few moments she almost forgets how desperately unhappy she is. She goes on humming for some time and then, pleased with the effect, suddenly feels moved to sing. Her clear young voice, though it is tremulous and sad, resonates in perfect harmony with the music in the air, and the fox waits for her as she stands still for a while, just listening and singing. The turmoil in her heart eases a little, and her voice becomes more full and vibrant, resonating through the forest and silencing the birds with its pure beauty. After a time, she continues in the wake of the fox, even deeper into the forest, and croons softly to herself as she peers through the half-light, looking for the source of the music.

She tries to keep track of the stream, but she is thoroughly lost and far from the familiar thicket where she began. Since she has no plans to return home, she hardly cares. After some time she hears the sound of rushing water, and it mingles with the notes in the air to form a breathtaking harmony. The fox has disappeared, but she follows the sound, which is quite close now, and finally comes to a wide clearing by a waterfall.

It is a place of tranquility and loveliness. A wall of rock faces her from across the clearing, and the sunset has dyed it a rich golden orange, while at the edges of the clearing, blue shadows are deepening. To her left, the waterfall pours down the cliff into a wide lagoon, giving rise to a light mist. Briar stops a moment to take it all in. She listens to the spellbinding sounds that fill the air, and she feels a response welling up from deep within herself.

Briar steps out into the clearing and begins to dance, her feet moving almost of their own accord. It seems as if her whole body is made of music. Her pain falls away, and she feels as free and innocent as if she had awakened from a bad dream. She sways and twirls and tosses her head, casting a long, dancing shadow while the sun slips toward the horizon and the sunlight on the wall of rock deepens to red. She feels that she is shining, radiant. Opening her arms to the sky, she reaches after an idea that is tickling at the edges of her mind. Some lovely thought is right there. She longs for it, but it is just out of reach, and it eludes her.

The sunset turns to violet, and the blue shadows lengthen. The music fades, and Briar slows and meanders to a halt. Sitting down in the middle of the clearing, panting slightly, the girl realizes how tired she is, and how hungry. Now she looks around in the gathering shadows and wonders what to do. She knows she can't find her way home, but somehow she no longer wishes to be devoured by wild animals. She wonders if she might spend the night in a tree.

As she sits lost in contemplation, she hears a rustling at the edge of the clearing and takes fright, raising herself to a crouch, getting ready to run. Out of the shadows comes Jack, her loyal squire of only a few hours before.

"God's feet!" he exclaims. "What a dance that was! If I could do that, I'd make me a livin' dancin' for the king and queen!"

Briar, who is both relieved and affronted by his presence, hardly knows how to respond.

"You saw, squire?" she says, not sure whether to be embarrassed.

"I couldn't help it! It was just that fine an' awesome I had to watch. Me ma set me to followin' you again when she seen you all alone and headed for the woods. She said it boded no good, an' I ought to bring you back. So I followed your singin'. It was like bein' under a spell, it was—"

"I am never going back!" Briar interrupts him. "I'll sit in a tree tonight!"

"Oh, that wouldn't do at all, miss! It gets damp and chilly at night here. Can't you feel it comin' on already? You'd catch your death! And, why, just think what would happen if you fell asleep. You'd fall right out of the tree and break your head! And won't everybody be lookin' for you an' wonderin' what's become of you?"

"No! Nobody cares a fig. Well . . . maybe one person," she says, thinking of Rose and the agonized expression in her eyes as

Lady Beatrice dragged her off. Then she starts thinking about her dear eccentric godmother, Hilde, and wonders if she has heard of Briar's crime and her terrible punishment, and whether Hilde still loves her. The queen too has often been kind. Would they care what had become of her? Not ready to think of home, she wipes her moist eyes with the back of her hand and pushes the thoughts from her mind.

"Why don't you come home with me, then?" Jack says. "Me ma will greet you kindly, though there ain't much to eat. Only you'd better decide quick, as these here woods will soon be dark, an' I've no mind to be caught in the deep forest at night."

It takes very little time for Briar to consider that this boy's home, however common, would be a better place to spend the night than the wild forest. "Your most gracious offer is gratefully accepted," she answers in her best court manners.

"Oh, are you still Sir Lancelot," he asks her timidly, "or should I call you something else?"

Briar shies away from introducing herself as Lady Briar. She instinctively feels it would be like bragging to this humble boy. "Just call me Briar," she says simply. "Lead the way!"

Taking her by the hand and leading her, Jack heads back toward the setting sun, into the woods, and onto a narrow path. They fumble between the trees in the dim light. Their ears are attuned to every sound, but it is twilight, the time when everything is draped in tints of cobalt blue and the creatures of the forest pause in their motions and pray. All is hushed except the noise of their own soft footsteps on the packed earth and the occasional swishing of ferns and small branches as they pass by. After a while they are walking in near darkness, but Jack is still able to make out the path. They continue on until they have reached the edge of the little thicket where they played that day. Suddenly Briar feels shy. How will Jack's mother react when she sees her face? She hesitates, but Jack pulls her along by the hand, saying, "C'mon! We're almost there!"

Out of the woods and up the road they go, and soon Briar makes out the dim shape of a hut in the gloom and a figure leaning out over the lower half of a door.

"Jack? My Jack? Is that you, son?" the figure calls.

"It's me, Mother. I'm back safe and sound, and I've brought someone with me!" Jack answers. He drags Briar forward to the door and on into the house, where his little old mother gets her first good look at the girl. She does not recoil or make the sign against evil or send her away like the other villagers did, but she takes a moment to adjust and then envelops Briar in her bony embrace, noticing as she does that the child winces with pain.

"Come in, come in, Little One. Thank heaven you are safe! There are wild beasts abroad in the night forest, you know! Come and share our fire—and welcome. I'm called Mother Mudge." In the feeble light, the woman's hollow-cheeked and careworn face glows with its own kind of beauty, transmuted by love and kindliness, and Briar feels welcome. She looks around her and sees two cows stabled at one end of the hut and chickens running loose about the one room, scratching in the straw spread over the earthen floor. One cow chooses that moment to lift her tail and expel a pile of dung, and Briar is struck by the strong smell that quickly permeates the air. As Jack and his mother take no notice of it, she does her best to ignore it too.

Mother Mudge leads her to the dreary peat fire that burns in the center of the room. The little woman sits on a three-legged stool and stirs something in a pot suspended above the fire. "You must be hungry," she says to the children. "Sit down. Let's get some food in you, and then you can tell me all about your adventure." She ladles the thin soup she is cooking into heavy wooden bowls for them as the children sit cross-legged on the floor. Briar thanks her most sincerely, as she has had nothing to eat since the blueberries earlier in the day and feels quite ravenous. She sees that the soup is made of beans and peas, with a limp piece of cabbage floating in it, but she is so hungry that she hardly cares, and she drinks it up eagerly. It is not very good. Still, she thinks she could easily consume another bowlful, but the pot is empty.

"But you didn't have any," Briar says, suddenly remorseful.

"Oh, I already had my fill. Don't you mind me!" she responds, but Briar doesn't really believe her.

"Thank you," Briar says again. "You are very kind."

They sit in comfortable silence while Jack sips slowly at his soup, trying to make it last as long as possible. The chickens cluck restlessly as the peat fire sizzles and smokes. When Jack finishes his paltry meal, Mother Mudge takes Briar's hand in both of hers and looks into her eyes. "Now won't you tell me your story, child? How did you come to be wandering in the forest alone at such an hour?"

Briar hesitates. This woman is a stranger, however kind she might be, and Briar, even aside from her fear of being returned to the castle, is still too hurt and humiliated to want to speak of what has befallen her. But as she meets the woman's friendly gaze, she sees only comfort and compassion.

"I got a beating!" she blurts out, her eyes tearing up. Her story comes out disjointedly, telling of the bishop's accusation and the others who joined in. Then she backs up to explain about what had really happened in the water with the Lily Maid of Astolat. Finally, watching Jack's mother for signs of judgment or censure, she ends up with her escape from the castle and the music in the woods that made her want to sing and dance.

"I didn't hear no music," Jack says. "Just your singin'."

"But it was everywhere!" Briar says, her eyes shining. "The most beautiful thing!"

Jack and his mother exchange glances and look at her in a peculiar way, until Briar, deeply embarrassed, thinks she shouldn't have spoken of it. Finally, Mother Mudge nods her head. "I have heard, long ago, of stories like this, tales of gifted ones who could hear the music of the spheres. The stories have it that such people, at times of great emotion, can hear music in the very air, a sound so heavenly that it has the power to heal the soul. Was it like that?"

"Yes, it was just like that," Briar whispers in awe.

"An' you should have heard her singin' and seen her dancin'," Jack says excitedly.

Mother Mudge thinks that this must be a very special child. Since she has always made it her business to know everyone in the village and everything about them, she has of course observed Briar and Rose on their expeditions to the woods. She knows full well that Rose is the princess, and she thinks that Briar might belong to the nobility in the castle, but she would never guess that they are sisters. The girl's fine manners and speech and the make of her ruined tunic and shoes give her away as well, but Mother Mudge gives no sign of her knowledge. She is very poor and very hungry, so it is understandable that she wonders if she might receive some sort of reward for returning the girl, but the castle drawbridge has surely already been drawn up for the night, and looking at Briar's trusting face, she concludes with a sigh that she will not compel the child to go back until she is ready.

"So you heard this music out in the forest?" Mother Mudge asks. "Have you ever heard it before?"

Briar thinks hard. "I've heard musicians play, but it didn't sound like that. I don't know how to say it. I wish it would come back."

"Never mind, dearie. Perhaps someday you'll hear it again. You've had quite a time, all told. I think what you need now is a good night's sleep."

Briar glances around quickly and sees that there are two straw mattresses rolled up in opposite corners, and she thinks she will have to sleep on the hard earth floor. But Mother Mudge discerns her expression and says, "I'm sorry, child, that we have no real bed to offer you. You wouldn't think it, but back when Jack's father was alive, we used to have a fine house, and nice things and real beds. That was a long time ago, before the giant began to rob us. Now we've become poor, forced to give half of what we own for the king's Giant Tax."

Briar looks at them in disbelief. "Half of *everything?*" she asks, having never before contemplated just where the offerings to the giant came from.

"It's true, child," says Mother Mudge mournfully. "Half our crops, half our silver pennies, and half our livestock, and just about anything that might be of any value. The soldiers come and collect it all, and what can we do? Then King Warrick gives it away to the giant—but this is no kind of talk for bedtime! Don't you worry yourself about that giant, dearie. Why don't you make yourself comfortable in the loft and think about better things? You'll find plenty of straw up there for your bedding."

Briar climbs the ladder to the loft, where the straw is indeed plentiful. She burrows into it, making a nest for herself. The straw itches and her back hurts, and now she is directly above the cows, so she smells their manure quite strongly, mixed with the haze of smoke from the peat fire. Though there is a hole in the roof for the smoke to go out, it takes a circuitous route, enveloping Briar and making her cough. It is the first time she can ever remember not sleeping in her own bed with Rose, and thinking now of Rose, she feels lonely and abandoned. Though Briar senses the difference between Rose's treatment and her own, it has never occurred to her to blame her friend for it. But she has just a sliver of hope that someone will listen to Rose tell the true story and that the injustice will be remedied.

There is a sudden hard knock on the door, and Mother Mudge, who was about to bed down herself, turns and opens it. From above in the loft, Briar is astonished to hear the low, clear voice of her devoted godmother, Hilde, asking if Mother Mudge had seen a girl child roaming alone in these parts. Briar is filled with warmth. Hilde still cares about her, cares so much that she is out searching for her, even after nightfall. Either that or Briar is in even more trouble than she thought. While Mother Mudge debates what to do, Briar climbs out of the loft and down the ladder and guiltily shows herself, head hanging as if she expects to be reprimanded.

"There you are, child!" says Hilde. "You've given us quite a worry! How did you come to be here, of all places?" Behind her stand two sturdy guardsmen with torches, looking on impassively.

Briar, gratified to hear that someone has been worrying about her, lifts her head hopefully and says, "I ran away. I was out in the forest until almost dark. Jack came and brought me back here."

"You went into the deep forest alone? Don't you know there are wild beasts and ogres and all manner of dangerous things there? Praise be to all the saints for Jack!"

"Mother Mudge too!" Briar adds. "She gave me her supper."

"A good thing for you that there are kind people in the world!"

Hilde asks to shake Jack's grimy hand. A moment later she shakes his mother's, and when Mother Mudge takes her hand away, there are three gold coins in it. Hilde gives her a warm smile. "You've behaved most admirably, and I thank you. The queen thanks you as well," she assures her. Hilde takes Briar's hand. "Come now, child, they've left the drawbridge down while I looked for you. We must hurry back."

Briar says goodbye and thank you to Jack and his mother. She is full of trepidation about going back to the castle, but though Hilde's manner is reassuring, it is also implacable, and Briar goes along without a peep. As they approach the drawbridge, she is full of wonder that it is down after nightfall, and because of her! She fears that she will receive another beating for being the cause of this, but she is comforted when Hilde says, "The queen herself insisted that you be found, my girl! I hope you appreciate it. Come, she'll want to see you. We'd better get you cleaned up first."

Back in Hilde's chamber, Briar's godmother calls for water

and clean clothing to be brought. She puts a soothing ointment on the child's bruises, hoping as she does that Bishop Simon will live to regret this day's work. She determines to tell the queen of the bishop's treatment of the girl.

Presentable at last, Briar is taken to Queen Merewyn's chamber, where the queen remains awake. She knows she must resist the urge to take her child in her arms and make much of her, though that is what she wants to do. Briar must never suspect that the queen is her true mother, and so Queen Merewyn only questions her gently. The girl confesses her terrible crime of playing in the water with Rose, expecting to be condemned all over again, but the queen, who has already listened to the story from Rose, is concerned primarily for the girls' safety. She upbraids Briar firmly for going into the deep forest alone and, furthermore, forbids the two girls from leaving the castle again for the remainder of the summer. This in itself is a terrible blow to the child's intrepid spirit, knowing it will take away not only the special spot she and Rose have adopted for their own, but will also deprive her of her discovery of the place by the waterfall. And what of her new friend, Jack? She lowers her head, staring at her feet, and tries not to pout, as Hilde has always warned her against this evil habit. Hilde thinks she detects in the girl's demeanor signs of incipient rebellion and holds on to the thought.

Meanwhile, Briar, despite the blow of this new edict, is still able to feel relief that the queen is not condemning her or accusing her of trying to drown Rose. Briar demonstrates her gratitude with a long, graceful curtsy. No questions are asked about the time she spent in the forest, and she does not volunteer anything, except to relate the kindness she received at the hands of Jack and his mother. The way those two had looked at her when she spoke of the heavenly music makes her reluctant to tell of it again. She is sent on to her room, accompanied by a guardsman with a torch, but Hilde and Queen Merewyn continue talking long after she is gone. Hilde lets the queen know of Briar's bruises at the hand of the bishop.

"I resent every blow he administered!" says the queen. "But I fear I have little power to prevent his abuses. I will speak to the king, though with little hope. If she is to be educated, Bishop Simon is the only person qualified to teach."

Over the years, the queen has listened to Hilde's counsel concerning the upbringing of the two girls, and the queen hearkens to her now.

"There is more to education than Bishop Simon can teach them," Hilde says. "I quite admire their striking out to have an adventure on their own. While I appreciate the importance of all that they are taught, I place more value on self-reliance! Given their freedom, that is something the children can best teach themselves."

"Surely," the queen responds, "you're not suggesting that I allow them to go drowning themselves in that stream."

"No," Hilde agrees. "But they are curious and spirited. Unless I am much mistaken, they will get into other scrapes. Perhaps you had best have them taught how to swim."

That night, the king and queen are preparing for bed. Queen Merewyn waits for the right moment to approach the king on the subject of Bishop Simon. At last she says, "Husband, it has come to my attention that the bishop is using a heavy hand with a cane to discipline our Briar, and for no good reason. I want you to petition the church to replace him."

"Petition the church to replace him? Why, it is only through his holy intercession that we have not been utterly destroyed by the giant's marauding! I can do nothing against the bishop, lest he cease to protect us with his special prayers and masses." He pauses, thinking about Briar, something he rarely allows himself to do. But though he is very careful to let nothing show in public, he does not deny his concern for his firstborn daughter to the queen. "Still," he says, "I'd give much to protect our child from his untoward punishments. He presumes too much."

"What, then, shall be done?"

"Only this that I can see: let the child take care that she does not give him cause to use the cane."

Chapter Three

HIGH IN THEIR ATTIC ROOM, Briar and Rose are reunited at last. Rose, having cried herself to sleep, awakens at the sound of Briar entering the room. Rose leaps out of bed and rushes to her side. In the flickering light of Briar's candle, Rose anxiously searches her face for signs of pain or anger or grief.

"Oh, thank goodness you're back!" she says. "Are you all right? Where have you been? Tell me everything. I've been suffering torments over you since we were parted!"

Briar smiles wanly, and though she is ready to collapse from fatigue, her head is still too full of the events of the day to rest. She wishes to unburden herself to her lifelong friend, but she has no words for what she has experienced of cruelty and of beauty. She has been stretched, and has grown larger and deeper, and there is a space now between her and Rose, a breach in their extraordinary connection that she does not know how to bridge. And there is the question: Did Rose defend her? Did she try? Trust must be restored.

As if she had somehow heard the question, Rose takes her hand and says, "I tried to tell them what really happened, but no one would listen. Then I threw a fit and demanded to talk to my lady mother, and *she* listened. She said you must be found, and she ordered a search of the whole castle and the village. We've been so worried about you! That horrible Bishop Simon is the one who should have been thrashed! He made everyone believe that you were trying to drown me. I do believe he hates you!"

Briar's eyes tear up, partly from relief at finding that Rose is still her faithful friend and partly from hearing the stinging truth that Bishop Simon hates her. She bows her head and sniffles.

"Oh, I am sorry! I shouldn't have said that," says Rose.

"No. It's true," Briar acknowledges with sorrow. "But why? I *try* to do everything he asks. He seems to get mad when I give the *right* answer!"

"I think he doesn't like it that you're so smart. Maybe he's afraid that you're smarter than he is! Can't you just try to pretend to be dull-witted for a while and see if it helps?"

"Then he'll sit me in the corner with the donkey ears on. And everyone will laugh. That pig Lord Henry will laugh and call me names. They all will."

"But it would still be better than making him so angry! When you know the right answer, just wink at me and then keep it to yourself. Let Bishop Simon think he's winning. Secretly you'll still know you're the smartest. And I'll know too. Maybe after a while it won't be so much fun for him, and he'll give up putting you in the corner. It's worth a try."

Briar agrees. Though she seethes with the injustice of it, the plan offers a shred of hope, and she likes the idea of practicing a subterfuge on the sadistic clergyman.

"But tell me now what happened—unless you don't want to. Was it terrible?"

Briar only nods, her eyes glistening with unshed tears. After a long silence she says, "I ran away. The villagers drove me out of town, and I went far into the forest, farther than we've ever gone. I wanted to never come back."

"But how would I ever have found you? How *were* you found?"

Briar's mind is flooded with memories of unearthly music, and of her astonishment at hearing her own voice sing with it and feeling her own feet dancing to it. She does not know how to express to Rose that she found *herself*. After another long silence she says merely, "Jack followed me. He took me home to his mother, and she was kind to me. And then Hilde came to their cottage, and she brought me back and took me to the queen. And the queen was kind to me."

"But is that all?" says Rose. She is left feeling unsatisfied by this account, which tells her so little. She senses that some great change has come over her dearest friend and that for the first time, she is being shut out. She reaches a hand to touch Briar's shoulder, but Briar winces in pain and the hand is withdrawn. Rose feels a flash of unreasoning anger, perceiving rejection where none was meant, and she turns away wordlessly to prepare for bed. Briar, unable to manage her own undressing, wears her clothes to bed, lying gingerly on her side, and Rose lies down facing away from her. They are both silent. It is a long time before Briar hears Rose's breathing become slow and heavy, and a longer time before she feels herself begin to relax. Despite her many hurts, her mind keeps harking back to the exquisite music she heard in the forest. Her whole body remembers what it felt like to sing and dance so joyously, and it seems now like an inexpressibly lovely dream. Yet she knows that it was real, and remembering it, she feels the same peace, the same delight that enveloped her then.

At last, she sleeps.

When morning comes, Briar awakens first, poking Rose's shoulder and calling her "lazybones." Her gestures quickly restore the happy normalcy of their old relationship.

Rose, all resentments forgotten, giggles and bounds out of bed. "I'll beat you downstairs!"

"No, you won't! I'm already dressed!" is the rejoinder. Briar splashes water on her face and lunges toward the door, though she is moving a little stiffly.

"Cheater!" cries Rose, struggling into her clothes as Briar exits the room and starts down the stairs. Rose finishes her toilette and runs after her, but Briar has stopped at the bottom of the stairs, unwilling to go any farther. Bishop Simon stands at the entrance to the chapel, oozing self-importance and universal condemnation. Rose sees the difficulty and takes Briar by the hand, keeping herself between her friend and the clergyman as they hurry past him into the chapel for the morning service. Briar finds it almost impossible to listen to Bishop Simon's voice as it drones on through the psalms and prayers. She thinks that such a man should not be allowed to speak those sacred words. She fervently prays that snakes and toads will come out of his mouth instead. Her wish is not granted, however, and she suffers through the service, repeating rhymes in her head so she does not have to listen. Already she dreads spending the morning under his tutelage.

When school begins, she sits on the back bench close to Rose and tries to blend in. Her breathing is ragged and uneven as she waits to see what Bishop Simon will do. For a time, he paces back and forth, conducting the students through numerous rhyming stanzas designed to teach them the rules of Latin grammar. His raptor eyes are squinting to observe the slightest wrong movement of the lips, his ears listening for the smallest mistake, waiting to heap his scorn on the first to falter. Lady Arabella, Elizabeth, and Jane, having heard about Briar's beating of the day before, sneak insulting looks at her as they repeat the required phrases, while Lord Henry and the other boys stare and snigger openly. Even so, they are all word-perfect in their recitations. Though the children have little idea of the meaning of the words they say by rote, they have become very good at parroting them. So the bishop is at first thwarted, for his true satisfaction lies not in the teaching, but in the refined art of shaming and punishing.

The lessons drag on, and Briar tries to make herself very small and unobtrusive. Bishop Simon acts as if she is beneath contempt, calling on everyone in the class but her. Briar, whose last nerve is on edge, withers under the strain. She picks at the skin of her cuticles until it bleeds. And so it goes. Each day, for weeks, the pattern continues, until she begins to let down her guard.

One morning, Bishop Simon seems to be in an exceptionally good mood. He drills the class on the times tables, up to ten times ten. Briar knows the times tables up to twenty times twenty, but he does not call on her. An hour passes while he reads out the names of the entire line of kings and queens of the Kingdom of Wildwick, then tests them on it. Briar knows them all by heart, but he does not call on her. Another hour passes while he fires Latin proverbs at them for translation, but he does not call on her.

"Repetitio est mater studiorum," he says loudly, and points to Bosley, the altar boy.

"Um, ah, repetition, um . . . is . . . is the mother, um . . . study . . . the mother of studies. Repetition is the mother of studies," the boy answers nervously. Bishop Simon glares at him, but makes no comment. Briar, following his every move and expression, sees that he is avoiding even looking at her. And so her guard is down when he turns on his heel and faces her with the look of a feral cat who has cornered a particularly juicy mouse.

Pointing his finger at her, he almost shouts the words, *"Sus laborem vestrum omni tempore!"*

Briar starts an involuntary smirk, but quickly suppresses it. The priest has made a glaring mistake, a mistake that nearly makes her laugh. She immediately realizes that he must have meant to say, "Sustain your efforts at all times," but she knows that instead of *sustineant,* the Latin word for "sustain," he has said only *sus,* the word for "pig." She nearly blurts the word out loud but bites her lip instead.

Too late.

"Is something *funny?*" Bishop Simon roars, flushed with anger. With his closed fists on his hips, he demands an answer.

Realizing the enormity of her crime, a terrible chill goes down Briar's spine and all through her. Rose takes a strong grip on her hand, serving as a reminder, if she needed one, that she must keep her knowledge to herself. "No, Bishop Simon," she quavers.

"Stand up when you speak to me!" the bishop bellows. "I saw that smirk on your face! Is there no end to your impertinence? Translate that sentence! *Sus laborem vestrum omni tempore!* What does it mean? Speak up!" His eyes boring into her, he grabs his cane and summons her to the front of the class.

Close to panic, Briar forces her body to move. Would he really beat her again, now that he has done it once? She thinks he would. Should she run from the room? But then would she ever be allowed back in? Would her education cease? Her brain strains to think of a safe reply, but her mind goes blank. Finally, she blurts out the translation for what she thinks he intended to say.

"Sustain your efforts at all times?"

The bishop, obviously furious that she has answered correctly, immediately looks for some other angle of attack. "A lucky guess! *Beware* the sin of pride, lest it be your downfall!" Ignoring all his own sins, the old villain slaps his cane against his palm, letting the moment stretch out while she stands there, frightened and tremulous.

Suddenly the air is split asunder by the loud, frantic clanging of a bell. The children and the bishop look up in alarm, as if the cause is written on the ceiling, and then there is the sound of running in the passageway outside, and a page thrusts his head in at the door and cries, "It's the giant's bell! He's coming down from the mountain! Get to the shelter!"

Bishop Simon forgets about Briar in an instant. In fact, he wastes no time on his pupils at all, but immediately begins gathering up the golden candlesticks and crucifix from the altar, along with every other loose valuable the chapel contains, while the class descends into chaos. Rose grabs Briar, and they rush away, along with the rest of the students. But while the others storm down the tower stairs toward the shelter of the cellars, Briar and Rose shrink back into a dark corner, first gasping at the timely reprieve and then stifling their laughter at the sudden opportunity. They have waited and planned for this moment, and they won't be huddling in the cellars. They will see the giant for themselves this day or suffer the indignity of breaking a sacred spit promise.

They wait until the rest of the class and Bishop Simon have all gone, and then they make their way down to the courtyard. Sprinting through the crowds of panicking people and livestock, they arrive at the foot of the bell tower and begin the long climb. The alarm bell sounds louder and louder to them as they labor up the two hundred steps toward the top, stopping several times to peer out the narrow windows to see what they can see and to give Rose a rest. When at last they reach the top, the sound is deafening. They cover their ears and nod to Jerold as he strains with his whole body to pull the thick bell rope. He tries to yell to them but cannot make himself heard, and Briar and Rose ignore him anyway.

They rush to the side facing the mountain to look past the crenelations and get their first glimpse of the giant. Peering into the distance, at first they see only the vast forest and the blue, cloud-topped mountain. Then Briar spots a movement, still very far off, a human form the size of a tree, pushing everything out of his way and heading toward them. She points it out to Rose, and they watch, engrossed, as the faraway form of the giant progresses. Then they look down and watch the tiny figures scurrying about in the courtyard below.

They can see the villagers streaming through the gates into the castle with their livestock, and Briar wonders whether Jack and his mother are in that melee. Coming from the farthest edge of town, they would probably be among the latecomers who would find no room left in the cellars. They would be forced to remain aboveground with the animals and the palace guard while the royals and nobles took shelter below. They might be safe enough within the castle walls, but no one really knows what the giant might be capable of doing.

Finally, Jerold stops ringing the bell, though the sound still reverberates in his ears, making him deaf. "What do you two think you are about?" he yells. "You should be down in the shelters."

"But Jerold," Rose responds, smiling her most appealing smile, blue eyes flashing, "we just came up to see how you were doing . . . and maybe see the giant too."

"Eh?" says Jerold. "See the giant? You'll see him all right! He's headed straight for us, he is, and you may wish you was down in the cellars right soon!"

"But we'll be safe up here, Jerold, won't we?" Rose asks sweetly. "We'll just peek over the edge and be very quiet and he won't even know we are here. We've never seen the giant before!"

"You two will be the death of me," moans Jerold, sitting down on the stairs and holding his head in his hands. "I cannot leave you here! If anything happens to you, it's my neck, sure enough!"

"Poor Jerold," Briar says, patting his back. "Just stay with us. We won't let you get in trouble. We'll tell everyone that you stayed here to guard us!"

Jerold only groans, and the girls go back to the opposite side of the tower roof and look out for the giant. Only the motion of many branches is visible now as he pushes through a forest of tall trees on the far side of the carefully plowed fields. The girls' attention is riveted, their eyes growing larger as the giant emerges from the forest and stomps across the fields, leaving deep footprints longer than the girls are tall. Soon he is approaching the castle wall, dragging a huge tree trunk behind him, each step making a resounding thump, like a drumbeat. He strides up to his ankles in the moat and stops. Though he is not as tall as the castle wall, he lifts the enormous tree trunk easily and holds it over his head as if he were about to knock the wall down. Rose and Briar quickly squat to hide behind the battlements, peering cautiously out through the crenels, both of them suddenly having second thoughts about this adventure.

The giant makes an indelible impression on Briar and Rose, not only with his huge proportions — five times the size of a tall man — but with his immense air of power and privilege. He carries himself like a jaded old despot, lazy but lethal. Though his head is gray and balding and his belly bloated, he is trussed up in rich clothing and wears an expression of careless cruelty.

"He's so *nasty!*" Rose whispers.

"Look, he's sneering, see?" answers Briar. "His mouth is all crooked on one side like when the dogs snarl at one another."

"Perhaps we'd better go down after all?" Rose suggests, eyeing the opening to the stairway. But before there can be any discussion, the giant opens his mouth and roars, "Bring me treasure! Bring me your harvests and your cattle! And be quick about it, or

I'll smash this wall into rubble!" Rose and Briar experience a thrill of terror, yet they can't look away. Rose wonders if her father will come out to parley with the giant. She sees a small contingent of robed figures ascending the stone stairway to the wall walk inside the battlements. They are too distant for her to make out their features, but she sees a flash of gold among them and thinks it is her father's crown.

It is indeed King Warrick, and he finds, as he is inexorably herded toward the giant by his bullying counselors, that the crown weighs heavily upon his head. Though he has been called upon to plead with the giant many times before, it still unnerves him to get close to someone whose grasping fingers can reach right up to the top of the castle wall. As the giant stands there with his tree trunk held overhead, even an accidental sneeze from such a titan could have terrible consequences. And it is unnerving to have to yell to be heard. *What is the point?* he wonders, despairing. The giant will do what he likes. Resistance would only make him angry. He will have his way in the end. The king lifts a hollow horn and yells through it for amplification. "Hello, friend Giant!" he calls out disingenuously. "We wait to serve you, as usual! Please give us a little time to gather our offerings . . ."

Briar and Rose can barely hear the king's speech, but they can make out enough of it to hear the desperation in his voice. Rose is shaken. She has always believed that there was no situation her father could not master with a few royal decrees. She wants to close her eyes but cannot tear them away from the spectacle. Briar sees the giant throw his purse over the wall on the end of one rope and a large empty sack on the end of another.

"Fill them!" he thunders, and the girls look on as the king turns nervously to consult with his counselors, only to find that they have backed well away. It is all up to him now, so he lifts his horn again to give the order to bring forth the offerings for the giant, and the courtyard becomes a hive of activity as soldiers run to the treasury vault, the larder, and the storage cellars to collect the goods. Soon they return with overflowing carts and wheelbarrows, lining up to unload them into the giant's bag. At least, the king congratulates himself, he has his own hoard of food and drink hidden deep below the castle, along with his own load of treasure. There is no danger that his nobles will ever go hungry, though the peasants grow sickly and thin. The king looks on as his men heap the fruits of the villagers' labor into the giant's big bag. For a moment, he spares a thought for his hungry subjects whose food is being stolen, then tells himself that there is nothing else he can do.

Across the courtyard, Jack and his mother also observe, shaking their heads sadly. They'd had no breakfast that morning, and their stomachs growl as they watch the food being shoveled into the giant's bag.

From the top of the bell tower, Briar and Rose can see a pair of soldiers struggling to carry a heavy chest across the courtyard and two more chests being carried behind them in the same manner. These are hauled to the edge of the giant's purse and emptied into it in cascades of gold and silver. The giant's cruel laughter rings out as he brings the tree trunk down on the castle wall, fracturing the stonework. "What goes on in there?" he growls. "Hurry! More! More!"

At this King Warrick finally protests, calling out to him, "Please, Your Honor, sir, we barely have enough to live on now! Paltry as it is, sir, we're giving you all our best! If we give you any more, we'll perish of starvation!"

"That's none of my business, now is it?" the giant roars. "Bring me cattle! I want three head of cattle! See to it!" The king gives a signal, and a group of soldiers rushes to commandeer three prime specimens from among the cattle, which had been driven into the castle for protection. Amid the wails of protest from their owners, they are herded out through the gatehouse and around the castle to where the giant stands. Not nearly satisfied with this, the giant draws up the rope with his purse on it and peers inside.

"Not much gold in there!" he growls. Then, looking at the king, he seems to have an inspiration. "That crown on your head is gold," he says pointedly. "Pitch it in here!"

King Warrick is appalled! How can he give up the symbol of his authority, the very crown that has been passed on from his own father and his father's father before him? Would his people lose all respect for him? He desperately racks his brain to think of something—anything—that might switch the giant's interest from the crown. There is one thing he can come up with. Though he has managed to save it from the giant so far, surely it is not too great a price to pay to hold on to his royal crown. He calls to a young soldier and tells him quietly what he wants, then turns to bargain with the giant. "Your Honor, sir, my puny little crown would do you no good. You couldn't wear it. Please allow me to show you something else that will entertain and delight you for years to come! So exquisite and cunning! You'll never guess!"

"I don't like guessing games!" the giant objects, but the desperate king keeps giving him tantalizing hints until the soldier arrives with a large bundle wrapped up in fine cloth. The king gently unwraps it, revealing a finely made harp with the head and arms of a woman.

"Not the harp!" Rose cries. She has listened, rapt, to the harp's lovely music many an evening of her young life, but her protest is borne away on the wind. Her father commands the harp to play, and so the hands pluck on the strings while the harp woman sings a hauntingly beautiful song. The giant is mesmerized, nodding his head to the rhythm of the music, and he waits until the end of the song to speak.

"I will have it!" he declares without ceremony. The giant's hand reaches up, and the harp screeches, "No! No! Master, save me!" Ignoring her cries, the giant grasps the harp with surprising delicacy and places it in his purse. Then, hauling up his bag of plunder, he announces to the king and all who listen, "Just remember, you and all your lazy peasants, this land and everything in it belongs to *me*. I allow you to live on it only as long as you make it worth my while!" With that, the giant picks up the tree trunk and slams it down on the wall with great force, ten feet from where the king is standing. Huge stones and rubble rain down into the courtyard, where several guards are injured and one lies very still. Then the giant attaches the purse to his belt, grabs the cows' ropes with one hand, and slings the bag of plunder over his shoulder with the other. He turns and stalks away through the village. Over his shoulder he calls out, "I never said I *wouldn't* knock the wall down, now did I?" and he sets off toward the cloud-topped mountain, laughing obscenely.

Briar and Rose watch him go, trembling with relief. Rose's legs will no longer support her, and she sits down abruptly, leaning her back against the battlements. Briar watches the giant's retreat, not quite trusting that he won't come back and wreak more havoc. She looks down into the courtyard, where the castle guard is already swarming to repair the breach in the wall, and she wonders where Jack and his mother are.

Jerold begins to ring the all clear, and the girls collect themselves and make a hasty departure down the two hundred stairs. They reach the bottom and find that all is chaos within the crowded courtyard. People are calling out to find one another, and animals are bleating, honking, and barking in the confusion. The girls see this as a great opportunity to lose themselves, hiding from grownups who might compel them to join the women in the stuffy confines of the solar. Now all the villagers and their livestock are thronging out through the gatehouse and across the drawbridge, heading back to their homes, or what is left of them. Amid the noise and turmoil, Briar and Rose hold tightly to each other's hand to keep from being separated.

Suddenly they hear Lady Arabella's voice behind them, full of assumed authority. "You'd better come with us, you two, before you get lost in the crowd!"

Rose turns to face her. "Get lost in the crowd?" she repeats, looking around her with exaggerated fear and then at Briar. "Oh no! Lost? Whatever shall we do?"

"Oh no! I feel myself getting lost!" Briar cries, her hands gripping her throat as she backs away from Lady Arabella and her cohorts, Elizabeth and Jane. Rose grabs her own throat, making choking noises, and follows Briar into the crowd.

"How rude!" Jane remarks.

"I'm telling!" Elizabeth calls after them.

Rose and Briar spot several of the queen's ladies in waiting trying to weave their way through the melee, but the girls dart behind a nearby cart before they can be seen. They make for the stables, intending to spend the afternoon in the more congenial company of the horses, when Briar spots Mother Mudge and Jack and calls out to them. Jack hears her call and looks for her face among the many others. Seeing the girls, he turns to his mother and pulls her sleeve to tell her something. A minute later Jack has caught up with Briar and Rose, and they motion for him to follow them. Keeping their heads down, they arrive at the stables unimpeded.

The horse marshal is nowhere in sight, and the grooms, along with every other able-bodied servant, have been called away to work on repairing the breach in the castle wall. Rose leads the way past the stalls to a small tack room. Making sure no one is around to see them, they dart inside and make themselves comfortable sitting cross-legged on the floor. Away from the noise of the throng, Briar breathlessly asks Jack, "Did you see him? Did you see the giant?"

"*We* did!" Rose says. "We watched the whole thing from the top of the bell tower!"

"Aw, you did not," counters Jack.

"We did too!" Briar declares. "We saw him, clear as day! He could reach as high as the castle wall, and he was all dressed up in fine clothes, like a king! And his face looked totally evil, like the Prince of Darkness himself!"

Jack, now convinced, is duly impressed, his eyes widening accordingly. "I couldn't see nothing," he laments. "I was minding the cows. We were the last to come in, so we were in back of the rest when the soldiers came around collecting cattle for the giant. Lucky for us, they passed right by! We'd likely starve without Lulu and Bess!"

"Why don't you buy some more cows?" Rose asks innocently.

Jack just stares at her blankly, struggling for words. Briar elbows her companion, but Rose looks back at her in surprise. "What?" she says.

"It's just—" Briar begins. "It's just—"

"We be poor people, miss," Jack says. "Not like you grand ladies."

"Why do you call us grand ladies?" Rose asks, jealously guarding the freedom her anonymity gives her.

"Me ma said you were. I sure hope I didn't give no offense to you the other day. I didn't know—I thought we were all just play-acting. I never looked to be above myself."

"Never mind all that," says Briar. "Just call me Briar."

"Yes, Lady Briar."

"No, just Briar."

"All right. Just Lady Briar, and Princess Ro—"

"Just call me Rose!" says Rose. "And don't go telling everyone we're grand ladies. It would spoil our fun."

"I'll keep mum, then. You can trust me. Honesty's about all I got, but you can't buy a cow with that. My ma's got to turn over half our silver pennies for the king to give to the giant, and we got none to spare. Nor does any of the folk I know of. They be hungry and barefoot, and some are sickly too."

"Well, that's terrible!" Rose responds. "That giant is a murdering swine!"

"He is! And a blackguard!" Jack agrees.

"He's a bloodsucking fiend!" Briar adds. "Someone ought to stop him! But what can we do?"

"Nothing," Rose says quietly. "Even my father can't do anything. He can't afford an army. He just gives the giant everything he wants."

"Well o' course he does," Jack points out. "The giant could smash the whole castle if he didn't, and everyone in it."

"But it's not right," Briar says. "We shouldn't give in. It's not right to give in to a great big bully like that. It's letting evil prevail. It's not honorable."

"Even the bravest knights could not hope to defeat him!" Rose objects. "What can *we* possibly do?"

The children look at one another, afraid to think about an answer to her question.

Finally, Briar says, "We are not knights, but we are pure in heart, aren't we? Hilde told me that sometimes the pure in heart can work miracles. I don't know what to do either, but surely we must do *something*. For our kingdom, and for our honor. I mean us. The three of us."

Jack and Rose stare at Briar, their mouths open.

"What do you want us to do?" Jack croaks.

"Maybe we can't do anything until we're older, but we've got to keep looking for any chance and asking ourselves how it might be done, thinking brave thoughts, you know? Building ourselves up so we'll be ready if the opportunity comes. Mostly, we must *believe* in it."

There is a terrible silence as the words touch their hearts and take root.

Rose is the first to speak. "Maybe it would make Father proud of me for something besides looking pretty. That's the only compliment he ever gives me. I think it's the only thing he likes about me. All he expects me to do is marry well. Just imagine if I helped kill the giant! I'd save the kingdom! He'd have to be proud of me then! Maybe I wouldn't even have to marry!"

"Wouldn't it just be glorious if we could do it?" Jack says. "Every year, the giant gets worse. All of us in the village are getting poorer and poorer. Just think if I could do something to save them! Do you think a peasant like me could ever do something glorious?" Jack sniffles and wipes his nose on his sleeve.

"You have a brave heart, and a true one, squire," Briar tells him. "You have shown it in time of need and proven yourself worthy. And as for us, now that we've seen how evil the giant is up close, we can't ever forget it!"

"We should swear an oath," Rose whispers. "A solemn oath."

"On our lives," says Jack.

Briar puts a finger to her lips. "Wait a minute. First we ought to have a name. What do you think?"

"We should call ourselves the Giant Killers!" cries Jack, shaking a feeble fist in the air.

The girls look at each other and nod in approval. "The Giant Killers!" each of them echoes, fists in the air.

"Yes," Briar continues. "We will be a secret society, with our own code of honor, like knights have." She looks off into space for a time, her lips moving noiselessly. "So listen, how about this for an oath?"

She clears her throat and begins. "We do solemnly swear to kill the evil giant, to stay true to our cause through thick and through thin, and to defend one another to the death."

"You forgot 'On our lives,'" Jack corrects.

"All right. We'll put that right in the beginning. We do solemnly swear *on our lives* to kill the evil giant. So. Are we ready?"

"We should hold hands," Rose says.

"Yes," the other two respond, and the three children stand and form a little circle in the quiet room strewn with hay. The rays of the sun come streaming through a window, shining on their earnest faces and turning the dusty air into gold as Lady Briar, Princess Rose, and Jack, the peasant, look one another in the eye and repeat the solemn oath, on their lives.

Chapter Four

SATISFIED THAT THEY HAVE BEGUN WELL, the three Giant Killers decide to adjourn to the kitchen for a little celebratory refreshment. Keeping to the shadows, they skirt the courtyard, making their way along the castle wall to the kitchen door. Here they stop, and Jack, hanging back, says, "They won't want the likes of me in there. I'll be in trouble for sure if they catch me pilferin' from the castle kitchen."

"You go," Briar says to Rose. "Allard likes you. He'll give you anything you want."

Rose recognizes the truth of this and, pinching her cheeks to make them pink, goes in to turn her charms on the unwary cook. Before long, she returns, smiling victoriously and holding something wrapped in a handkerchief. The three find a shadowy corner to sit in, and Rose hands out fresh blueberry tarts, still warm from the oven. This is a once-in-a-lifetime treat for Jack, who bites into it carefully, as if it will prove to be unreal when he actually tries to taste it. The girls watch him openly, intrigued by the sheer joy written on his face. A broad, juicy smile spreads across it, and he is just going for another bite when a tall boy wearing an embroidered doublet and silk hose saunters up to them and sneers, "Well, what do we have here?"

Startled by Lord Henry's sudden appearance, the three Giant Killers get to their feet, with Briar and Rose closing ranks in front of Jack, who drops his tart in the shuffle.

"The women have sent everyone out looking for you! And here you are, stuffing your faces, in company with this—" He pushes his way between Briar and Rose and stops at the sight of Jack with blueberry jam on his face. "This! You're keeping company with a *peasant!* Isn't that rich! Where did you pick him up? He's so dirty he smells! Have a little pride, you two! Stick to your own class!"

"He's got a brave heart and a true one, which is more than you do!" Rose says. "Go mind your own business and leave us alone!"

"I'm not going anywhere until I've taken you to the queen. If you don't have any sense of what's right and fitting, I do! Get rid of this knave and come with me now, or I'll tell everyone what you've been up to."

The girls look at each other and then at Jack. Briar hands Jack her own half-eaten tart, and Rose follows suit. Jack, who had been on the verge of tears over the loss of his tart, accepts their offerings with a smile. Turning back to Lord Henry, Rose tilts her chin up and announces, "We were just leaving anyway, so you needn't make such a fuss about it!" The girls bid Jack goodbye. Then, ignoring Lord Henry, they stalk off ahead of him, toward the castle keep, their backs erect and their noses in the air.

When they reach the solar, Lord Henry, wanting to get full

credit, announces loudly that he has found the two girls, but true to his word, he does not tell what they were doing.

"You're a good boy," says Lady Beatrice, as Lady Arabella, Elizabeth, and Jane suppress their giggles.

"I told on you," smirks Elizabeth. "I said I would!"

Briar and Rose are greeted with widespread reproach by all the ladies in waiting, who are increasingly swayed by Lady Beatrice's assertion that Briar is leading Rose astray. Word has gotten around about Briar's beating, and the popular opinion is that she must have deserved it. The queen looks up, stopping conversation, and merely tells the two girls to be seated.

"Why don't you sit there next to Lady Arabella, Princess?" suggests Lady Beatrice, hoping to separate Rose from Briar and put her in the sphere of influence of the older, more befitting companion. Lady Arabella gives Rose a tentative smile. She has never understood what Princess Rose sees in Briar, or why Rose shuns her own company. She is obviously so much more suitable than the ill-favored companion the princess clings to. Lady Arabella, who carefully imitates the manners and aristocratic bearing of the queen, would dearly love to be the princess's bosom friend herself. She can imagine taking the unruly girl under her wing and making her ladylike and proper. How proud she would be to fill that role, if only the princess would turn to her. But Rose pretends not to have heard, finding a place for Briar and herself to sit together. She does not see Lady Arabella's look of disappointment, and indeed it would not occur to her to give the older girl a second thought. Lady Arabella turns away, her feelings hurt once again, laying the blame on that other one, the ugly one, who alone stands in the way of her ambition.

As Rose and Briar pick up their needlework and begin to sew, they find their own topics to discuss under their breath. They call to mind that it is only a week until Midsummer's Eve, though Bishop Simon insists on calling it St. John's Eve. He preaches that it should be an occasion only for fasting and keeping vigil. But the villagers have no respect for his opinion and resent his interference, and so, in spite of him, they secretly cling to their old ways of celebrating. While the bishop is holding his services at the chapel, the peasants will be dancing around a bonfire and making merry, and Briar and Rose want to be there to see it. As they hatch their plans, Briar, who can't bear the monotony of shoving her tiny needle in and out of her sampler, twitches with impatience. Her only relief from the tedium of sewing is to see how fast she can do it. Paying more attention to their budding scheme than to her stitching, Briar stabs her own finger with her needle. A drop of blood oozes out onto her sampler, staining it.

"God's thumb!" she mutters.

"You cursed! I heard you! I'm telling," Elizabeth says.

"Oh, really?" Briar responds. "What did I say?"

"God's thumb!"

"Did I? Well now you've said it too. Be sure and tell on yourself."

Elizabeth is temporarily flummoxed by this, missing her chance to be the center of attention, and her mouth shuts with a little pop. But Jane, who has been listening, chimes in, "You started it, Lady Briar, and *I'm* telling!"

"I'll put a stop to this," announces Lady Beatrice and, taking Briar by one arm, separates her from Rose, sitting her down among the older women, where her every move will be watched. Now Rose has only Lady Arabella to talk to, which suits Lady Beatrice very well. Lady Arabella is conscious of her dignity. She sits quietly and makes neat, regular stitches on her sampler. From time to time she looks up to smile condescendingly at her younger companions, managing to communicate with half-closed eyes and an upward tilt of her chin that she is far above their juvenile concerns and has long since given up all childish things. Princess Rose and Lady Briar, meanwhile, have developed a method of biting down on their lower lips and expelling air out of one cheek that sounds perfectly like a fart, and with each of their heads bent over their work, they practice this with great subtlety from their respective sides of the room. The elegant ladies, both offended and embarrassed, suspect one another but are too polite to mention it. And so the girls go on amusing themselves.

Only later that afternoon do they meet in their attic room and explode with pent-up laughter. It makes a welcome release from the seriousness of their thoughts earlier in the day. But though Briar and Rose laugh, they have not forgotten their earnest vows to destroy the giant. Their promises are alive within them now, wherever they may be or whatever else they may be doing.

The queen, however, observing their behavior in the solar, is not so ignorant of their antics as she might have seemed. She recalls her own girlhood and the tricks she played on her nursemaid. Still, the girls are nine now, certainly old enough to have acquired some self-control and a sense of what is fitting. She shakes her head and stifles a laugh. There is still time. They can enjoy being children yet a while, she thinks. Little does she realize that the three young children have committed their lives to doing what none of the adults could even imagine.

A week later, Briar and Rose have escaped again from the confines of the castle. Collecting Jack from his cottage on their way to the thicket, they hold the second meeting of the Giant Killers' club under the huge old oak tree, which they have claimed as their own. This time, the girls have thoughtfully provided a small repast of bread and cheese. Seeing how Jack's eyes light up at the sight, the first order of business is to eat. Only when their stomachs are full do they begin to discuss their new organization and its pressing issues.

"Shouldn't we have a code of honor," Briar says, "like the knights do, to keep us pure in heart?"

"The knights have valor, most of all," says Jack. "They have to be brave to fight. Our code of honor should start with that!"

Rose's face falls. "What if I don't have any valor?" she asks. "I think I used it all up watching the giant from the tower. My knees still feel kind of shaky when I think about it."

"Mine too," Briar admits. "Maybe valor is something we can build up to. We can practice on little things and work our way up to giant-size valor. All right?"

Rose and Jack nod solemnly, if a little uneasily.

"All right, what else?" Briar continues. The three Giant Killers go on proposing different virtues for their code. They finally settle on a short list: Valor, Faith, Loyalty, Hope, Sagacity, and Truth.

About this last one there is some hesitation.

"Wouldn't that mean we would *always* tell the truth, even about our secrets? Even to someone like Lord Henry?" Rose asks.

"We can't do that," Briar objects. "We should only speak the truth to people who share our cause."

"Well, we'd better leave truth out, then," says Rose.

"It's too bad," Briar responds, shaking her head. "It's in the knights' code. We'll just tell the truth whenever we can. I think we have enough now, don't you? We'll have to commit them to memory. And we'll need a secret signal or maybe a handshake, or something. Something we can always recognize or do, no matter where we are."

"A hand signal, maybe?" Jack asks.

"Something simple! Maybe like this," Rose proposes. She spreads the first two fingers of her hand apart in a *V*, with the rest tucked under. "*V* for valor!"

"And then we could use just those two fingers to shake hands! We would just shake fingers," Briar offers, "when we want to meet back in the tack room."

"But how will I know?" asks Jack. "I'll be at the other end of the village."

The girls look at each other. "We need a special signal for Jack," Briar acknowledges.

"Something he can see from far away. Can he see our attic window? It's high at the top of the castle keep, and it faces the drawbridge . . . What do you think, squire? If we hang our red blanket out the window, could you see it from outside the castle?"

"Don't know," Jack responds. "We'd have to try it."

"I'll sneak up and hang out the blanket," Rose says. "You can go with Jack and point out our window, and then we'll meet in the stables. All right?"

Without too much difficulty, the experiment is proved successful. Jack and Briar spot the window with the red blanket—and Rose's small arm, waving—high on the castle keep. Afterward, in the stables, the three Giant Killers meet again, congratulating themselves on their sagacity.

"Now to get down to real business," Briar says. "What about the giant?"

"We should figure out where he lives," says Jack.

"When Jerold spots him from the tower," Rose puts in, "he

comes from the direction of Cloud Mountain. He must live up there somewhere. But that's such a big mountain and such a long way away! He could live anywhere."

"Somebody'd have to track him. But how?" asks Briar. "None of us could do it. It would take a knight on horseback, and there's no telling how far it would be or how long he'd have to be gone for—if he ever came back."

"That's something we'll have to think about when we get older," Rose says. "Or *maybe* we could convince one of the knights to go?"

"How could we do *that?*" asks Jack.

"They'd just laugh at us," predicts Briar. "If they even listened to us at all. Besides, we'd be revealing our secret cause to the grownups. We should add that to our code of honor: no grownups. Agreed? They would ruin it."

"Agreed," say the others. "No grownups."

Midsummer's Eve arrives, and all the women of the court search the fields and glens for the special herbs to place beneath their pillows in order to bring on important dreams, perhaps dreams of one's future husband. Rue and vervain, trefoil and Saint John's wort, and roses, which can substitute for any other ingredient in a pinch. Lady Beatrice has collected and traded for a handful of each, and she gives some to Rose, repeating the proper instructions. Rose, in turn, gives some to Briar.

"I don't need this," Briar says, disgusted. "I'm never going to have a husband!"

"You never can tell," Rose responds.

"Well, I don't want to think about it."

"Me neither," Rose says, tossing the herbs aside. "I already know I'm going to have to marry whomever Father chooses, maybe some rich old king from a neighboring realm. I just hope he's not a scoundrel or a brute. Let's talk about something else."

"Do you think there will be a Maypole?" Briar says.

"There was last year. And mummers. Maybe they'll do the play of Saint George and the dragon. That's my favorite!"

"Do you suppose we can stay up tonight and watch the wakefire? Lady Beatrice says there will be spirits abroad!"

The girls' eyes sparkle, and they smile wordlessly to each other in perfect understanding. If there is a way, they will find it.

Slipping quietly through the gatehouse and across the drawbridge, they stroll through the village. There they find everything in a pleasant confusion. It is a day of rest from labor, and the scrawny, miserable villagers do their best to summon some holiday spirit as they go from house to house collecting wooden items and bones to burn in the bonfire. The air is filled with the aromas of baking, of savory stews and sizzling fowl. Though goods are scarce, those who have little share with those who have even less. Children are at play with hoops and sticks, riding barrels, and practicing on stilts. The elders sit together and look on, gossiping and nodding, chuckling at the children's antics.

Briar and Rose meander through the melee until they spot Jack with a cluster of other ragged children gathered around a spinning top. The girls flash the secret hand signal at him, and he trots over to them, flashing the signal back.

"Are we having a meeting, then?" he asks, *sotto voce*.

The girls realize that the holiday makes a perfect opportunity to slip away for a meeting. "Yes," answers Briar. "We'll meet you at the drawbridge just after supper, if we can. Will you come?"

"I'll try. If I'm not there by the time they ring vespers, don't wait for me."

Four hours later the girls have changed into their old, ruined clothes, their heads covered with scarves, their faces smudged with dirt. They are tiptoeing down the circular stairs from their attic room, hoping to evade detection but also sneaking just for the fun of it. There are numerous dangers to be avoided. The main difficulty is to get past the chapel, where the adults are gathered for their St. John's Eve vigil. As quiet as butterflies in flight, they take off their shoes and touch their toes to the cool stone floor, all the while trying to stay out of sight and keeping a sharp lookout.

At last they believe they are out of danger, and they run down the next flight of stairs. But they have picked up a tail; out of the shadows slips Lord Henry. His curiosity aroused by the girls' sneaking manner, he follows along some distance behind them, hoping to catch them in some misdeed. He stalks them out of the keep and into the courtyard. Meanwhile, he himself has been spotted and pursued. Elizabeth, Jane, and Lady Arabella also want to enjoy the evening's festivities, and when they see Henry slinking in the shadows, they immediately sense some intrigue going on. Like three curious cats, they pad on quiet feet after him.

Briar and Rose creep along the wall of the keep, then dash across the courtyard and hasten into the doorway of the kennels. There they stop to peer cautiously out and check behind them, spotting Henry in a moment.

The two girls, who frequent the animals' various dwellings at every opportunity, are familiar with all the ins and outs of the kennels, the stables, and the mews, as well as all the various back ways and hidden doors of the castle. They are prepared to lead Lord Henry on a merry chase. Briar pauses just long enough to be sure he has seen her, and then they disappear into the recesses of the kennels and go through the rear passageway, which leads to the stables. Finally, they peek back out the front door of the stables in time to see Henry entering the front door to the kennels where they have just been. Then they spy Lady Arabella, Elizabeth, and Jane following a little way behind Henry. Seeing that the chase is on, Rose and Briar spend the next half hour weaving in and out of doorways, skittering along dark corridors, and finally taking refuge in a long-disused hidden stairway. After some time, they feel it safe to come out. Seeing no sign of the others, they make for the spot near the drawbridge where they had arranged to meet Jack.

Lord Henry, having lost the trail, is set upon by Lady Arabella, Elizabeth, and Jane, who demand to know what he is about, sneaking around the castle like a thief.

"Never you mind!" he replies.

Lady Arabella, who will not be so easily deterred, says, "Oh, come on, Henry! Whatever you're after, why not let us help?"

Not usually prone to sharing anything with a gaggle of girls, he realizes that the four of them have a better chance of finding the fugitives than he does alone, and so he enlists their aid. Lady Arabella, though she seems to go along with him, is really alert for any opportunity to further her own plans to win Princess Rose's friendship. Elizabeth is already anticipating her moment of glory telling on Briar and Rose for whatever they are up to. Jane, too meek to make a decision of her own, simply copies the others as she always does. They split up and search all over the castle, while Briar and Rose have already escaped from it.

Jack finds Rose and Briar at the agreed-upon spot and, seeing that they have come in disguise, invites them to join in the games of the commoners' children. Since all the village children know one another, Jack introduces Briar and Rose as servants' children from the castle. At first the peasant children stare and point at

Briar's face. Briar is ready to run away, but Jack takes her by the hand and keeps her by his side, as if to announce that she is under his protection. Soon the two girls are accepted into the game of tag that is already in progress. The children are all playing at being fairies of various colors, and the one who is "it" is the evil gray fairy who chases them. The girls quickly forget about Lord Henry and the others as they lose themselves in the fun. The adults look on fondly, well aware of Princess Rose's identity but determined that her evening of freedom shall not be spoiled by having it revealed.

Meanwhile, Lord Henry and the three other girls, not thinking to go outside the castle and look among the commoners' children, wander about in growing frustration until the trail goes cold. Lady Arabella, Elizabeth, and Jane become distracted in the courtyard by the Morris dancers, who have bells jingling on their shins and handkerchiefs flying in their hands. The three girls have all but given up the chase when they notice Lord Henry slipping sur-reptitiously into the mews, and they wonder if he has picked up the trail once more. Quickly making their way through the crowd surrounding the dancers, they start shadowing him again. And so the chase continues.

Rose and Briar play happily until eventide; then they watch with Jack as the wakefires are lit and the cattle are blessed by lead-ing them sunwise around the fires. The streets are lit with lanterns on poles, and the three children join those garland-bedecked villagers who are wandering from one fire to the next.

Soon there is a competition among the boys as to who can jump the highest over the bonfire, and Jack lines up to try. He gets a running start and makes a mighty leap, but he gets one foot singed for his trouble. He cheerfully leaves it to the bigger boys, for the height of the highest leap is said to determine the height of the year's crops.

As daylight fades and bedtime approaches, Briar and Rose are missed. Lady Arabella, Elizabeth, and Jane are also missing. Lady Beatrice suspects that something is afoot. She is certain that Briar will lead Rose into some kind of trouble, and perhaps the other three girls as well. She has raised the alarm, and servants have been sent out to search for them.

Briar and Rose hear their names being called, and they look about for a place of safety. Just as Jack is leading them to hide behind a nearby cottage, a voice calls out, "Oh, *there* you are, my naughty little elflings! The dragons are looking for you. Would you like me to make you disappear?"

The girls see that it is Zane, the jester, and they laugh. "Yes, make us disappear!" they both say.

"Ah, but first you must answer my riddles!"

"How long will that take?" moans Briar. "We're in a hurry."

"Never fear! I'll give you three easy ones. Pay attention, now!"

Zane admonishes them, bopping each of them lightly on the head with his baton. "The first. Answer me this: What always weighs the same, no matter how big it gets?"

"I know that," says Briar. "It's a hole!"

"That's it—very good! Hmm. Now tell me this: What runs around the cow pasture but never moves?"

"A fence!" says Jack. "I've heard that one before!"

"So you think you have gotten the better of me. I'll give you a harder one. Let's see . . . How about this, my clever young rascals. What has a hole in it, but holds the weight of the world?"

Briar and Rose and Jack look at one another and shrug. "We're stumped," Rose admits.

"Come on, Zane, tell us," Briar says, "before somebody finds us!"

"Ah, well then, I'll take pity on you, since your poor brains are so feeble. What has a hole in it, but holds the weight of the world? A crown, my fine clotpoles, a crown! Now come with me and I'll show you the secret of invisibility."

"We want to get back into the castle and hide out in the stables."

"All right, here's the trick, elflings," whispers Zane. "You're rather big to disappear, so find someone bigger than you to hide behind—someone who's going your way—and stay in their shadow. It only takes a bit of practice. There you go. Poof! Disappear!"

Rose immediately spots a large woman near the edge of the

road, heading in the direction of the drawbridge. Rose falls in step on the far side of her. Briar attaches herself to a burly man while Jack, having no need to hide, keeps a lookout. The way is treacherous — the searching servants seem to be everywhere — but with a bit of skill, darting from person to person, shadow to shadow, the children gradually make their way undetected back through the gatehouse and into the castle courtyard. From there it is but a short dash to the stables, where it seems that everyone is out taking part in the celebrations.

They hurry to the tack room to convene the third meeting of the Giant Killers' club. But once again they have been observed. Lord Henry, still watching for the pair, catches sight of them slipping into the stables, and he sneaks in after them. Lady Arabella, Elizabeth, and Jane observe him on the move and follow along, tiptoeing into the stables behind him. They catch up with him outside the tack room. Seeing them, Henry puts his finger to his lips in a signal for quiet, and they all creep into the empty stall next door.

"We have to find out where he lives," they hear Briar saying. "There may be some way we could follow him and do it there."

"Yes. Maybe poison his food!" says Jack.

"But it must be such a long way away, all the way to the mountain, and we don't know how far up he goes," Rose says. "Besides, we could never keep up with him."

"No, but maybe he's worn a path. His footprints must be clear enough to follow," says Briar. "But you're right; it's awfully far. None of us have ever taken a journey like that. It could take days to get there, maybe even a week. We'd have to take all kinds of provisions, maybe even a packhorse or two. Nobody would let us."

The children sigh heavily. "But maybe when we're older, we could," says Jack. "Or maybe—"

"Maybe what?" Rose asks.

"I'm just thinking. Maybe we could poison the food he takes from here!"

"How would we do it?" Rose asks. "It would take an awful lot of poison to kill a giant."

In the stall next door, Henry and the girls look at one another, wide-eyed. Henry, without hesitating, bursts into the tack room and blurts, "You think you're going to kill the *giant?*"

Lady Arabella, Elizabeth, and Jane follow after him with gasps of astonishment.

"Who asked you?" Rose exclaims, near tears that their secret has been discovered. "This is our club, and we don't want you in it, so you can all stop following us and go away!"

Henry, ignoring her, says, "You can't go poisoning the giant's food! Suppose he doesn't eat enough to kill him. You'd just make him very sick, and very, very mad! He'd probably flatten the whole village, and maybe the castle too! Don't you think if it was that easy to get rid of him, they would have done it already?"

"Have you got a better idea?" asks Briar.

"Well, I wouldn't get us all killed, to begin with."

Lady Arabella's mind is working feverishly, trying to calculate a response that will be most likely to please Rose without seeming to approve of the preposterous venture. "Um . . . I'm sure it's very brave of you to even think of killing the giant, but please tell me you don't intend to really try it."

"Yes, we do!" exclaims Briar. "Maybe not today. Just someday, but we've got to start planning. We are the Giant Killers' club, and that's our only aim, to someday kill the giant."

"And if you thought about it for one minute," adds Rose, "you'd see that it's the only way to save the kingdom from that terrible old monster! The grownups have given up. Papa can't afford a whole big army. It's up to us now."

"That's ridiculous," Elizabeth insists, "and I'm telling!"

"Me too!" echoes Jane.

Lady Arabella turns on the two and warns, "If you do tell, then you're not my friends anymore!"

Elizabeth and Jane look as if they've been slapped by the older girl, and they close their mouths and stand back.

Lady Arabella has seen the belief in Rose's eyes, and figuring that it will cost her nothing to seem to go along with the princess, she says, "I want to join your club. I want to kill the giant too. What do I have to do to join?"

Briar, Rose, and Jack look at one another; they huddle in a circle for a whispered conference, then nod. "You may join," Rose announces, "if you take the oath and uphold our code of honor."

"Wait a minute," Lord Henry says. "You mean *he's* in your club? That peasant? I'm not joining if he's in it!"

Jack, who has recognized from the first that these other children must be nobles, hangs his head and is silent.

"This is Jack," Briar says, "and he is noble in spirit. He is one of us."

"Well, you'd better keep him away from me. Just make it clear that if I'm joining, I'm in charge."

"Nobody's in charge," Briar responds. "Everybody's the same."

"If I'm not in charge, I'm going to tell everyone what you're up to, and they'll never let you out of their sight again," Henry says, folding his arms.

At this, Briar, Rose, and Jack go into another huddle, which lasts for some minutes. Finally, the three stand before the others and Rose announces that they will all be allowed to join. But only with the understanding that anyone breaking the oath will face terrible torments and suffer the curse of the Giant Killers from that day forward.

"What is this oath, then?" demands Henry.

Rose clears her throat, puts her hand on her heart, and says, "We do solemnly swear on our lives to kill the evil giant, to stay true to our cause through thick and through thin, and to defend one another to the death.

"That's the oath," she pronounces, "if you have the courage to take it. You probably ought to think about it first."

"I'm not afraid to take it," insists Henry, "as long as everybody knows that I'm in charge."

Rose reports their decision that Lord Henry may consider himself in charge. This is not quite the same as saying that he is actually in charge, but Henry does not notice the difference, and he assumes a look of puffed-up pride.

Rose turns to Elizabeth and Jane. "What about you? You don't have to join, but if you ever speak of this to anyone else, you'll suffer unspeakable torments."

"Well, what if I don't want to swear 'on my life'?" says Elizabeth. "What if we aren't brave or stupid enough to try to kill the giant? What could *we* do anyway?"

"What can *you* do?" scoffs Rose. "Probably nothing! But if you can't do anything else, you can keep your mouths shut. Agreed?"

Jane and Elizabeth look to Lady Arabella, who lifts her chin and says, "Come on! I'm joining. Are you?"

The two girls are less afraid of the giant than of losing Arabella's patronage. They hold each other's hands for courage and nod in unspoken agreement.

"All right then," Rose says, pleasantly surprised. "A moment of silence."

The moment passes, and she says, "Now repeat after me . . ."

The oath is administered, the new initiates repeating the words with appropriate gravity if not the deepest conviction.

"And then there's the code of honor," Briar adds, and she goes down the short list of virtues that they've chosen as their guiding principles, with the others echoing them.

Finally, the secret hand signal and handshake are revealed. By now, Henry, Lady Arabella, Elizabeth, and Jane are beginning to join in the spirit of the thing.

"Maybe we could make up our own language!" offers Jane, this being the first original idea she has ever expressed in her life. Briar and Rose, who have always had their own private sign language, exchange glances, both subtly shaking their heads in the negative, signaling their agreement that they will not share their secret language with the others.

Henry, catching on to Jane's idea, says, "Yes. We ought to have a sign for danger."

"And maybe another sign for if the danger's passed?" Lady Arabella suggests.

The little group experiments a bit and settles on a pair of signals; then Henry says that it's time to discuss the giant.

"We ought to be finding out everything we can about him. We'll have to keep track of when he comes and what he takes and everything he says."

"We can tell you about the last time he came! We saw it all,"

Briar says. She and Rose quickly recount everything they observed on the giant's last raid, including the fact that he had carried off the magic harp from the royal treasury. The other children volunteer their own thoughts about the giant and his habits, and much discussion ensues.

"Couldn't we dig a deep pit, disguise it so he couldn't tell it was there, and make him fall into it?" says Elizabeth.

"We couldn't dig a pit deep enough, silly. Besides, how would we make him fall in it?" Henry asks.

"Maybe he could get struck by lightning?" Lady Arabella offers. "If we could just get him to come out during a thunderstorm."

Briar, Rose, and Jack come up with a few half-baked ideas of their own, only to give them up again, and the excitement wanes.

"Well, that's all I can think of for now," said Henry, beginning to lose interest. "You must know that we can't do much of anything until we're older. It would be suicide to even try."

"Yes," puts in Lady Arabella, "let's not do anything dangerous. We'll have to have a foolproof plan before we do anything, right?"

Elizabeth and Jane agree with this wholeheartedly as they back out of the room and turn to go.

Henry hesitates, then fires one last shot. "Just remember, *I'm* in charge now!" He smiles triumphantly and departs.

Lady Arabella flashes the secret Giant Killers' signal for Rose's benefit and follows the others out.

Left to themselves, Briar, Rose, and Jack wait silently until

Briar sticks her head out the door of the tack room and finally turns to say, "They're gone."

"Well . . ." breathes Rose. "Now what?"

"I say we invent a new secret signal," Briar responds, "one that's just for the three of us when we want a private meeting."

Jack laughs. "And we didn't tell them about the red blanket at the window signal, so we can still use that." They decide to use a circle, formed with the thumb and forefinger, as their private sign; then they consider other places to hold their meetings, finally settling on a storage shed behind the kitchen.

"Now we can go on the way we were before, and Henry can think he's in charge," says Rose.

"Well, at least there are more of us now to fight the giant," Briar observes.

"Do you think they'll really help?" Rose asks. "I wonder."

"But they took the solemn oath—on their lives!" Jack protests. "I could find you a whole bunch of my friends who would take the vow in a minute. And they would mean it! Only Lord Henry would never let them."

"Lord Henry would never have to know," says Rose, smiling.

"Could you really find so many who would want to join?" asks Briar. "Even with the danger?"

"They hate the giant," Jack declares. "He takes everything we have, an' we go hungry; then he smashes our houses an' anybody who is in them, just for spite. Nobody hates the giant more than us village folk."

Briar and Rose look at each other, communicating silently, nodding. Briar says, "Go ahead, then, Jack. Give the oath to all your friends, and all their friends too, if they're really sincere. We'll have a whole army of Giant Killers!"

Jack smiles. "Yes, Lady Briar."

"Just *Briar!*"

Night has fallen. Outside the stables, the children can hear the merrymakers laughing and shouting, and the servants still calling their names. The girls tell Jack of their plan to stay up and watch the wakefire all night. They invite him to join them, but Jack replies that his mother will be worried if he does not go home. He quickly takes his leave. Shortly thereafter Rose and Briar sneak out of the stables with all the secrecy and guile they are capable of.

"There you are!" Lady Beatrice's voice rings out behind them almost immediately. "I might have known you'd be leading her astray," she snarls to Briar, "when she should be in bed!"

"And look at you!" she exclaims to Rose. "Where did you get those ragged clothes? You're a fright! And your face is dirty! How can you be the prettiest princess with dirt on your face?"

"But Lady Beatrice—" Rose objects, or tries to.

"Don't 'but Lady Beatrice' me! Come with me now! Don't you

realize that there are evil spirits roaming about? The veil between this world and the next is very thin on Midsummer's Eve. You can't be too careful! Hurry, now!" She grabs each of them by an arm with a firm grip, propelling them along bodily, and she doesn't let go until they reach the foot of the circular stairs to their attic room.

"Now go on with you, and don't bother trying to sneak down again! I'll be standing right here."

Halfway up the stairs, Rose whispers, "This calls for desperate measures!"

"Yes!" Briar agrees. "On to the secret passage!"

Halfway up the stairs, the two miscreants had recently happened upon one of the castle's hidden doorways concealed in the staircase to their attic room. They had found that it opened into a dank, narrow passage, which they had not yet had the chance to explore fully. On their way up the stairs Briar borrows a candle from a wall sconce as Rose pushes on the wall next to it until the door gives way. Inhaling the smell of damp mold, the two girls enter the secret corridor that lies beyond.

"There might be a way to the outside here somewhere," Briar speculates. Closing the door behind them, they go along single file through the dark, ominous passageway, trying not to touch the slimy walls. They shiver as they brush aside cobwebs. Following some twists and turns, they carefully climb a flight of uneven stairs. This brings them to the last spot they had explored, where they had discovered a small peephole, just at the right height for a grownup to reach but too high for either of the girls. They hear the murmur of deep voices on the other side of the wall.

Briar sets the candle on the floor with care. "Scoot down," she says in hushed tones, "and let me sit on your shoulders."

"No. I want to go first!" Rose says.

"You went first last time," Briar says.

"But it was just a boring meeting of the counselors."

"Well, maybe it's just another boring meeting of the counselors, but it's my turn!"

"Oh, all right, but tell me everything you see," Rose insists.

The feat is accomplished with the ease of practice. Rose squats down while Briar gingerly clambers up to sit on Rose's shoulders, both of them pushing their hands against the wall for balance. Rose, using the strength of her legs and back, stands up so that Briar can see through the peephole.

"It's your father's counselors, all right," Briar whispers. "I think all of them are here."

"What are they saying?"

Briar turns her ear to the peephole and listens while Rose strains beneath her weight. Briar hears someone comment that the king and queen are still attending Bishop Simon's St. John's Eve vigil. Then the talk turns to the purpose of their meeting, which seems to be to discuss a demand for higher pay. The conference heats up as the counselors air their grievances. Several insist that the king can certainly afford to increase their pay, for he can always raise the Giant Tax. This degenerates into a squabble about the kingdom's finances.

"What is it?" Rose asks.

"Something about the royal treasury. I don't understand much. Wait a minute!" Briar's attention is arrested by the words ". . . and young Rose's loveliness will be a sure enticement for some wealthy king to join himself to our failing kingdom, even without a dowry. In fact, for a beauty like Rose, he should *pay* such a bride price as to turn around the dwindling fortunes of our beleaguered kingdom."

Another voice says, "Better yet, the entrancing Rose might be able to induce a powerful husband to send his own mighty army to deal with the giant once and for all."

There were sounds of approbation all the way around.

The first voice spoke up again. "And no one need ever know that Rose is not the true heir—"

Another voice silences the first. "Stop right there! You know it is death to speak of it! You endanger us all."

Briar gasps, not knowing which is more horrifying, hearing that Rose is not the heir, or the warning that to speak of it is death. Was Rose not the rightful daughter of the king? How terrible for her to find out! And death to speak of it! For both reasons, she decides on the instant that she can't tell Rose what she has heard.

"What? What is it? I can't hold you much longer!" Rose objects.

"Put me down, then," Briar says, her voice and her whole body shaking. Her mind is spinning. If Rose wasn't going to inherit the kingdom, who was? Was it such a terrible secret that even a court counselor would be put to death for speaking of it? What would happen to her if they knew that she had heard? She suddenly feels exposed and vulnerable, as if her very thoughts might show on her face and betray her. She clambers off Rose's shoulders, and afraid of what the candlelight might reveal in her own countenance, she quickly suggests that Rose should carry the candle.

"What did you hear? Come on, tell me!" Rose implores.

"Nothing. They just stopped talking, is all."

"Give me a turn, then. Let me listen."

"I can't. I feel a little dizzy. Let's go back. I think I want to go to bed now."

"But what about staying up til dawn to watch the wakefire? I'm sure we could sneak back out if we tried. Lady Beatrice isn't going to stand down there *all* night!"

"I'm tired. I just want to go to bed. C'mon, let's go. This place is giving me the creeps."

Rose sighs, just loud enough to signal her frustration, and picks up the candle. "All right, then, we'll go back, but next time we find something interesting, I get the first turn!" She leads the way, Briar following, brushing away sudden tears. Rose is not the heir! Briar must carry the dreadful secret now, even though it means lying to her bosom friend, a lie that has already come between them. She tries to lock away the awful truth in her heart, hoping that in time she can forget it.

The girls settle into bed that night, neither wanting to put Lady Beatrice's herbs beneath her pillow to bring on dreams of what may come. The roses and rue and trefoil lie scattered on the floor, waiting in vain to tell of a future that no one imagines.

PART TWO

THREE YEARS LATER

Chapter One

DEEP IN THE ENCHANTED FOREST, far from the edge of town, a waterfall cascades down a wall of rock, a fine spray blowing into the contorted face of a twelve-year-old girl. She sits on a rock on the shore of the clear lagoon, trying to make out her reflection in the shallow water. The face that looks back at her reminds her, as if she needed reminding, that she is not like other girls—and never will be. Just now, it is not the protruding brow or the sagging eyelid or the crooked nose alone that she observes, but the grimace of sadness written there.

Even so, this glade is her place of comfort and strength, and she looks up as she listens to the music of the falling water. And to something else. She perceives an otherworldly harmony in the air, which only she can hear, something like harps and tiny bells and lovely voices singing. It lifts her spirits as nothing else can. Briar has come again to the one enchanting spot where she can feel relief or joy. It has become her habit to take flight to this refuge whenever her troubles become too much to bear.

Like today. She has long been accustomed to teasing from the other children or to being blamed or slighted or ignored by adults, but she has no defense against the special torments Bishop Simon keeps in store for her. Though she has learned, by feigning to be meek and slow-witted, to evade much of the clergyman's more predictable wrath, today's offense was not immediately obvious to her. He had been pontificating on the seven deadly sins. He had made the children repeat them after him: wrath, avarice, sloth, pride, lust, and envy, and just when he got to gluttony, she had looked up at him, at his great girth, and looked straight into his eyes, unthinking. He had caned her for insolence.

She is calm now, the tears having been dissolved away by the spray from the waterfall, and in the beauty of the music she is moved to sing. Her voice wavers at first, then strengthens and soars to match the magical notes that fill her ears, and the birds hush their singing to listen.

Someone else listens too. Catching the melody from some distance away, someone comes closer to hear, and hiding in the thick undergrowth of the forest, someone watches with avid eyes as Briar begins to dance. She sways and twirls, her body expressing both sadness and joy, entwined together in wild abandon, and still she sings. Someone watches on. Listens on. Time seems to stand still while the girl turns her most heartfelt emotions into song and movement. At last she steps slowly and lights on a tussock of grass. She feels at peace, yet she has the familiar feeling that there is something, some idea or realization, just beyond her reach.

"What is it?" she says aloud. "What?"

She hears only the enchanting music, fainter now, like a sweet whispering, and so she stares up into the clouds and listens, hardly aware of the lingering pain in her back. Someone's eyes watch her for a minute more, and then someone slips silently away.

It is a long time before Briar allows herself to think of going back to the castle. The shadows grow slowly longer. The afternoon light makes the great rock wall glow as if lit from within. Finally, driven by hunger, she leaves her secret haven and follows the path toward home, hoping she doesn't have to face anyone. When she reaches the courtyard, she hangs her head so as not to meet anyone's eyes, but she feels a sudden tap on her shoulder and looks up. There stands the jester in his ridiculous particolored costume, bopping her lightly on the head with his baton.

"Zane! Go away. You'll draw too much attention to me."

The jester looks over his shoulder, then over his other shoulder in an exaggerated manner. He salutes her and says in a loud whisper, "I spy no dangerous enemies as yet, Captain! Let us retreat before we are besieged by the goblin hordes!"

Briar shows the hint of a smile, then takes his hand and makes straight for the kennels. There they are greeted by a horde of happy dogs, among them the faithful greyhound Toby. Toby jumps up on Briar, a paw on each of her shoulders, and licks her face affectionately. She scratches behind his ears until he calms, and she and Zane spread their attention to the other dogs until they finally become calmer too. At last Briar flops cross-legged onto the floor. The jester salutes her again, twirls in a circle, and flops down next to her.

"Now what will it be, my captain?" he says. "A joke? A story? A bit of juggling? Or shall I just do this?" He reaches over and puts his two forefingers at the corners of her mouth, spreading them wide to make her grin.

Briar shakes her head free of him and says, "I don't want anything like that."

"In that case, how about some victuals? Art thou hungry?"

"I am hungry. I missed supper. You would get me something to eat?"

"Of course! We are sorely outnumbered, and the odds are against us. We must stick together!"

"Zane?"

"Yes, my captain?" he responds, saluting.

"You're a peach."

"Yes, my captain!"

"Would you find Rose too? And send her here?"

"At once, sir! Could you just give me a small smile before I go on this dangerous mission?"

Briar can't help but offer him a smile.

Zane smiles back. "I believe we have the enemy on the run, sir!" he says as he leaves.

A few minutes later Master Twytty, the kennel master, comes in and, finding Briar with the dogs, says, "Lucky for us you've dropped in, my lady. Old Toby here has been wanting his stomach rubbed, and you're the only one he'll allow to do it!"

As he looks on, Briar makes a fuss over Toby and gives him an extra-long tummy rub. A brief time later, Rose appears with a bag stuffed full of good things to eat. The dogs crowd around her excitedly, snatching at the good-smelling bag and making Rose afraid. And so she suggests that they remove to the tack room in the stables next door. There Rose sits down beside Briar. "Are you all right?" she asks, her eyes full of sympathy.

"I will be," comes the answer.

"Someday Bishop Simon will roast in those eternal flames he's always telling us about."

"Won't he be surprised? I almost wish I could be there to see it."

"I've been looking for you for hours. Where were you?"

Briar, who for reasons she can't articulate, has never told Rose about her secret place by the waterfall, merely says, "I was in the woods."

"You should have seen Bishop Simon after you left. He was so angry I thought he would combust."

"Well, what else can he do to me? I'm becoming quite used to his beatings. Wouldn't he be stymied if I got to liking them?"

"At least it doesn't happen very often."

"That's easy for you to say! You've never had a beating in your life. No one beats a beautiful princess."

"I'm sorry," Rose says, not meeting Briar's eyes, "but I can't help it, you know."

"I know you can't," Briar agrees, but in her heart, a little more bitterness grows. Sometimes, when she is very hurt and angry, a memory comes unbidden to her of a disembodied voice saying *Rose is not the heir,* but she quickly squashes the memory down deep and tries, yet again, to forget it.

The girls are quiet for a time while Briar makes short work of the bread and cheese Rose brought. Then they have a long talk concerning what they would like to do to Bishop Simon and bad names they would like to call him.

"I'll tie him up and let him starve while I eat in front of him," Briar says. "The dog-hearted maggot-pie!"

"He's a paunchy, onion-eyed footlicker!" Rose adds vengefully.

"He's a vain, puking gudgeon!" Briar says.

"He's a surly, toad-spotted miscreant!"

"A churlish maltworm!"

"A villainous, boil-brained measle!"

This cheers Briar up enough that she feels she is ready to face the world again, so they dust themselves off and decide to go and see Hilde about some salve for Briar's bruises.

On the way, they encounter Lady Arabella and her followers, Elizabeth and Jane. Lady Arabella smiles engagingly at Rose and invites her to join them for a game of backgammon in the great hall. Rose, having lately been harassed by Lady Beatrice into accepting a few such invitations from Lady Arabella, has found the girl to be surprisingly good company. She is skilled at games and laughs easily. Despite the many rebuffs Rose has given her, she calmly extends the hand of friendship over and over again. And though Rose has little use for Elizabeth and Jane, she at least finds them pleasantly respectful. With them, she is the leader, the smart one whose ideas are followed. Responding at last to Lady Arabella's proffered friendship, Rose has begun to question some of her own assumptions about the girl. And so Rose offers Lady Arabella an affable response to her invitation, but replies that she and Briar have already made plans.

"Another time, then?" asks Lady Arabella.

"Yes, another time," responds Rose, and so they part.

"I notice she never invites me to her games," Briar says.

"I'm sure she meant both of us!" Rose assures her. "Do you think Lady Manners would be rude enough to stand there and invite me and not you?"

"I think she might, yes."

Rose, trying to be fair, says, "You just don't give her a chance. She's not so bad. You should get to know her."

"No, thank you," Briar mutters, and the matter is dropped.

At the top of Hilde's tower, they knock tentatively. There are strange noises behind the door, too loud to be any of the small animals Hilde leaves running loose in her quarters. Finally, Hilde opens the door, looking flushed and disheveled, a butterfly net in her hand.

"Ah, it's you," she says. "You've arrived in the nick of time. Come in!"

The girls enter Hilde's inner sanctum and find it in a terrible state. Mice, rabbits, hedgehogs, and a panic-stricken tortoise are scrambling at full speed all about the floor, bed, and table. Bottles, jars, and vials have been knocked over, and some lie broken on her table. Her carefully sorted herbs, usually put away in her special cupboard with all the separate compartments, are scattered and mixed up in a mess of enormous proportions. And the wildlife climb up the compartments as if they are on rungs of a ladder in what appears to be a desperate attempt to get away from something—the girls cannot immediately perceive what. As Hilde shuts the door behind them, they see the something speed by them in a blur just above the floor. It looks to be a very small, reddish infant with wings and barely discernible horns and a tail.

"What is it?" cries Rose.

"An imp!" answers Hilde. "It just hatched. And here I thought I had a griffin's egg! We've got to get him out of here. Take these," instructs Hilde, handing them each a net similar to her own. "See if you can catch him—but watch out if you do! That little tail can deliver a nasty sting."

Briar and Rose immediately station themselves at opposite sides of the table while Hilde takes a position by the door. After a few tense minutes and many near misses, Rose plops her net directly over the little creature and catches it in mid-flight, whereupon it immediately lets loose the loudest, most aggravating wail the girls have ever heard. The other creatures stop their mad race and freeze.

"Hold that net down! Don't let him escape. I've got to mix up a quick potion. Let's see, angelica, wormwood, basil—where did the spotted thistle go? Oh, dear, is this the arnica or the henbane? I *must* find the garlic!" While Hilde quickly mashes the ingredients with a mortar and pestle, the girls examine the angry imp baby as he struggles to get away. He is rather adorable despite his disgraceful behavior.

"You'd better hurry up, Hilde!" calls Briar. "I think he's eating the net!"

Hilde hurries over with a bowl of something, saying, "I hope this works. I had to use snail oil instead of snake." Then she dribbles the substance liberally over the captive imp, while reciting,

> *"Calm and sweet,*
> *Head to feet,*
> *Transformation now complete.*
> *Abracadabra!"*

The imp stops its noise and begins to gurgle happily. Hilde removes it from the net and tosses it out the window.

"That should hold it for a few days, by which time it will be far away from here!"

"But it was so cute!" Rose protests.

"And you just threw it out the window!" cries Briar.

"It can fly," her godmother comments drily. "Make yourselves useful, and help me clean up this mess. Don't touch the herbs! I'll have to sort them all out again. And my alchemy experiment is ruined. I'll never change straw into gold at this rate."

Rose and Briar stoop and begin the long, arduous process of picking up and setting things to rights. It is nearly evening before they have restored all but the scattered herbs to order.

"I'll have to replace half of these," Hilde complains. "Perhaps tomorrow afternoon I can take the two of you out to gather fresh ones for my collection. Come to me after the midday meal. I will account for you to the queen—

"Briar, you're moving very stiffly," sharp-eyed Hilde adds. "Have you gotten into trouble with Bishop Simon again?"

Briar nods wordlessly. Hilde removes a small jar from a drawer in the cupboard, takes the lid off, and sniffs it. "Still good," she announces. "Try this on your bruises—but sparingly! I calculate it might have certain side effects if used too liberally."

"Like what?" Briar asks, taking the jar.

"It might turn your skin thick and leathery and could numb all feeling where you spread it too heavily."

"You mean permanently?"

"That's a good question. I can't look it up in my book of spells. I invented the recipe myself."

Briar looks at the jar, thinking she might be willing to take her chances with the side effects being permanent, when Hilde continues, "Oh, and it's got essence of pond scum in it. It might turn your skin green. And warty. Maybe for an hour, maybe forever. You're old enough to decide if you want to take the chance."

"Thank you," says Briar. "I think." With that, the girls make their departure, and later, at bedtime, Rose asks Briar how much of the magic salve she wants spread on her back.

"All of it," comes the reply.

"Are you sure?"

"I'm sure. If I get the side effects, then Bishop Simon can't hurt me anymore. That's worth turning my back green. And warty. I'll never be beautiful anyway."

"But your back—"

"Go ahead. Make it numb. Make it green. Just do it."

It is morning. Amber light shines through the solitary window of the small attic space where Briar and Rose rest, and it illumines their sleeping faces. Briar awakens and, giving Rose a poke on the shoulder, says, "Wake up, lazybones!"

Rose's eyes flicker open. Immediately she turns to Briar and says, "Roll over. Let me see!"

Briar turns her back to Rose and lifts her hair. Rose peeks under her shift and sees bright chartreuse skin. With warts. She pokes Briar's back and asks, "Can you feel that?"

"Feel what?" Briar responds.

"It's happened! The side effects. Just like Hilde said!" Covering Briar's back quickly, as if someone might see, Rose asks, "How are you?"

"I'm just fine!"

A short while later they take their places in the chapel. While Bishop Simon conducts the morning service, Briar tries to suppress a smug little smile. During breakfast, Rose reminds her in hushed tones that they don't know how long the effects will last. Briar thinks only that she has become invulnerable. She is almost tempted to try to provoke Bishop Simon into another beating, just to enjoy the fact that he cannot hurt her. She sits through the morning's lessons, itching to call out the answers to the questions the clergyman poses to the class. Finally, thumbing through a book on geometry, he calls on one of the older pupils with a difficult question, hoping to embarrass the boy when he's unable to answer.

"Calculate the area of a triangle with a base of seven cubits and a height of three cubits, and state the formula," he demands.

Briar, who makes it a habit to listen in on the more advanced lessons to the older students, knows the answer immediately. Without thinking, she blurts out, "The area is half of the base times the height! Half of twenty-one is ten point five square cubits!"

Bishop Simon looks down at the book to check the answer, then slams the book closed and looks up at her wrathfully. "There is nothing so terrible as a *cheat!*" he thunders. "What manner of trickery or magic is this? Admit your guilt now, quickly!"

"But I'm not guilty! Honestly I'm not," Briar says. "I just . . . I just spent a lot of time studying last night." Briar knows that it sounds like a lie, and in fact it is. But she hopes it sounds more believable than telling him she is really the smartest person in the class, which is the actual truth.

"Cheat!" he bellows, getting red about the face. "Was yesterday's chastisement not enough for you?"

Briar, all too aware that the effects of Hilde's magic salve might wear off at any moment, decides that there is no safe answer to this, and she keeps silent. She cannot bear to think of getting another beating, and she immediately regrets her outburst. But Bishop Simon is relentless. Picking up his cane, he flexes his arm and snarls, "You will observe, class, what happens when people are caught cheating! Come here and take your punishment, wretch!"

Briar knows that she has no choice but to obey. Immediately, Bishop Simon lifts his cane and rains down blows on her back. But as he strikes her, her back feels nothing. All she feels is the humiliation and injustice of being struck and punished for no reason, and that is painful indeed. But she does not cry, and she does not cry out. Bishop Simon, getting no satisfaction from his futile exertion, finally slows to a stop, and glaring at her with his small, piggy eyes, he banishes her from the classroom.

Only too glad to leave, she stands outside the door and makes an effort to calm herself, closing her eyes and breathing slowly in and out. She waits there until school is over and Rose emerges.

Not sure whether to offer her friend sympathy or congratulations, Rose asks, "Did it work? Did you feel anything?"

Briar does not want to explain her feelings, so she merely says, "No. I didn't feel a thing," and quickly changes the subject. "Let's go eat!"

"Absolutely!" replies Rose, and they take a detour to the great hall, where a sumptuous midday meal is being served. The harvest has been a good one this year, and the giant has not yet come to make his demands, so for a short time, meals are plentiful. The girls share a trencher heaped up with beans, squash, and carrots, until, well satisfied, they excuse themselves and make their way up to Hilde's aerie.

"Ah, here you are, my dearies," she greets them. "We're to go herb picking today. Come. Everything's arranged." Hilde furnishes each of them with a wicker basket and leads them back down through the castle proper, out through the gatehouse. They make their way through the village, where Princess Rose is lovingly watched over by the villagers, who are proud of her beauty and enchanted by her sweet innocence. Once free of the castle and village, the girls' mood lifts, for the air is fresh and sweet and there is no one to observe or hamper them. It is an idyllic afternoon. As they proceed down an overgrown lane through the forest, Hilde leads them in a number of choruses of "The Maid and the Goose." It is a charming old ballad in which a goose falls in love with a maid and argues with her through thirteen verses that she should marry him rather than cut his head off and have him for dinner. In the end he fails to convince her, and in three-part harmony, they cheerfully sing the final chorus: "And she choked on his meat and died, tra-la. She choked on his meat and died."

By this time they have reached a wide glade, a perfect place to look for herbs. Hilde sets the girls to hunting for the little daisy-like flowers of chamomile while she searches for mint and mugwort and anything else of interest. When they have examined the whole glade and collected what they can, they move on through the forest to a broad hillside meadow by a rock face riddled with small caves. From there they can see the castle and most of the village. At this distance the village appears tranquil and charming, with no hint of the terrible toil and struggle of its people; their cottages have become more dilapidated, and they seem to grow thinner and more ragged as each year passes. But for this lovely afternoon, such thoughts are far away. The girls are engrossed in their tasks of looking for herbs, happy to be free of the castle and all its constraints and cares.

"What do you use mugwort for?" Rose asks Hilde after a while.

"It repels insects and wild animals. It must be boiled slowly into a potion."

"Can we help you make it? I'd rather learn that than more etiquette or needlepoint."

"Oh, yes, dearies. I'd say a basic knowledge of herbs and their uses should be part of a royal education. Even a queen should know that sage wards off evil. You never can tell when you'll need such knowledge."

"What is chamomile for?" Briar asks.

"It induces sleep. Comes in very handy sometimes," Hilde says, putting her arm around Briar and giving an affectionate squeeze. Briar takes in these lessons as naturally as food or drink or sunshine, for she looks up to her godmother and wants to emulate her in every way. Hilde is the one adult in Briar's life who acts as if she adores the girl exactly as she is, and that makes for a powerful bond indeed. Even Rose has noticed that Hilde has a soft spot in her heart for Briar, but she tries not to resent it.

The three make their way slowly across the hillside, foraging and talking desultorily under the cobalt sky. Their fingers are stained green from picking. Their baskets are slowly filling up. The hot sun shines down on their heads while they listen to bird-calls and swat away insects. Finally, Hilde signals them to halt, cocking her head to one side and putting her finger to her lips for silence. Suddenly she looks up. "It's too quiet! The birds have stopped chirping. Even the insects are silent." She pauses, then exclaims, "The giant's coming! I hear his footsteps! Quick, we must hide! Into a cave! Over this way!"

Briar and Rose do not move at first, frozen with fear, but Hilde gives them each a push, and then another, until they start to run. She shoves them into the first cave she comes to, and, seeing that the cave is quite deep, she takes the girls by their hands and goes back as far as there is light to see. They hear the footsteps more loudly now. The two girls can't tell if the earth is quaking or if it is their own bodies shivering with fright as they imagine how easily the giant's feet could trample them. His steps come closer and closer, and then his feet, in his cuffed boots, are visible just in front of the opening of the cave. They hear loud sniffing noises, and the giant, talking softly to himself, says, "I smell *human! Cursed* if I don't!" Then, louder, "Come on out, you! Come out and face your doom! Ha ha ha!" He gives a mighty stomp, shaking the earth and causing small rocks to come loose around the terrified girls. They huddle together and stifle the urge to scream.

"Lily-livered, eh?" the giant bellows, and he stomps once more for good measure. There is a prolonged, tense silence. Then, crouching down on the side of the hill, he begins to sniff among the rock formations.

As he sniffs, Hilde and the girls inhale his odor, which is so noxious as to suggest that he left off bathing in the previous decade. Hilde and the girls are barely breathing. As they hear the giant's sniffing coming closer, they inch farther and farther back into the darkness and crouch down behind a large boulder. Finally, the entrance to the cave is blocked by the giant's nose and mouth, and he thunders, "Aha! I smell you now, and I'm going to squash you till your guts come out! Ha!" He sticks his hand into the entrance of the cave and reaches back as far as his arm will admit him, his fingers curling and uncurling, grasping thin air. Briar smothers a gasp as one of his fingers grazes her shoulder. The three all back up even farther into the utter darkness behind them, fearing at any moment that they might step into a hole or fall into a pit. Hilde whispers to the girls to stop. Setting down her basket, she draws something out of the leather pouch attached to her waist. It is a black powder, which she rubs thoroughly all over her hands. "Stand back," she commands, and she clears her throat and pronounces an incantation.

> *"When circumstances grow too frightening,*
>   *Change this powder into lightning!"*

With that, a mighty clap of thunder is heard, and lightning bolts shoot out of Hilde's hands, striking the giant's grasping fingers with a jolt of searing white heat, filling the air with smoke and the smell of singed flesh. The giant lets out a yelp that is heard all the way to the castle, and he pulls his hand out of the cave so fast that he falls on his backside.

Purple with rage, the giant scrambles to his feet and cries out, "Sting me, will you? Canker blossom! I'll teach you your last lesson!" He stomps his foot down on top of the cave opening until he has dislodged a landslide of stones and boulders over its entrance. "Now you can starve, slowly, in the dark! Ha ha ha!" he bellows, and inside the cave, they hear his muffled voice.

In the sudden darkness, Hilde's hands, still glowing from the just-released lightning, give off enough light for them to see dimly.

Terribly frightened, Rose asks, "What do we do now?"

"Yes, what?" cries Briar.

"Calm down, dearies," comes the reply. "Let us be still and breathe deeply and think. Thank all the saints I had my lightning powder with me for emergencies. My hands will glow for maybe half an hour now, so we've got some time. Let's see . . . We can't get out the way we came. There may be another entrance somewhere in the other direction. Now, if we can only look for it without getting lost." Hilde stoops, picks up a charred stone, and draws a big X on the cave wall. "Here, dearies, place your left hands on the wall of the cave, like mine, and keep them there no matter what, unless I say otherwise. We're going to follow this wall and see where it takes us. Come, quickly."

Outside the cave, the giant, his burnt fingers in his mouth, kicks the rocky hillside once more in a rage, then cries, *"Aargh!"* and becomes twice as angry about the self-inflicted pain in his toes. He stomps away toward the castle, looking for something to smash. He easily uproots a tree taller than he is, breaks the branches off the trunk, and drags it along behind him.

High in the castle watchtower, Jerold has spotted the giant and rings the massive warning bell. King Warrick takes a moment to stand behind his throne, his face in his hands. His counselors will be waiting for him, and he will have no choice but to climb up to the wall walk, try to negotiate with the rapacious giant, and give in to his demands. Of course, the king will never surrender his secret cache of food and money, but still it pains him to have to give away so much that could otherwise have made him so rich. He even spares a little pity for his peasants, who have been so poor for such a long time. His counselors have told him that the villagers grow increasingly restive about the Giant Tax, and ominous murmurings have been reported in the streets. The king shakes his head. He will not think about that now. He straightens his crown and mounts the stairs to the wall walk.

At that very moment comes the furious giant, thirty feet high and looking to unleash his pent-up wrath. He steps into the moat and, lifting the tree over his head like a cudgel, slams it down onto the castle wall. Stones and mortar crumble and fall into the courtyard, raining death and destruction on those below. Though the king is unharmed, two men lie crushed by the rubble, and many more are injured. It's all the king can do not to turn and run, but instead he calls for aid for the fallen men, then commands that the usual offerings be brought forth — and quickly! Below, in the courtyard, men come with stretchers and bandages to tend to the injured and evacuate the area. The giant, peering through the ruined wall, snorts and says, "Peasants! Bah! There are always plenty more!" He throws his bag and his purse over what is left of the wall and cries, "*Fill them!* Hurry, before I smash something else!"

Soon parades of people come with sacks, wagons, and carts of goods, loading them into the giant's bag. Their faces are lined with grief, for they know their own families will go without. A dozen of the king's men drag chests of gold from the treasury and dump them into the giant's purse. The three bravest villagers deliver three frightened head of cattle to him, then turn and run away. Meanwhile the giant leers through the hole he has made in the wall, shouting, "More! More!" as people scurry around in terror. As has become his habit, the giant's last demand is for the king to give him his crown. He has learned that the king will offer some special prize from him in trade rather than give it up. This year he is not disappointed, for King Warrick offers him a very special hen — a hen that lays golden eggs! The giant demands a demonstration before he agrees. He knocks down more of the castle wall so that he can put his head in and watch. The king on the wall walk shouts, "Lay!" and the hen complies with a pure golden egg.

"Ahh! I will have it!" roars the giant. He reaches in, taking the hen's cage carefully in his two-foot-long fingers, and tucks it inside his doublet. With that, he has finally been appeased. He ties his purse to his belt, hauls his bag of plunder over his shoulder, and turns to retrace his steps back to the distant mountain, leading the cattle along behind him. On his way out of town he kicks down several of the villagers' cottages for good measure.

Back inside the cave, the light from Hilde's hands has grown dim as she and Rose and Briar have come to a dead end, and they are making their way back to the point they started from. At last they find the X that Hilde scratched on the cave wall, and they stop to confer.

"All right," Hilde says. "Don't be discouraged. We'll try following the other wall." Switching her hand to the opposite wall, she instructs the girls to do the same and follow her. And so they set off again.

"I can hardly see your hands," Rose says, worried. "We're going to be in the dark soon. What will we do then?"

"We'll continue just as we are and go on by feel. There's got to be another entrance here somewhere. There's fresh air coming from this direction. I can smell it!"

The girls try to take courage from this as they listen nervously for noises that might indicate that they are not alone in the cave. As utter darkness overtakes them, Briar, who is last in line, reaches out to hold on to Rose's belt, startling Rose so that she gives a little cry and turns around, letting go of the wall.

"It's all right!" Briar reassures her. "It's just me. I want to hold on to you."

"Where are you?" Rose calls out.

Hilde says, "Wait! I smell—" Before she can finish her sentence, there is a great rush of noise, and suddenly they are surrounded by a cloud of flying bats. The girls scream and crouch down with their arms over their heads, but they soon realize that none of the bats are touching them. They stay huddled on the floor of the cave and wait it out, until finally the bats seem to have gone and all is quiet.

"Bats," says Hilde. "I smelled bats. Rose? Briar? Are you all right? Where are you?"

"Here," they answer. "Where are you?"

"Stretch your hands out and come toward my voice. It's good that we found bats. That means there must be an entrance nearby. In fact, I think I see a little light up ahead."

They muddle around blindly for a while until they have found one another's hands; then Hilde leads them carefully toward the tiny scrap of light, which does indeed prove to be an opening.

"Oh, thank goodness!" Rose exclaims.

"Hurrah for Hilde!" Briar adds. "We're saved!"

The girls want to run forward, but Hilde cautions them to stay well back. "I'm going out to look around and see if the giant is returning," she warns them.

"I hate that giant!" Rose says. "He's a monster and a brute! I can't wait until we—"

Briar yanks Rose's hand and squeezes it tightly in warning, and Rose, suddenly mindful that Hilde is listening, adjusts what she was going to say. "I mean, I hope he chokes on all that food!"

No sooner has Hilde gone out to explore than Briar says, "You almost gave us away!"

"Sorry. I wasn't thinking. We've managed to keep the club a secret for all this time. This is the closest we've ever gotten to the giant. Much too close! Wait till we tell the others!"

Briar and Rose confer over this until Hilde returns to the cave, out of breath, apprising them that the giant is swinging toward a more southerly route and will likely miss them. As they retreat well into the tunnel, they can hear the distant pounding of his footsteps. They get louder as he comes nearer, and then they sound farther and farther away. The little party breathes more easily and creeps out of the cave, drinking in the fresh air and daylight. The danger finally being over, Briar and Rose recover their composure quickly. "Just think what a story we'll have to tell!" Rose says.

They come upon one of the giant's footprints, marveling at the proportions. "Look!" says Briar, placing her own foot down next to it, "I'm a bug!"

"Come. We must get back to the castle straightaway," Hilde warns. "They'll be worried about us."

"We lost our baskets in the cave when the bats came through!" bemoans Briar.

"We'll have to leave them. We're lucky to be going back with our skins!"

And with that, they head off for home.

Some time later they arrive at the castle, where all is chaos and woe. All able-bodied men have been conscripted to aid in the repair of the castle wall. Many are at work building scaffolding or hauling the big fallen stones back into place, working under the master mortar maker or the master mason. Some carry water or bring carts of sand and lime for the mortar. All will be working as long as there is light to see by and will start again at dawn, and on and on for as long as it takes to rebuild the wall. It is backbreaking work, but they are used to it. Half their harvest is gone, but they are used to that too. There is nothing for them to look forward to but more of the same, and they are used to it. But in their desperation, they ask themselves, *How much more can be borne?*

Chapter Two

MOTHER MUDGE LEANS OUT over her half-door, passing the time with her oldest friend, Granny Beasely. "They say poor Mrs. Dunlop is inconsolable," Granny says dolefully. "She's taken to her bed!"

"Aye," says Mother Mudge. "And her whole sickly brood are in a bad way. I don't know how they'll manage without the man of the house. None of 'em are fit to work in the fields. The Greers and the Wallaces are just as bad off. You'd think the king would do something for 'em, after the giant's gone and killed their menfolk. All he's done is raise the Giant Tax again."

"We neighbors will have to look out for each other. That's always the way of it. I can spare some beans for Mrs. Dunlop's soup, and a few others can pitch in. They'd starve waiting for the king to help them."

Just then the baker's wife, scraggly and careworn, comes up to join them. "Ah, me," she says.

"What's the matter, Agatha?"

"Why it's old William, the freeholder, and his whole family. They're giving up on the place altogether and movin' on. Can't make a livin' here, what with the giant an' all. Can't sell his land, as there's no one who can afford to buy it, so he's just walkin' away with the family and the shirt on his back. Most of us in the village wish we could do the same, but bein' bound to the king, we can do nothin' but make the best of things. It is our lot in life, more's the pity."

The other women moan softly in agreement. Mother Mudge looks thoughtful for a time, then says in a voice just above a whisper, "P'raps there's a limit to how much folks can bear! And the bishop, he's no comfort to the afflicted. He just tells us that it's all the fault of our own wickedness. Imagine saying such a thing to the bereaved! I know every family in this village, and I hear things. There's trouble brewin'! P'raps the king should pay more attention to the sufferin' of his people."

Granny Beasely and Agatha nod sagaciously, but Jack comes along, just in from working in the fields, and they quickly drop the subject. Mother Mudge asks Jack if he's hungry for a little pottage, and Granny Beasely and Agatha say farewell and move on.

Jack is tired and hungry after hours of backbreaking work, but he barely pauses long enough to wash his face and hands. Then he gulps down the pottage and goes on his way, walking through the little village to the castle, as he usually does about this time, to look for the Giant Killers' signal. He gazes up at the topmost window of the keep and spots the old signal for a meeting, the red blanket hanging from the window. He and Briar and Rose have managed to maintain the utmost secrecy for their private meetings of the original Giant Killers' club for the past three years.

Occasionally other meetings include Lord Henry, Lady Arabella, Elizabeth, and Jane, but usually it's only Jack, Briar, and Rose who convene in the storage shed behind the kitchen.

There are scores more youngsters of Jack's acquaintance who have taken the solemn oath to uphold their ideals and kill the giant. His neighbor, Arley, and Arley's little sister, Bridget, were the first to join, their eyes filled with zeal and their hearts full of hope. They spread the word to Dudley and Jarrett, Bertha and Quentin, Maddox and Emma and Marian, and they have spread the word to others, until every last child in the village over nine years of age has taken the oath of the Giant Killers and can proudly recite their code of honor. Jack acts as their secret representative and reports back any new developments to Arley and Bridget, who spread the word to Dudley and Jarrett, Bertha and Quentin, Maddox and Emma and Marian, and all the others. And so it goes, all unperceived by the adults around them.

Jack makes his way to the stables first, as they are closest. If this meeting is to include Lord Henry, Lady Arabella, Elizabeth, and Jane, they will be there, or if it is a private one, Briar and Rose will be waiting at the storage shed farther on. Knocking the Giant Killers' secret knock, three hard knocks and four soft ones, Jack is admitted to the tack room, where the larger party is already assembled.

"Did anyone see you?" inquires Briar.

"I don't think so," Jack replies, shutting the door behind him.

"So what is this great revelation you found out about the giant?" Lord Henry quizzes Rose. "I'm dying to hear it."

"It's just this," she responds. "He has a terrific sense of smell. We were hidden inside a cave and he still smelled us. If we're ever going to sneak up on the giant, that might be important to know."

"Sneak up on the giant? What good will that do us? How is that ever going to happen? We don't even know where he lives! He just heads off toward the mountain. He might live anywhere up there."

"Maybe it's time we found out!" Briar says. "We're not little kids anymore. There must be a way!"

"I can find out where he lives!" cries Jack. "Just give me a packhorse and some supplies. I'll follow his tracks up the mountain and see where they lead. I'll go."

Lord Henry, Lady Arabella, Elizabeth, Jane, Briar, and Rose all look at Jack, and at one another.

"Are you serious?" asks Rose.

"Do you really think you can do it?" Briar asks. "What about your mother?"

"My mother keeps telling me I'm the man of the family. I'll just have to tell her I'm going on a man's business and leave it at that. And you would have to promise to take care of her while I'm gone—and . . . if I don't come back. None of you could disappear for even a day or two without causing a major crisis. I'm the only one who can go."

"What if there is more than one giant?"

"That's one of the things we need to find out."

"What if he smells you?"

"I wouldn't get that close."

"He'd smell you even if you didn't get close. That's the whole point."

"Maybe Hilde has some bear grease or skunk oil or something we could snitch that would mask his smell," offers Rose. "Just in case. But whose horse could we give him?"

"Wait. We're not really talking about sending him out to find the giant all on his own, are we? He might get killed!" objects Briar.

Rose, and therefore Lady Arabella, and therefore Elizabeth and Jane, all agree.

Jack, who has never had enough to eat, is the smallest among them. Nevertheless, he takes Briar's hand and looks calmly into her eyes. "I can do it," he says. "We couldn't do it before. We were too young. Now, if you can get me a horse, I can go. It's time. I should go soon, while the tracks are still fresh."

Lord Henry looks on, an expression of reluctant admiration struggling with his habitual contempt. He notes the respect with which the other youngsters are regarding Jack. Suddenly, in a burst of uncharacteristic generosity, he blurts, "He can use my horse." Almost immediately he wants to take it back, but everyone's eyes are upon him now, and he enjoys their looks of approval so much that he quickly improvises a plan. "I'll ride out and meet you beyond the far field; then I'll walk home and say that Baxter threw me and ran away. Of course, I might get in trouble," he adds with a self-important air, "but then when you return, I'll 'find' him again, and it will all be smoothed over. Did you ever ride a horse, boy? Do you know how to take care of one?"

Jack, getting over his surprise, responds, "I've ridden Farmer Oldham's plow horse and taken care of him all right."

"Well, my Baxter is no plow horse. Do you even know how to saddle a horse?" Lord Henry asks with enormous condescension.

Jack, who is meek enough to accept this without resentment, responds, "Maybe you could show me? I've only ever ridden bareback."

"Baxter is used to being ridden with a saddle," Henry says, the truth being that Henry himself has never mastered riding bareback. This only increases his loathing for the boy, which shows all too clearly on his face and in his tone of voice.

"He'll do fine with the horse," Briar says confidently. "But how will we get his supplies?"

"We'll all have to help," Rose answers. "We'll each of us have to pilfer whatever we can from the pantry and storerooms, and I'll see what I can get from Allard. We should plan for a week, just in case."

They continue to work out the details until everyone is sure of their roles. Jack, Briar, and Rose seem lit from within. Their voices are animated, their eyes sparkling. Finally, all the talk is resulting in a course of action, and they are able to do something. The others go along. Though they have no great belief in the project, they are interested to see what Jack can do. With one last admonition to Jack that he must keep his distance from the giant and not try any heroics, the meeting of the Giant Killers is adjourned.

Sometime later, Rose and Briar meet up with Lady Arabella, Elizabeth, and Jane again.

"Have you heard the news?" Lady Arabella asks excitedly.

"What news?" Rose responds.

"You mean, you haven't heard?" says Elizabeth with a superior air. "A master painter has arrived at court. He'll be painting portraits of all the most important people, and my papa says that I may have lessons!"

"*My* papa says *I* may have lessons too!" adds Jane.

"If he *gives* lessons," says Lady Arabella. "And if he does, it will probably only be for the princess, not for the steward's daughter or for a knight's daughter, you know. So you may as well forget it."

Elizabeth's face falls, and Jane sulks.

Rose, who feels guilty at the girls' disappointment, nevertheless is filled with delight at the thought of having lessons from a master painter. Like her mother before her, she has an inchoate longing to create something beautiful. Her embroidery, when she takes the trouble to do it, is perfectly lovely, but still she yearns for other means of expression and has only dreamed of such an opportunity. "I must see Papa about this, immediately," she says eagerly and, excusing herself, goes to find the king. Lady Arabella, Elizabeth, and Jane ignore Briar and move on, their noses in the air.

Briar, left on her own, contemplates sadly that the painter will certainly not be wanting to paint *her* portrait. In search of comfort, or at least distraction, she effortlessly climbs the steps to Hilde's high tower room. Experience has taught her to listen at the door for signs of trouble before knocking, and she hears crashing sounds within. Though she can't make out the words, she also hears the unmistakable lilt of Hilde's enthusiastic cursing. Waiting for a lull in the commotion, she finally decides to knock. Hilde jerks open the door, her broom in her hand, saying, "What do you wa— Oh, it's you, dearie! Come in, come in. Don't be afraid, It's just the imp. He's come back to his hatching place, with friends. An infestation, I'm afraid. Here, hold the broom while I look for the incense. Just wave it at them if they come too close. They're nesting up in the rafters!"

Briar looks up and sees a cluster of small reddish bodies buzzing around the ceiling like inflamed cherubs. She knows how much trouble they can cause, but she must admit they're cute.

"What are you going to do?" she asks, slightly worried.

"Smoke 'em out!" comes the reply. "Ah, here it is! Skunk scent? No, they'd probably like that. Maybe something sickeningly sweet.

Yes, honeysuckle!" Hilde sets seven little brass bowls out, spreads them around the room, and puts a little chunk of incense in each, lighting them and gently blowing on them. Soon, wisps of smoke rise up like attenuated ghosts, curling and swaying, ascending to the ceiling and there melding into a sweet-scented fog. Gradually it fills the whole room, and the imps begin to choke and splutter. Down they come, one by one, until the entire flock of them are fluttering about just above the floor, coughing and mewling. Hilde is holding a cloth over her own nose and mouth, and she's given one to Briar. With her free hand she catches an imp and tosses it out the window. Briar tries this and finds it pretty easy while the imps are incapacitated. Soon there is just one imp, which has stashed itself in behind the cupboard and won't come out with either coaxing or threats. Finally, Hilde and Briar stand by the window, resting and breathing deeply. They have given up on removing the last imp.

"What do we do now?" asks Briar, her eyes still watering from the incense.

Hilde sighs heavily. "Well, there are times, dearie, when there's nothing to do with a problem but learn to live with it. I suppose this is one of those times."

Briar smiles. "So you're going to keep him?"

"Oh, no. You can never 'keep' an imp. They stay with you only if they want to, and they only want to if there is plenty of trouble for them to get into. I'm afraid there's endless trouble for him to get into here. Oh, my spells and potions! This is not going to be pretty."

Briar chuckles. She feels a warm camaraderie with her godmother. Briar thinks that she herself has a *lot* of problems that she just has to learn to live with. Sometimes, when Bishop Simon is berating her or the other children are making fun of her or the adults are blaming or ignoring her, she imagines that she is back at her beautiful haven by the waterfall, listening to the celestial music, dancing and singing away her pain. Only Jack knows about it, because he had found her there once, and Mother Mudge, to whom she had artlessly confessed the whole thing after that first time. But they hadn't heard the heavenly music. When she told them of the music, they looked at her the way people looked at old Mad Godwin as he went gibbering down the street. She has never told anyone else about it again, wanting it to be hers and hers only, safe and secret. But now she finds herself alone with Hilde, who has been her comfort and refuge all her life, and she longs to be really understood.

"Do you want to know something?" she says haltingly.

"Yes. What?" is the plain answer.

Briar proceeds to pour her heart out, telling Hilde everything —from following the red fox through the deep forest to discovering the waterfall, up until her last magical afternoon dancing in the clearing, feeling as earthy as a drumbeat and as light as a hawk gliding on a warm updraft. Hilde's face at first reflects her surprise, which is replaced shortly by the deep satisfaction and joy of finding some long-awaited treasure.

"Ah. The gifts," she says under her breath. "They've come to fruition, then, and all in secret. Lovely. Lovely."

"Gifts?" Briar asks, her hearing too acute for her own good.

"Yes, dearie. This music you hear—it's the music of the heavenly spheres. Only a few can hear it. It is a great gift. And the singing and dancing are gifts too. You are very blessed." She does not mention that these were the gifts of the fairies, intended for her sister, for how could she explain that?

"What does 'fruition' mean?"

"Why, nothing, child. I was just mumbling to myself." Hilde wonders then about the other gifts, the first gift, the gift of wit, rife with possibilities, and the last gift, of strength. "Why don't you come over here," she suggests slyly, "and help me move this chest under the window."

"I can do it all by myself!" Briar assures her, and proceeds to demonstrate the fact, bending to grab the sides of a small but heavy chest. She lifts it with powerful legs, her strength seemingly greater than that of a full-grown man rather than that of a twelve-year-old girl.

"Oh, well done! Have you always been so strong?" Hilde asks.

"I don't know. I guess so. I always beat Rose up the stairs anyway. She gets tired."

"And how are you doing in your studies?" Though Briar's

intelligence is obvious to Hilde, she does not know how to account for the poor reports the queen gets of the girl's progress in school. She and the queen have long suspected some questionable accounting on Bishop Simon's part.

Briar is quiet and thoughtful for a minute before she answers. "Bishop Simon thinks I'm a dimwit. Rose and I thought up this plan for me to pretend I'm not very smart so Bishop Simon won't get mad when I give too many right answers."

"He punishes you for giving the right answers?" Hilde asks, her mind filling with things she would like to do to the old villain.

"He used to. All the time. And for asking questions. Now I just nod to Rose when I know the answer. It's our secret."

Hilde is beside herself with delight. Briar sees only that Hilde is happy with her, and it inspires such confidence that she wants to share that other thing, that terrible thing she has shoved down into a hidden corner of her mind and tried so hard to forget. Once again, she remembers the slime on the damp walls. And the peephole. And the secret. Ever since that night when she and Rose explored the hidden passageway and she listened in on the meeting of the king's counselors, she has been afraid even to form the thought. But it comes to her now, hovering on the tip of her tongue. *Rose is not the heir.* Could she finally unburden herself and lay down her anguish in the lap of her trusted godmother? Did *she* know who the 'true' heir was? But the fearful admonition surfaced once again in her memory: it was death to speak of it.

Perhaps if Hilde knew the truth, then *her* life would be in danger. Briar shuts her mind against the possibility. There is nothing else she can do or say, so she closes her lips and swallows hard.

"So serious, you are," says Hilde. "What troubles you, dearie?"

"Oh, nothing," Briar answers, her secret throbbing in her heart like a caged bird trying to get out. *Rose is not the heir.*

Hilde, too, holds tightly to her secrets. *You are the firstborn, blessed by the fairies.*

Only a fragile membrane of silence keeps them both from the truth, but it might as well be a stone wall. They harbor their secrets alone, side by side, as the evening light fades.

"I better go." Briar sighs. "It's nearly suppertime. Do you need any more help?"

"That's all for now. I'll just put away my breakable things. You go on. Thank you, dearie."

Hilde embraces the girl warmly, then watches her go, her own thoughts turning dark as she is reminded of the evil gray fairy and the spell *she* cast when Briar and Rose were infants. Hilde couldn't even guess which girl had been touched by the gray fairy's curse, having switched the two of them at the very moment the gray fairy pronounced it. Perhaps it would be both. Perhaps neither. Hilde only hopes and prays that it will not be Briar who is condemned to sleep until awakened by a kiss, for who would fall in love with her poor, misshapen face and kiss her? Hilde fears that King Warrick's command to destroy all the spinning wheels in the kingdom will be of no avail when the time comes. If the evil fairy chose to, she could conjure a spinning wheel out of nothing! Or she could choose to recant her terrible spell and save both girls from harm. But how likely was that?

High in a black tower on a lonely hill, the gray fairy gazes into her crystal ball. At first she is calm, then she groans, then something like a growl emanates from deep in her throat as she conjures images of the past in the crystal ball. Her face is suffused with rage. Her eyes flash, wide and bloodshot. The small sparrows she has suspended upside down from each wrist flap and squawk pathetically as she moves her hands over the ball.

The image that appears is a scene twelve years old, but ever fresh in the gray fairy's mind, for she renews it nightly and will never let it fade. It is the scene of her public rejection and humiliation, and she has nursed it in her memory until its importance has grown to disastrous proportions. It is the scene of a great gathering of the nobility and every other important personage in the kingdom, all present to celebrate the birth of an heir to King Warrick and Queen Merewyn. The scene includes eight fairies of the kingdom: pink, green, white, blue, purple, yellow, red, and gold. But not gray. No, not gray. She, only she, was excluded. Only she was shunned. The insult still burns like acid, and her hatred flows continually from the wound. Reliving the episode again and again, she observes herself turning inward, sinking down to her own darkest side until her hatred finds a focus, a perfect target to take revenge upon them all: the beautiful, innocent babe, Princess Rose. What better way to hurt the king and queen and all who rejected her than to spoil their joy at the baby's birth?

She lets out another low growl. "And look what I did!" she gloats. "Well, what did they *expect?* Those proper people? Their *royal highnesses?* Lords and ladies of the court?" Suddenly she lifts up her chin and laughs bitterly. "They'll never forget me now, not as long as they live! I'm the most terrible, the most powerful, the most brilliant!" She picks up a black book with strange symbols on its cover, sets it on a table, and opens it up. She thumbs through it slowly, muttering to herself. "Those interfering fairies — that gold fairy who tried to undo my curse — I'll get them if it takes all the dark arts to do it!" She closes the black book and sets it down carefully.

"True love's kiss!" she cackles. "The fools! Do they think I'll let anyone get that close to her? Wait till they see all the havoc I will unleash! I shall rattle the very heavens! Ahahaha!" On and on the gray fairy raves, until sparks fly from her fingertips and ignite small fires in the straw spread on the floor. She stamps them out quickly, screaming with frenzied laughter.

Abruptly her laughter ceases. Rubbing her hands over her crystal ball again, she summons a different image, a view of young Rose as the girl goes about her day. Rose is surrounded by adoration, beloved by the whole court. "Wonderful! Wonderful!" says the gray fairy. "Let them all adore you! The greater their adoration, the greater their suffering when you meet your doom!"

The gray fairy follows Rose's movements and listens in on her conversations as she meets up with her friends, then asks her father if she may have lessons with the new painter. Her wish granted, she goes to the kitchen and charms the cook out of a snack.

"That's right, pet," the gray fairy snarls. "Make the most of your charms. Make them all love you, for it will make my revenge all the more brutal!" And she laughs her horrifying laugh until the air around the tower crackles with it and birds and beasts flee. The small birds suspended from her wrists have stopped fluttering, for they are dead.

Jack straightens up from his bent-over position and wipes his perspiring forehead with his sleeve. He claps his hands together to loosen the dirt on them and futilely tries to rub it off. He has weeded the whole croft garden and tended to all his other chores in preparation for his journey up the mountain. Now, with the sun high overhead, the time has come. Fixed in his resolve, he says a brief but firm goodbye to his mother, leaving her calling after him.

Meanwhile, the saddlebags hidden away in the tack room have grown full as each of the Giant Killers has made their contributions to the provisions. Even Lady Arabella and Elizabeth and

Jane have done their part, more to please Rose than for any other reason.

At the appointed time, Briar and Rose sneak the bags out of the castle and make their way to their rendezvous with Jack and Lord Henry beyond the far field. Henry is holding tight to Baxter's bridle, reluctant to give him up. Having taught Jack the finer points of saddling Baxter, he lectures the boy about things Jack already knows as to the proper care of a horse. Jack patiently nods in agreement. When the girls come up to them, there are some last-minute doubts.

"You're sure you really want to do this?" Briar asks.

Jack, who has had nightmares of being chased by the giant, nevertheless puts on a brave smile. He claps her on the back, leaving a dirty handprint. "I'll be fine," he reassures her. "Just like you said. And so will Baxter," he promises Henry. "I'll just do a little lookin' around and come right back."

Henry reluctantly hands Jack the reins, then fastens on the saddlebags. Jack leads the palfrey to the fence and climbs on his back. Baxter turns his head, as if to see who is riding him. Seemingly satisfied, he responds to the hitch of the reins and the pressure of Jack's heels and his soft "Tchk-tchk," and he trots off across the meadow.

"He'd better bring my horse back," Henry says, hands on his hips.

Henry and the girls turn to go, but it is decided that they

should not be seen returning together. So Rose and Briar wait for Henry to go on ahead of them while they travel home by a different route.

Master Nilson Olyver is a man of great talent. Gray of hair, lean of body, he has the penetrating stare of a man who could paint one's soul as well as one's likeness. He sits on a stool before a blank canvas in the anteroom that has become his studio, awaiting the arrival of the princess.

Master Olyver was struck dumb at his first sight of Rose. Her sprightly personality, her perfect features, her glowing complexion, her bright blue eyes and silky golden hair have overwhelmed him with the urge to pick up a brush and start painting. When it was proposed to him that he take her on as a pupil, he humbly suggested that if Rose were to pose for him, there would be no charge for her lessons. In the end, the king, always eager to practice any economy that did not affect himself, was only too happy to grant his approval. Now, at the appointed hour, Rose, accompanied by Lady Beatrice as her chaperone, arrives in Master Olyver's studio. He greets her formally with a bow.

Rose responds, "My mama says that we must dispense with etiquette and you must treat me as you would any other student. So please call me Rose."

"Excellent, Rose," says the artist. "This is my apprentice, Lanford Cole." He points in the general direction of a sturdy young man who has a head full of unruly black hair and green eyes that seem to laugh at everything.

"Call me Lan," he says, smiling. Lan takes in the image of the lovely princess, who is expensively clothed and spotlessly clean. He thinks he has never seen anyone quite so beautiful, but he wonders how long that fine dress is going to stay immaculate. He imagines wryly how she will react to getting paint stains on those porcelain hands.

"If you'll please sit over here, my dear," Master Olyver suggests. "I'd like to get started with your portrait while the light is good."

Rose, disappointed that the posing is going to come first, nevertheless does as the painting master says. She suffers his further directions patiently as he has her turn this way and that to find the very best angle. Although Rose seldom thinks of her own looks, she is aware that even at twelve, she is the center of attention in any room she enters. It is a power she has barely begun to exploit. Though sometimes she shyly wishes for anonymity, still she takes it for granted that she will usually get her own way with her bright smile and dazzling blue eyes. Most things come to her so easily, in fact, that it is surprising that she is not as yet spoiled. Perhaps her friendship with Briar, whose experience and expectations are so different from her own, serves to keep her sweet and natural. Or perhaps some of the pink fairy's ill-fated gift of sweetness has come through after all.

Rose endures the ordeal calmly while Master Olyver directs Lady Beatrice to arrange her hair and clothing just so. Every view of her is so sublime, the painter has trouble deciding on one, but at last he positions her with her face turned slightly to the side. The three-quarters view shows the perfection of all her features. Concentrating, he sits down in front of his blank canvas to work. First he makes a quick sketch. Then he blocks in large, simple shapes of harmonizing color, starting with the darks. Then on to the bright gold of her hair and the folds of her blue dress. An hour passes very quickly for Master Olyver and very slowly for Rose, who has several itches she'd like to scratch. Finally, Master Olyver says the word, and she is free.

"Is it time for my art lesson now?" she asks, trying to hide her impatience.

"Of course, of course, my dear," the old painting master assures her. "But what are we going to do about that dress?"

Lan, who has been waiting for this moment, pipes up. "You'd best wear this," he says, picking up a large apron that is encrusted with splotches of every color of paint, and he waits with some amusement to see her reaction.

Lady Beatrice looks on with disgust. "Haven't you got a clean one?" she demands.

Rose smiles eagerly, saying, "This one is just fine!" Taking it from his hands and putting it on, she turns her back to him and says, "Tie it up for me, would you?" as if she wore it every day. Lan, pleasantly surprised, reaches around her and awkwardly grabs the apron strings, fumbling them about and finally tying them.

Master Olyver looks at her critically. "We must do something about the sleeves," he says. When Rose puts her arms out, her voluminous oversleeves hang down, as is the fashion. The master approaches her and rolls one sleeve back as far as he can, Lan following suit with the other.

"Ahem!" Lady Beatrice clears her throat in warning, unsure whether to object to the indignity or approve of the saving of Rose's beautiful blue dress. Finally, she decides on the latter and sits down to do her needlework, one eye always on the proceedings.

"Now," says Master Olyver, "to begin at the beginning."

"Will you teach me how to make paint?" Rose asks eagerly.

"It's not an activity for fun, young lady. It's a very delicate process. A drop too much beeswax, a dribble too much linseed oil, and the whole batch may be spoiled. Worse than that, some of the pigments are quite poisonous and must be handled with extreme caution. Lan has learned to mix many of them for me, but the more hazardous ones, like king's yellow, I make for myself. This is where the paint is ground." He leads her over to a broad table covered with jars of different sizes and shapes that are filled with powders, paints, and oils, all laid out in an orderly fashion, and a number of tools, pots, and other objects. In the middle of the table Rose sees a large marble slab, with a muller—a club-like stone instrument shaped like a rounded wedge—and some spatulas, and she yearns to get her hands on them.

"I'll have you mix some of the safer ones, just to know how it's done. You must follow directions exactly. Lan, start her off with yellow ochre."

Lan proceeds with exaggerated patience to demonstrate the various stages of paint making to the enthusiastic Rose. First he gently heats the linseed oil over a flame, stirring in a few drops of beeswax to make the binder. Leaving that to cool, he picks up a jar of ochre pigment, measures some out on the slab, forming a little well in the middle, and sets Rose to work with a spatula, mixing dribbles of oil and a sprinkle of water to the powder. She continues for some time, until the pigment forms a crumbly paste. Then Lan judges it is ready to mix with the muller.

He shows her how to add in the binder a little at a time, grinding and coating every particle of pigment on the marble slab over and over again; then he turns the muller over to her. It is tedious work, and Rose crushes and scrapes until her arms ache, and still she keeps working, with a smile on her face, while Lan looks on with the hint of a laugh in his eye, waiting to see if her enthusiasm will wane. Finally, her face shining with slight perspiration and her cheeks beautifully flushed with exertion, she produces a smooth, buttery paint. He inspects it closely, then nods with real approval and stores it away in a corked clay pot.

Afterward, Rose unties the apron and looks at her hands. They are covered with ochre-colored spots suggesting some exotic disease, a fact that amuses her immensely. Lan, pleased by her sanguine attitude, shows her how to clean her hands with mineral spirits and soap until they are mostly restored to their naturally white state. There are only a few spots of paint on her sleeves, and they don't show when she rolls the oversleeves back down.

Lady Beatrice, seeing that there is still paint under the girl's fingernails, gives a derogatory snort. "Hmph! A fine pastime for the prettiest princess! Now she has the hands of a common laborer!"

Rose blushes with embarrassment, but she knows it is pointless to argue with Lady Beatrice, who has her own strict ideas as to how the "prettiest princess" should look at all times. The other ladies of the court too would doubtless give her trouble over her painter's hands.

Master Olyver, who was working on another painting, turns to Lady Beatrice and says, "On the contrary, my lady, she has the hands of an artist! A grand and noble profession, sought after by kings!" On hearing this, Lan stands up a little straighter and puffs out his chest.

"Hmph!" Lady Beatrice repeats. Rose allows herself to be shepherded away, with only a backward glance at Lan.

After the evening meal, Briar and Rose find themselves at large, with nothing to do. Before anyone can discover them and assign them some unwanted activity, they head up the circular staircase to their attic room. Much to their annoyance, they realize they are being followed by Hilde's imp. He hovers in the air just above their heads and makes little farts.

"Ugh! Go away!" commands Rose. But he does not go away. He bobs up ahead of them and stops, hovering in a shadowy corner and scratching at what looks like a slight crack in the wall. The girls know this place. It is the entrance to the secret passageway where they still sometimes try to listen in on castle business. Just then, they hear Rose's name being called at the foot of the stairs. They look at each other in alarm, Rose's face suffused with resentment.

"What do they want *now?*" she says disgustedly. "It's always something!"

Then the girls look at the imp, who seems without words to beckon them onward. As if drawn by some force, they rush to the crack in the wall and push on it. The wall swings inward, and the secret passageway opens up. The imp leads them into the dank darkness, and Rose grabs a candle from a wall sconce and follows, with Briar coming along behind and closing the door.

"Oooh!" Rose says as she touches the damp, slimy walls and blunders through sticky cobwebs. The imp leads on. They climb the flight of uneven stairs and come to the place where the small peephole opens in the wall above them. Even though both girls have grown since last they visited the place, neither girl is quite tall enough to reach it on her own.

"It's my turn to listen," Rose whispers.

"But I never hear anything interesting. Either it's just boring stuff or there's no one there," Briar whispers back. Briar always does her best to discourage Rose from listening, in case she hears something she shouldn't.

"That's not my fault. It's still my turn," Rose insists.

"Oh, all right then!" says Briar, bending down. "Get on."

Rose sets down the candle and, hiking up her skirt, climbs onto Briar's shoulders. Briar braces herself against the wall and straightens while the imp flutters above them.

Staring through the peephole, Rose quickly sees that her father and Bishop Simon are alone in the room next door. She turns her ear to the peephole to listen. For a while she hears nothing but dull castle business, but then she hears the bishop making a demand for new golden altar cups for the chapel.

The king answers with a plea. "You must know, Your Grace, that we're running short of gold. What we have, we use to appease the giant."

"Never forget," responds the bishop, "it is only through my holy intercession that the giant is kept from destroying you utterly! And remember that it was I who placed the crown upon your head. I am the head of the church in this kingdom! Only through me can you save your immortal soul from the eternal flames!"

The king replies, "Of course, *of course,* Your Grace. You will have your golden altar cups. I will make the arrangements at once." But there is an edge of resentment in his voice.

Listening, Rose hears the irritation in her father's words. She thinks he's been backed into a corner and unwillingly seeks to appease the bishop. She finds the whole exchange disturbing. Does Bishop Simon bully even the king then? Surely that is not the rightful role of the head of the church! She listens some more, but the men seem to have left the room.

Briar hisses, "Get down! I want to hear," and the two of them accomplish this with practiced ease. "My turn," Briar whispers.

"They're gone now," Rose replies, but she relates the conversation as accurately as she can, especially the end of it. "And then my father said, 'of course,' as if the bishop can always have his own way no matter what!"

"He's a bad, nasty bishop," Briar says. "He shouldn't be a bishop at all!"

They hear a small giggle above their heads and look up at the little red imp. He flutters there, giggling, until Rose tells him *"Hush!"* Then he flies toward what appears to be the end of the passageway, turns, and disappears.

"What?" cries Briar, picking up the candle and following. "Where did he go?" The girls make their way to what has always looked, in the dim candlelight, like a dead end. The imp appears

again out of the side of the passageway, and they finally see that it is not the end after all. It is just a sharp corner into an even narrower hallway.

"Come on!" says Briar, "Let's see —"

"— where it goes!" Rose finishes her sentence.

The two girls trail after the imp through the narrow corridor for a long, long way, going around several more turns until they have lost all sense of direction. Finally, they follow him up another stairway, where he stops and hovers next to a spot on the wall. As Briar draws nearer, she holds the candle up and whispers, "Look! It's another peephole. Quick, lift me up!"

Rose complies with a minimum of trouble, and Briar puts her eye to the hole and says, "This must be your parents' room, but nobody's here. You might as well put me down."

When this is accomplished, Rose asks, "Do you suppose the imp led us here for some reason?"

"Only trying to cause trouble! I'm sure we'd be in a lot of trouble if we got caught listening in on the king and queen's private conversations."

"Who's going to catch us in here? I'm sure nobody else uses these passageways, or there wouldn't be all these cobwebs."

"It's a good thing, too! I think whoever built this passageway must have died and never told anybody about it."

"Or maybe he was killed by some long-ago king in order to keep it a secret!" Rose holds up the candle and looks at the end of the passageway, which has been bricked over. "Or maybe he was walled in and left to die!"

"Oooh," Briar breathes. "Maybe his bones are around here somewhere!"

Then the girls abruptly agree that it's time to leave. On their way back to the entrance, they tell each other ghost stories until they are deliciously spooked. Then Briar asks, "What if the gray fairy lurks in these passageways?"

Rose squeals and says, "Don't even think about it!" And they speed up, hurrying back the way they came, panicking somewhat when the door to their stairway won't open. Finally, with Briar applying all her strength, it gives way, and much relieved, they and the imp go about their business.

The next morning, Briar swings a bag full of food back and forth jauntily as she makes her way through town to Jack's cottage. She is keeping her solemn vow to Jack to provide for his mother in his absence, faithfully delivering a bag of food collected by the Giant Killers for this express purpose. Just now Briar is having difficulty with the local dogs, who smell something delicious in her bag. They leap and yap after it, but she holds it close and tells them, "Shoo!"

Ahead, she sees Mother Mudge leaning out over her half-door, calling to her. Briar smiles. She knows she is always welcome at Jack's cottage, even if he's not there. Over the last three years she has become a frequent visitor, like one of the family, and now that Jack is away, his mother looks to Briar to tell her where he has gone. Briar feels terrible having to tell Mother Mudge that she doesn't know where Jack is. This is technically true, as she does not know his exact location, but in any case, knowing that he was stalking the giant would not make his mother feel any better. Briar promises to keep a lookout for him every day from the top of the high tower, and this comforts Mother Mudge somewhat.

Briar has also taken on the role of emissary to the village children, that other branch of the Giant Killers' club, all of whom know of Jack's mission and all of whom keep it quiet. Jack had long ago introduced Briar to his neighbors, Arley and Bridget, and they introduced her to Dudley and Jarrett, Bertha and Quentin, Maddox and Emma and Marian, and a host of others. None of them tease her anymore about her looks or call her names, for she has become a friend. And she holds no grudges. As she passes, they flash the secret signal for the Giant Killers, the circle with the thumb and forefinger, and she flashes it back. The village children also take turns looking out for Jack at the edge of the far field, anxiously awaiting his return.

Today Briar walks out to the far field and meets with Arley and Bridget, who are keeping watch for Jack.

"What do you suppose he'll find up there?" Arley asks, staring hard at the cloud-topped mountain.

"Well, if he finds the giant's house," Briar responds, "it would have to be pretty big. Maybe as big as the whole mountaintop! Or maybe it's a cave—a huge cave—or even a palace. With all the gold the old villain has stolen from the treasury, he probably eats off golden plates and drinks from a golden cup!"

Little Bridget's eyes grow wide. "Really? And does he get enough to eat and everythin'? I wish we could get enough to eat! Food has been awful scarce since our pa got sick."

Briar feels a pang of guilt over the breakfast she just enjoyed. She thinks she should bring an apple for Bridget the next time she sees her, but then she thinks that she should bring one for Arley too, and one for Dudley and Jarrett, and Bertha and Quentin, and Maddox and Emma and Marian, and all the others, and suddenly she is overwhelmed because she knows she cannot feed them all. For a moment Briar wishes that Hilde had some medicine that would make her aching heart as numb as her green-and-warty back. She looks into Bridget's big brown eyes, thinking she could at least bring a basket of food for her suffering family, and she silently vows that on the day they kill the giant, things will be different.

Chapter Three

JACK IS HALFWAY UP THE GREAT MOUNTAIN. The trees are thinning out, and he notices the stumps of some that have been cut down. Finally, he comes to a clear stream and stops for a rest, leading Baxter to drink, then dunking his own head in the cold water. The going has been rough and is becoming even more so; the land is getting steeper now, and he and Baxter are tiring more easily. Still, the giant's footprints make a plain path up the slope, and Jack is eager to see what there is to see above the clouds that encircle the mountaintop. He shakes the water from his head like a wet dog does and decides to proceed on foot, leading the horse by his bridle. It will be slower, but Baxter will be more sure-footed without the added weight.

Several hours later, they reach the misty underside of the clouds. Baxter seems nervous, prancing and whinnying in the white vapor. Jack stops again, tying the horse to a tall standing rock. He makes up his mind to go forward by himself. He fixes the knot for Baxter's reins so that if he doesn't come back, the horse can eventually pull himself free. "Goodbye, Baxter, old friend," he says, giving him a carrot. "You're a good horse."

Not knowing what lies ahead, Jack feels that it's wise to put on the appalling skunk oil that Briar gave him to disguise his human odor. It makes it almost impossible to breathe, but it may save his life, so he rubs it into his skin and clothes until he positively reeks with it. Squaring his shoulders, he goes on his way.

As he continues upward, the cloud closes in around him until he can see only a few yards ahead. He can still hear Baxter whinnying nervously, the sound eerily muffled in the thick mist. Finally, the cloud becomes so thick that Jack can no longer see where he's putting his own feet. Everything around him is white, and he has lost all sense of direction. He proceeds blindly until the surface he's walking on begins to feel soft and spongy, and he sees a hint of blue sky ahead. In another minute he emerges from the cloud and a cold wind whips his hair over his eyes. When he brushes the hair away, he is amazed to see that he has strayed far from the side of the mountain onto the cloud itself, which seems to be the only thing holding him up!

He stomps a few times to be sure of the terrain and finds that it's much like walking in snow, only squishing slightly with each step. He looks about. Behind him is the mountaintop and the afternoon sun. All around him is the azure sky and, stretching away as far as he can see, the white, fluffy top of the cloud that he has just climbed through. And there in the east, away in the distance, is a big, grand giant's house—sitting right on the cloud! Jack wonders if there is some kind of powerful enchantment here to make a cloud hold up a house, but he knows nothing of clouds and even less about enchantments. All that matters is that this cloud holds him up.

Considering what to do next, he swallows hard as he reluctantly concludes that he will have to get closer to scout the place out. His skunk-scented disguise does not give him much confidence, as he doubts that many skunks come up here. Nevertheless, there is still a light mist about chest high, which hides him somewhat. If need be, he can go belly down and crawl. He turns to look at the mountaintop and chooses a certain rock formation in the west, directly under the sun, to mark his place for the trip back. Then, crouching until he is almost covered by the fog, he proceeds awkwardly due east toward the house.

After a long trudge through the spongy terrain he can see a little better, and he notices a great pile of something near the house. It looks like a stack of cut trees lying on their sides. He moves closer again, then stops suddenly at the sight of a large figure coming out of the door. Even at this distance he can make out the dissolute form of the giant, potbellied and lumbering. Frantically Jack stoops down into the mist, hoping he has not been noticed. It looks as if luck is on his side, though, for the prevailing wind blows his odor away from the giant, who is grumbling under his breath and seems not to have sensed anyone's presence. The giant, still muttering, separates one large tree from the pile, and, picking up an enormous ax, he begins to chop the tree into pieces.

While the giant is busy, Jack thinks he might be able to look around and discover if there is a way to get into the house without being seen — not that he plans on attempting it, but for future reference. Cautiously, he begins to make a wide circle around the structure, taking note of all the ground-floor windows and doors from a healthy distance, listening intently in case the chopping should stop. All in all, he counts ten windows on the ground floor of the side facing him, the ledge of the lowest one at least a dozen feet higher than he could possibly reach. With nothing nearby to climb on, it looks to him as if there is no hope of getting in that way.

In back of the house he spots another door, tightly shut, and counts five windows on one side of it and four windows on the other. He debates whether to circle to the far side of the house, as that would bring him upwind of the giant. Jack goes just far enough around the corner to see that this side also has ten windows, like the first, and one of them is open. He judges that it is not so high that a good, long ladder wouldn't reach it, but where would he get one? There might be enough lumber in the giant's woodpile, but there would never be enough time to make one, even if he had the tools, and it would be impossible to drag one here from home. His heart sinks as he realizes that there is no way to sneak in. He is about to turn and retrace his path when he hears the giant's voice calling out from the front of the house. Instantly, Jack hides himself in the mist and listens.

"Woman!" the giant bellows. "Cook my supper! And make it quick!"

Jack can't see the giant from his hiding place, and he dares not go any closer, but at least now he has some useful information: there is someone else within the house — the giant's servant, or perhaps his wife? Is she a giant too? Realizing that she may see him through a window, he continues to make his way arduously back around the house, slinking along the foundation. This time he observes one window, much smaller than the others, down at ground level, nearly obscured by the mist. It has bars over it, like a dungeon. Jack goes right up to it and peers in. He makes out a small, dark room and notices with some frustration that the bars are too close together for him to fit through them. He makes a careful mental note of the location of the window, then follows his own route back. After some time, he returns to approximately where he started.

Jack can see that the giant is still busy chopping wood, and it's obvious from the curses he's muttering that he is in quite a bad temper. Jack knows he's been lucky so far, and that his luck may run out. Part of him wants to turn and run while he still can, but another part wants to wait and observe whether the woman will come to the door. It is while he's deciding that the giant suddenly roars, "Ugh! What is that stench?"

Jack sinks down and freezes, suddenly afraid that the wind may have changed. He raises his head just enough to reconnoiter and then begins to crawl back toward the mountaintop on hands and knees. This is difficult in the soft surface of the cloud, but at least he can count on the mist to obscure him. Far behind him he hears the giant again, yelling, "Skunk! That's what it is! Phew! How did it get up here?"

Terrified, Jack realizes that he is trembling. He gets to his feet and, back bent over, breaks into a kind of ungainly run, his feet sinking slightly at each step. He proceeds this way as fast as he is able, listening for sounds of pursuit. Finally, he hears the giant exclaim, "It's out there somewhere! *I'll* take care of the stinking thing!"

Jack dares not lift his head to see where the giant is, but he hears strange, squishy thuds that he thinks must be the giant's footsteps, and then a louder *WHAM-splat,* with the giant shouting, "There! Take that!" This happens again and again: *thud thud thud thud . . . WHAM-splat!*

"Where are you, you blasted rat?" the giant bellows. *Thud thud thud . . . WHAM-splat!*

Jack knows that the next blow of the ax could be the end of him. Silently he repeats the only prayer he knows: *Thank you for the world so sweet, thank you for the food we eat—* Then he realizes that *he* may be the food that's eaten, and he chokes. He hears the giant coming closer—but then getting farther away. Then closer, then farther away again, as if he is just wandering randomly. Jack feels a flicker of hope. Maybe he's still downwind after all.

As he hears the giant get farther away again, Jack lifts his head for a few seconds to take his bearings, then quickly resumes his awkward, bent-over run. This goes on for what seems like an eternity, with his muscles screaming their objection and the thudding and whamming and bellowing always behind him. He tries to remember how long he traveled to get to the giant's house from the mountain, and then he faintly hears a woman's voice call out, "Master, your supper's ready! It's getting cold!"

Jack risks putting his head up once more to see if he can observe the female, and there is, indeed, a figure standing at the door, though he is far away now and can barely make her out. She looks to be a giant too, but much shorter than *the* giant.

"Bah!" growls the giant. "Can't find the putrid thing anyway!" His rampage is over as suddenly as it began. Jack watches, disbelieving, as the giant stomps back to his house, dragging his ax behind him.

Still shaking, Jack turns to the west and scans the mountaintop for the rock formation he memorized when he first arrived. Spotting it, he heads straight for it with hope in his heart. After what seems like an eternity, the mist rises higher and higher over his head, and once again he becomes lost in the cloud, with no sense of direction.

Finally, he calls out for Baxter and hears the horse's faint whinny somewhere ahead. Repeating this periodically, he follows the sound until the mist begins to disperse somewhat and he can make out a path and feel solid earth under his feet. And there, away down the path, he can dimly see Baxter. Nothing has ever looked so good to him. With a final burst of strength, he runs the rest of the way and gives the surprised horse a hug.

Briar is at the top of the watchtower, keeping a lookout for Jack. She breathes in the cool, crisp air. The landscape spreads out before her: the long, thin strips of fields, empty now after the harvest; the forests saturated in orange, red, green, and gold; the stream winding its way through the woods. She looks up at the clouds surrounding the mountaintop and wonders once again what lies above them and whether Jack is safe, wherever he is. She turns to Jerold, the lone soldier stationed at the top of the tower, and asks, "Do you see anything out there?"

Jerold, who has the sharpest eyes in the kingdom, peers out at the countryside for several minutes; then, pointing toward the farthest field, he says, "Look over there! Something's moving just a bit, maybe a person, maybe a horse—can't tell at this distance. It's heading toward the castle—still a long way off."

"Oh, Jerold!" Briar cries. "I *love* you!" And she kisses him on the cheek, then rushes off down the two hundred stairs. In no time at all she is across the courtyard and into the gatehouse, while Jerold is still rubbing his cheek and laughing.

As Briar runs past Durwin, he calls out to her with a smile, "Where are you off to in such a hurry, my fine lady?"

"To meet a friend!" she replies, barely slowing. While she

rushes through the town, several children silently drop what they are doing and follow, picking up others as they go, until half the children in the village are quietly hurrying toward the farthest field. The adults look after them, mystified. Ignoring the stitch in her side, Briar pumps her legs, making her way steadily onward until she arrives at the edge of the far field, where she meets up with Dudley and Jarrett, the two boys whose turn it is to keep watch.

"I think he's coming!" she gasps. "I saw something from the tower."

The other village children soon catch up, and they all wait, straining to see in the direction of the mountain, passing the time until at last they spy someone on a horse coming around a bend in the road. They all run to meet him. Jack, not knowing what to make of this, slides down from the horse's back and waits for them. Only as they approach him do the children smell the awful skunk scent. They all come to a sudden halt, some of them actually backing away but still calling out his name. "Jack! You've come back!" and at the same time, "Jack, what is that terrible smell?"

Jack, suddenly realizing that this is a welcoming party, grins widely. He apologizes for the foul odor. Turning toward the nearby stream, he asks if someone could bring him some lye soap, an item that nobody thought to provide for his return trip, and some clean clothes. Briar goes at once to Mother Mudge to deliver the news that Jack is back and to pass on his requests. Half an hour later, he has bathed, delivered his report to Briar and the village Giant Killers, and returned to his mother's open arms.

"Jack, Jack!" she cries. "Don't ever scare me like that again!" But Jack can't make such a promise.

Briar finds Lord Henry and advises him that his horse is back, safe and sound, and Henry goes to the edge of the far field to retrieve him, making himself a hero with the horse marshal. Indeed, his whole circle of friends is so impressed by his supposed deed of horsemanship and skill in finding the lost horse, he quite begins to think of himself as a kind of hero and almost forgets that Baxter was never really lost.

Later on, when the castle members of the Giant Killers' club convene in the tack room, Jack, who still has a bit of skunk odor about him, recounts his story to Rose, Lord Henry, Lady Arabella, Elizabeth, and Jane.

"I'm afraid there's no way into the giant's house," he says dolefully, "and it's quite a long run from the house back west to the mountaintop. It was just luck that kept me downwind of the giant. If he had had my scent, I'd never have been able to outrun him! I'm afraid it would be impossible to get at him in his house. Not and live to tell about it. Not without help. We'll have to think of something else."

"It's too bad I couldn't have gone," Lord Henry repines. "I'm sure *I* could have found something." Then, seeing the looks of censure on his fellow Giant Killers' faces, he adds, "But I suppose you did the best you could."

"Yes," Jack answers quietly, "I did."

"Of course, you couldn't have done it without my horse."

"Baxter's a fine horse. I was most grateful for him."

Henry, having established his superiority — at least in his own mind — favors them all with his mature opinion. "This whole thing gets more ridiculous by the day!"

Briar challenges him. "Ridiculous to get rid of the giant?"

"Ridiculous to think we can do it ourselves!" says Henry. "It would take an army — a big one — to bring him down, and maybe even they couldn't do it."

"If that's what you believe, then you've broken the oath of the Giant Killers and besmirched our code of honor."

"Oh, grow up! We've been meeting like this for years, and what have we accomplished? It's just a lot of daydreams."

"We've only just started," Briar says. "At least we know where the giant lives now — and that there's a giant woman there too. That's progress."

"Not much," Henry says, heading for the door. "Tell me when you've got something more impressive to share! And forget about using *my* horse for any more of your useless schemes!"

Lord Henry leaves. Lady Arabella, Elizabeth, and Jane soon make their excuses and follow him, leaving Briar, Rose, and Jack to make what they can of the situation.

"They think it's hopeless," Briar says. "They've given up."

"But you never know what *will* work," Jack says, "and there are still all the other Giant Killers in the village. They won't give up hope. It's all they've got! They're all practicing with slingshots, just waiting for the chance to get the giant between the eyes! They'll never give up. And I won't either. Someday I'll find another way to go back to the giant's house, and I'll think of something!"

"Maybe," Rose says. "You never can tell."

"There's got to be a way—" chokes Briar. "There's just got to be!"

By the next day, the excitement over Jack's return has died down. Briar and Rose have escaped the confines of the castle and retreated to their little thicket by the stream. They sit side by side on a low branch of their favorite tree. It is the ancient oak, gnarled and crooked and perfect for climbing. They are surrounded by curtains of spectacular fall foliage swaying and rustling in the chilly breeze, while below them lies a fragrant carpet of fallen leaves. They are discussing Great Philosophical Questions. They have discussed them often before, but not so frequently now as they once did.

"I don't know . . ." Briar trails off. "I can be good when good things are happening, but I want to be bad when bad things are happening. Like when people are mean to me, I think of *really* bad things to do or say. Do you suppose it counts if you think bad thoughts when people are being mean to you?"

"Bishop Simon would say so," replies Rose, "but he's evil himself. What if everything he says is a lie? Would you still want to be good? What if there's no reward?"

"I still would. Just so I wouldn't be like *him*."

"But what if everybody else was evil?"

"I'd go off by myself and just be normal."

"What do you mean?"

"Like mostly good but sometimes evil, but just by myself so it wouldn't matter."

"So it wouldn't matter if you were evil by yourself?"

"No, because nobody else would be affected by it."

"But what about you? Would you be affected?"

"Who would care?"

"I would care."

"But you wouldn't be there."

"Yes, I would."

"Don't be silly. If I'm alone, you can't be there."

"I would be with you in spirit, and I would care."

"Well, then I'd try harder to be good."

"So would I."

"Well, that's settled," says Briar. "I'm hungry. Are you hungry?"

The girls agree to go and get something to eat. On their way through the village they stop at a street market and buy some bread and some fresh-picked apples from a vendor—and an extra one for Durwin at the gatehouse. At twelve, they are not forbidden to leave the castle unaccompanied. Still, it doesn't hurt to be nice to the porter, just in case they might want to stay out late sometime, playing with the village children.

Rose does not participate in these games as often as Briar does, as she increasingly spends her free time playing chess or backgammon or dice in the great hall with Lady Arabella and the other girls. Lady Arabella has slowly but surely won her way into Rose's confidence. Rose finds that she actually enjoys the time she spends with the older girl, and even with Elizabeth and Jane, all of whom treat her like a princess. Besides, it is a relief not to have Lady Beatrice nagging her over the company she keeps. And who else is there for her to keep company with while Briar goes off on her own, as she increasingly does? Rose knows what horror Lady Beatrice and the other castle ladies would express if she were found to be spending time with the peasants, as Briar is free to do. Rose would never hear the end of it.

Briar, however, as time goes on, feels herself to be ever more distant from Lady Arabella and Elizabeth and Jane. They sometimes make a perfunctory effort to include her, but she feels the falsity of it. She feels that they are judging her. She knows they think her inferior, and even waspish, having regularly fallen prey to her sharp wit. At the same time, she is judging them, finding them shallow and self-centered. For her it is easier to go out and be with Jack and her friends in the village or to go into the forest or to her secret place by the waterfall and be alone.

And so it is that the girls part company at the castle keep, with Rose going in to be with Lady Arabella and her friends. Briar goes on to the kitchen, where Hilde, upon Briar's request, has ordered a basket of food prepared for the girl to take to Arley and Bridget's distressed family in the village.

Briar cheerfully retraces her tracks to deliver the heavy basket to their cottage. She knocks on the door, then starts to leave the basket there, intending to depart quickly before they can thank her. But she is observed by Bridget's mother, who answers the door and invites her in. The woman smothers Briar in an embrace, crying, "You dear, good child! You couldn't have come at a better time! Come in! Come in and share with us!" She picks up the basket in both hands and leads Briar into the small home. It is much like Jack's home, but more crowded. There is a straw mat in one corner, upon which the father of the family lies, coughing feebly. A number of children cluster around their mother, including Jack's friend Arley and young Bridget, who both know Briar well from meetings of the secret club. Their big, round eyes are riveted hungrily on the overflowing basket, but they hang back politely.

Bridget, doing her best to observe the niceties, says, "Briar, this is my mum. And that's my pa in the corner. He's very sick. And you know Arley. And this is my brother James, and this is Silas, and this is my sister Edwina and my other sisters, Flora and Kate, and this is baby Jenny."

Briar smiles shyly. "I'm very pleased to meet you all. I just thought you might be able to use this, with your pa so ill. It's nothing really."

She begins to unpack the basket, passing around several loaves of bread first, which everyone takes a bit of and shares. Then she brings forth a whole feast of cold mutton and cheese, followed by a goodly supply of fresh vegetables and even a few pieces of fruit. The children ooh and ahh at each new gift to come out of the basket. Bridget's mother instructs them all to sit down while she parcels out some of the food. She immediately sets a pot of water to boil for a stew, adding vegetables and a small amount of the precious meat.

From the bottom of the basket Briar takes a small flask. "This is for your da," Briar says, handing it to Bridget. "It's a special tonic my godmother makes to help sick people get stronger."

Bridget takes the flask, tears coming to her eyes. "Oh, tell your godmother thank you! Pa, look what you've got!" she cries, and her father brightens up a bit and says, "Bless you, child!"

Briar stays for a little while, enjoying watching the children's happy faces and their parents' even happier ones. She is treated as a friend, and no one seems to bother about her appearance.

As time goes on, deeds like this become Briar's regular habit, with Mother Mudge always letting her know about certain families in the village with illness or injury and Briar bringing baskets of food to them, being welcomed into their homes, and getting to know the families. And none of them seem to care how she looks, and none of them ever forget the kindness.

Rose sits impatiently posing for her portrait while Master Olyver tries to capture her delicate gradations of peach-pink and white skin. A hint of dragon's blood red, a dab of king's yellow, mixed in with titanium white for the highlights and the barest touch of green for the shadows. He pats the brush on the canvas with such a featherlight touch that no brushstrokes are visible. So intent is he on his work that he keeps Rose in position long after her time is over, an unforgivable breach of conduct to Rose's mind. She deliberately breaks her pose and makes a silly face, bringing the session to an end.

"Isn't it time for my lesson?" she insists.

Lady Beatrice, who is always nearby, helps her roll up her sleeves, and Master Olyver sits down with the girl and begins to teach her the rules of perspective, how to give the appearance of depth to a flat drawing. To begin with, he teaches her to place the horizon at eye level, find the principal vanishing point, and draw receding lines from an object in the foreground to that vanishing point.

"Any parallel lines in nature will appear to meet at one and the same point on the horizon," says the master. "Lan will demonstrate this for you and guide you in making your own drawings of a three-dimensional box, as examples, from different heights and positions."

Lan shyly takes Rose aside to a worktable and shows her how it's done. For a long time they confer with their heads together while Lan sneaks admiring looks at her and she barrages him with questions. In answer, he covers her hand with his own and guides it to make the drawings. Rose finds it suddenly difficult to concentrate. She thinks of pulling her hand away, but doesn't really want to. She watches his lips move as he carefully explains each step, but the words seem to be in some unknown language. She is suddenly fascinated by the way his dark hair falls down over one eye.

"Wait. What did you say?" she asks, her heart beating a little too fast, her breathing a bit irregular. "I didn't quite get it."

Lady Beatrice looks on with a sour face. She voices no objection, but listens with half an ear while she stitches away at her sampler.

"It's simple," Lan reiterates. "Anything above the horizon is going to slant down like this, so you see the bottom of it, and anything below the horizon will slant up, so you see the top. Here's a square. Now draw a line from each corner to the principal vanishing point and connect those lines to make it look like a box." He releases her hand so she can do the assignment herself, and her breathing returns to normal. She uses the ruler and tentatively draws her receding lines, then looks to Lan for approval.

"That's right," he says, a broad, slightly idiotic smile on his face. He stands there smiling a few beats too long, as if he had forgotten what he was going to say, and Rose smiles back at him. Lady Beatrice clears her throat loudly, and Lan suddenly recalls the power of speech.

"Here," he says quickly, "let's try it again. I'll draw a square up here this time, like so. You make it into a box."

They practice drawing together for the next hour, talking and sometimes laughing very softly so as not to arouse Lady Beatrice, who seems to have fallen asleep on duty. Rose peppers Lan with questions, some about art and some more personal.

"How long have you been studying with the master?" she asks.

"Oh, about two years. My mother gave me to be apprenticed when I was ten."

"And have you made any paintings of your own?"

"Master Olyver lets me copy other paintings for practice. He says I show signs of promise, but I have a lot of hard work ahead of me. I don't mind, though. I like it. No matter how much you accomplish, there's always something new to learn."

"You're so lucky to be able to become a painter. I wish I could be one!"

Lan is temporarily speechless. Finally, he says, "Yes, I guess I am pretty lucky—but you'll be a queen someday!"

"That's no guarantee of happiness," Rose says sadly. Then, wanting to change the subject, she asks, "Did you travel much before you came here?"

"Oh, a lot. We've been all around the countryside doing portraits of lords and ladies, but now that Master Olyver has been made court painter, we'll be staying here."

Rose smiles shyly, unaccountably pleased by his answer.

Despite Lady Beatrice's sleeping presence, they continue their quiet conversation for some time. Lan is full of stories about his adventures with Master Olyver: accommodating the eccentricities of the gentry, traveling to cities and towns, making narrow escapes from highway robbers. Rose, for her part, tells him about seeing the giant from the watchtower.

"He has a snarl like a mad dog," she tells him, "and there's no telling what he will do. I was safe enough up in the tower, but it was still very frightening!"

"We've heard terrible tales of the giant," Lan concurs.

"And you weren't scared off?"

Lan hesitates for just a moment, then scoffs at the suggestion. "Not us! Master Olyver and I can look out for ourselves."

Rose thinks about this for a minute. She checks on Lady Beatrice and sees that she is still napping. Then she makes a decision. "Well, if you're not afraid," she says in hushed tones, "then there's something I want to tell you."

"Yes?"

"Some of us—I mean a few of us from the castle and lots of boys and girls from the village—we've formed a secret society. We call ourselves the Giant Killers. We're going to find a way to kill the evil giant!"

"Really?" Lan looks at her with barely contained surprise and a new respect. This is the last thing he would have guessed Princess Rose would be involved in.

"Yes. And one of the village boys—Jack—tracked the giant up the mountain to his house. Jack was very brave, even though he couldn't find a way to get at the giant."

Lan immediately thinks that he would like to be the one she called "brave." On the spur of the moment he asks, "Can I help? I'd like to join."

Rose smiles. "I'll bring you to the next meeting."

Lan smiles too, though he belatedly has enough sense to wonder what he might be getting himself into.

Just then Lady Beatrice wakes up with a snort and pretends that she has been looking down at her stitching. "Well, I declare, it must be time to leave!" she says. She crosses the room, links arms with Rose, and pulls her away from Lan. Rose casts a speaking glance over her shoulder at him as she turns to go, but sharp-eyed Lady Beatrice notices it.

As soon as they are out of the room, Lady Beatrice hisses into Rose's ear, "What a nerve that boy has, acting so familiar when you're the princess and he's *nothing. Less* than nothing. He's a mere *underling!* Not fit to touch the sole of your shoe! You, my dear, are destined for great things — a great future. Never forget your own importance!"

Rose hears, but she does not listen.

It is nearly Christmas, and Briar and Rose are helping with the decorating, draping evergreen boughs, ivy, and holly on every surface and hanging mistletoe from the doorways. Whenever they get the chance, they sneak into the kitchen, smelling all the wonderful aromas wafting about, anticipating the sumptuous Christmas banquet to come. They stick their fingers into the various pots for a taste — until they are shooed out of the way by Allard and several assistants.

Darkness falls early, and outside, white flakes are wafting down in a desultory way. Snow sticks like frosting to the battlements and every tree and twig. It drifts gently around corners, filling up hollows, making everything soft and rounded, sparkling like earthbound stars. The girls don their cloaks and venture out to the stables to take some apples to the horses. Briar wants to make a stop at the kennels first. Rose, still secretly afraid of dogs, is less enthusiastic, but rather than show her fear, she agrees. There they find that the dogs have picked up the excitement in the air. Even the docile greyhounds are agitated. The barking is deafening, and an enormous greyhound jumps up, puts its paws on Rose's shoulders, and licks her face. She tries to turn away, feeling her pulse quicken and sweat popping out on her brow. Meanwhile, Briar laughs and scratches behind the dogs' ears and calls them by name. They are all frantic for attention and hoping for treats. Briar sinks into the fresh straw and loses herself in the pack of lively dogs, speaking soothingly to them and waiting for them to calm down, as Rose looks on. For years Rose has gone along with Briar's love of the dogs while pretending to like them herself, but she finds that she is tired of pretending.

"Don't you mind them jumping all over you and licking your face?" Rose asks a little impatiently, as if she has wanted to ask this question for some time.

"I like it," Briar responds, turning her face aside to get a few words out. "They only do it because they love me. It's nice to be loved." She takes Toby's head in both her hands and kisses him firmly on the snout.

"There are plenty of *people* who love you, and they don't jump on you and lick your face."

"Really? Name five."

"Well, there's me. And Hilde. And my mother."

"Your mother?"

"You know she's always very kind to you."

"That's just because the queen is a kind person. She's like that to everybody."

"Well, that still counts. And then there's Jack, and his mother. That's five."

"They're friends, that's all. Think of two more."

"Well . . ."

"Well, you can't. So leave me to my dogs. They're settling down now. Come sit with me and relax."

Rose sighs deeply and sits down next to Briar, her lap immediately crowded by two noisy beagles and a small eager terrier. She forces herself to pet them, watching out for their teeth, and tries to talk to them the way Briar does. Then one of the bloodhounds puts its head over her shoulder and slobbers all over her. This is more than she can bear.

"Now look what he's done!" she cries. "There's drool all down the front of my cloak."

"Here," Briar responds, "use some straw to wipe it off. What's the matter with a little drool?"

"He got it in my *hair!* "

"When did you get so fussy?"

"I can't help it if I don't like it," objects Rose as the dog hovers over her shoulder. She pushes it away, trying to cover up her fear. "Besides," she splutters as her excuse, "I'm supposed to stay clean. I can't stand to listen to another one of Lady Beatrice's lectures!"

"Why do you listen to her, anyway? You're the princess, not her."

Rose stands up and brushes herself off, avoiding the dogs. Suddenly Briar's criticism is too much for her. It's not enough that she is constantly criticized by Lady Beatrice! "I can't just do anything I want because I'm a princess!" she yells. "Mother expects me to mind Lady Beatrice and all the other ladies of the court. You don't know what it's like, with everyone watching me like a hawk all the time, talking about how I'm supposed to be the prettiest princess. I have to keep up a certain appearance."

Briar promptly blows a raspberry. "You don't need to take yourself so seriously. You never used to. Do you think people don't look at me and judge me all the time? That's what's nice about dogs; they don't care about appearances."

"You and your dogs! I think you actually prefer them to people! I'm going to the stables to see the horses. At least they don't jump up and slobber on you."

"Go ahead! I'll stay here with my *friends*." Briar deliberately kisses the bloodhound on the end of its drooling face.

"Ugh. Stop that, will you? Now you're just being difficult on purpose."

"Oh, now I'm difficult?" Briar says, standing up. "You'll have to excuse me. I'm just one of the dogs, and I don't know any better."

Rose stomps to the doorway, where she turns and cries, "All right, *act* that way! See if I care. I'm going!"

"Then I'm staying!" Briar retorts, dropping back down in the middle of the pack of dogs, who immediately resume climbing on her and licking her face.

Rose leaves, and soon Toby and the others are licking salt tears from Briar's cheeks. She feels keenly that the friendship at the center of her life is slipping away from her, and she cannot understand the reason why. As she tries to think it through like a math problem or a particularly complex Latin phrase, it seems to her that the disagreement over the dogs is evidence of some sea change taking place. *There's* the root of it: Rose is changing; she is going her own way. Their days of easy camaraderie are growing fewer and farther between. Rose has other friends now, pretty friends—not like Briar. To Briar's mind, this is the obvious cause, and she tries to bear it stoically. It is her lot in life, one of those things Hilde speaks of that cannot be changed and so must be lived with.

Rose, less analytical but more temperamental, goes on to the stable by herself, hurt by what seems to her like Briar's willful refusal to understand her. She can always count on Lady Arabella, Elizabeth, and Jane to do so. She knows that the three girls regard

Briar with pity and some disdain, and she angrily wonders why she bothers to defend her to them. Yet she deplores the fact that she and Briar have argued.

Still, giving a little shrug, she decides that it will all blow over by bedtime anyhow.

PART THREE

Almost Four Years Later

Chapter One

NOTHING HAS CHANGED, thinks Briar as she stalks through the great hall, fuming with anger.

Turning her head, she shouts, "Well I *do* prefer dogs to people! What of it?" making sure that Rose hears her as she heads for the door. Briar is also heard by everyone present in the hall, including Lady Arabella, Elizabeth, and Jane. Lord Henry and a host of other boys are sniggering at the scene as well.

Lady Beatrice, observing the tiff, makes it her business to grab Briar by the elbow and tell her in acid tones that such displays are not appropriate for a young lady of nearly sixteen years. She admonishes her to sit down and be quiet. Briar forces out a "Yes, my lady," but then turns on her heel and walks away, leaving the officious Lady Beatrice behind. Some part of Briar hopes that Rose will follow her out, maybe even apologize and make up with her, and all will be well again, but the hope is feeble and quickly fades. These days, all their disagreements seem to end in sad stalemates awash with hurtful feelings that only intensify with each new clash.

Holding her head high, Briar walks across the courtyard and on out of the castle, heading toward the one place where she always feels safe and happy — her glade by the waterfall. She makes the trip unnoticed and unhampered, accompanied by a red fox and a chorus of songbirds as she walks down the forest path. Stepping at last into the lovely glade, she is ready to forget her quarrel with Rose. Her vexation falls away, like dead leaves in autumn, as she is suddenly surrounded by music, and she begins to sing softly to herself. Before long, she is singing aloud to the sweet open air and the fox and the birds.

But as she sings, someone hears. Someone follows the sound and watches as she begins to dance. Someone listens from the shadows as she sings her love of the earth and the sky and the waterfall. Someone's eyes follow her with infinite patience as she dances about the clearing, lost in her own world of rhythm and music. And when she finally slows to a stop, that someone slips silently away.

Briar, her heart lighter now, feels again that longing for some tantalizing idea, as if she were reaching for some lost part of herself. The music seems to promise something—something wonderful. But what? The music lingers, then slowly fades. Briar wanders dreamily along the shore of the lagoon until she comes to a smooth inlet. Sitting on a familiar rock there, she pulls back her hair, gazing at her reflection in the water as she often does, looking for some sign that she is growing out of her ill looks. If only the pool reflected the person she really was! A person with her own strengths, her own keen perceptions and deep feelings. But she observes what she always has: the protruding brow and sagging eyelid, the crooked nose, the asymmetrical face. She calmly contemplates that she has never seen anyone else so ugly. After nearly sixteen years she should be used to it. She should be used to people staring and pointing, calling her cruel names. She knows that look of shock when some people first set eyes on her. She sees the way they quickly look away, making the sign to ward off evil, then furtively look back again. And then there are the others who don't stare, who have long grown accustomed to her but judge her solely on her unsightly face. People who should know her better.

She lets her hair down, and turning back to stare at the soothing motion of the falling water, she contemplates her morning. It began with such promise: a clear spring day, the warm breeze heavy with a thousand wild scents. Briar had rushed through breakfast and was suffering through the morning's lessons. Bishop Simon, balding now and more obese than ever, was still enjoying his reign of terror over his students. His pleasure in inflicting pain had only grown with the years. His thrashing arm was still strong and ready for the slightest provocation—this being his favored method of inculcating learning—but many of his pupils were now too big to beat. He made up for this with ever more complicated cruelty, divining each student's weakest points and sensitivities and then making a public and painful mockery of them. As the day grew closer when Briar would turn sixteen and her lessons would at last come to an end, he seemed to make a special effort to embarrass and berate her while he still could. She dreaded this as much as any beating. She had been hiding her intelligence from him for years in order to escape his cruelest punishments, trying at the same time to avoid being mocked as a dunce. It was a nerve-racking struggle, each day a new trial, and she has withstood it by telling herself that she would soon be done with his lessons forever.

But that morning, something within her had finally rebelled. Though she had resisted the urge to really misbehave, she suddenly found it impossible to put on her act of stupidity for one more day. When Bishop Simon posed questions in astronomy, she blurted out the names of all the heavenly bodies. In geometry, she called out the proper formulas and then did the calculations in her head and called them out too. In history, she named the entire line of kings and queens of the Kingdom of Wildwick for the past ten generations, while avoiding the growing menace in Bishop Simon's cold stare. His condemnation, when it came, had been stark and pitiless.

"Cheat!" he cried, pointing his finger into her face. "Abomination!" He began slapping his cane into his hand and glaring at her with fire in his eyes, and she wondered if he would beat her after all. Hilde's magic salve had finally worn off. The green had mostly faded, the warts had gone away, and she had feeling in her back again. But it was not the physical pain she dreaded so much. It was the humiliation that would be more than she could bear.

"Cheating is a terrible crime," he had observed. "One that deserves *eternal* punishment!" He articulated each of his words, as if to sharpen them into weapons.

"I never cheat!" she had the nerve to say.

"Lies! Insolence!" he roared. "I expect no less from the devil's own spawn! I know not what manner of black magic or trickery you have used, but it is a surety that you do not possess the intelligence to perform so well without one or the other!"

His face turning red and mottled, the clergyman stood and wheezed for a minute while he tried to think of something else cruel enough to say. His small eyes narrowing, he pointed at her and said, "Look at you, misshapen thing! You are a *mistake!* You have no place here, except that the king and queen wish it. And see how you reward them. You are naught but a changeling! A demon! Begone with you!"

Briar had gotten away quickly, before he could change his mind, and though she felt physically unharmed, she smarted from his poisonous verbal attack for a long time afterward. Remembering it now, she thinks it might have hurt less to be struck than to be called a misshapen thing, a mistake.

She brushes away unwanted tears.

She remembers waiting a long time outside the room for Rose. She had been eager to leave the confines of the castle, as she so often did to get away from her troubles, but she hoped that Rose would come with her that afternoon. She imagined that they could retreat to their thicket or do some berry picking and forget the morning's disaster. But when lessons were over and Rose finally emerged, she was talking and laughing with the other girls, Lady Arabella, Elizabeth, and Jane. Briar paused, knowing she could not invite Rose without also inviting the other three. She fully expected that the other girls' attitudes toward her would be insufferably condescending, especially after Bishop Simon had so utterly vilified her in front of everyone. But if that was the only way to spend time with Rose, she thought maybe she should just do it anyway, in the hope that this time it would be different. And so she had finally decided to be generous and had invited them all.

"Oh yes, that sounds like fun," Rose had answered, giving her a sympathetic look, as if trying to make it up to her for Bishop Simon's abuse.

Lady Arabella stalled for time. "Oh, you mean right now?" she asked innocently. "We're sort of busy right now. We were going to have a game of backgammon."

"Oh, come on," Rose responded. "We can do that later. It's such a nice day. Let's go out!"

"All right then," Lady Arabella had agreed with a sigh. In truth, she was irritated beyond measure that Briar might still have more influence over Rose than she did.

Briar understood Lady Arabella's meaningful sigh immediately, but Rose, already imagining what fun they would have, seemed not to notice. In truth, Rose read the sigh as a sign of

Arabella's continued intolerance of Briar, but she hoped that the proposed outing might provide an opportunity for them to get to know and like each other better. Briar ignored Lady Arabella and forced a smile.

Lady Beatrice, who had come looking for Rose, overheard their plans. She immediately interjected that they *must* have the usual accompaniment of a dozen guards and a chaperone to go outside the castle. It was no secret that the beautiful Princess Rose, having blossomed into young womanhood, was considered by the king to be the treasured jewel of his court. It was common knowledge that her eventual marriage was the last, best hope for the survival of his failing kingdom. Therefore he had decreed that she should never be outside the castle walls without a guard. He had delivered this royal edict, curtailing Rose's autonomy "for her own good" when she turned fourteen. She had accepted it with poor grace, fiercely resenting the loss of liberty, especially since Briar had complete license to come and go as she pleased. No one feared that *she* might be carried off or suffer from unwanted romantic attention.

With Lady Beatrice insisting on the proprieties, the simple outing had gone forward, including the guards and the chaperone. The five girls had spent the afternoon—under guard—picking blueberries. But Lady Arabella, Elizabeth, and Jane firmly planted themselves beside Rose at all times, thus keeping Briar away from her. Briar found that whenever she tried to get next to Rose, one of the other girls would maneuver into her way, and whenever she tried to speak to Rose, one of them interrupted with silly comments or loud laughter, so that Briar was the odd one out. She had borne this with all the patience she could, until the outing was over and they returned to the great hall of the castle. Then she managed to get Rose aside and upbraid her.

"So I invite you for an outing and you don't even talk to me!"

"What do you mean?" asked Rose. "We were all talking!"

"No. Every time I tried to talk, your friends interrupted me. It was more than rude."

"They wouldn't do anything like that on purpose," said Rose, disappointed that her hopes for the afternoon had not worked out. "I'm sure all you had to do was speak up. You're being too sensitive."

"You'd be sensitive too if they ever treated you like that. A dog wouldn't treat me that way!"

"I can't believe you're going on about your precious dogs again! You really do prefer them to people, don't you?"

That had been the final straw, the reason for Briar's open declaration that she actually did prefer dogs to humans, and she had meant it, wholeheartedly. But now, staring down into the water, she knows that her musings must come to an end. She must leave her secret haven and go back and face everyone, and she can just imagine the teasing that is to come. She plans out how she will respond. She imagines herself dignified and above it all, ignoring everyone with an unconcerned air. She has practiced this technique often and finds it a better solution than trading insults. In any war of insults she inevitably wins, as she is able to think up far better and more imaginative slurs than anyone else, but she has found it to be a hollow victory. It merely serves to reinforce a wall of bad feelings in her opponents, which makes her feel more alone in the castle than she already does.

She sighs heavily and stands up to go, giving one last, fond look around, her eyes resting on the spreading ripples in the lagoon. She breathes in slowly, as if to inhale the beauty of the place and make it part of her. A smile plays at the corners of her lips, softening the irregularities of her face. Her tormentors are not the only people in her life. She still has friends, and she resolves to meet with them.

As she walks by Jack's house on her way back, she sees Jack, bent over, working in his mother's croft garden, and she calls to him. He looks up and smiles, trying to brush off his dirty, calloused hands, comparing them with Briar's smooth white ones. Jack, having grown up perpetually hungry, has matured into a gangly young man, though he is still a bit shorter than Briar.

Looking around the small yard, Briar notices that there are no more chickens. She knows that one of their cows died last winter and that the garden crops won't ripen for another month. She worries, as always, that there is not enough to eat in Jack's house. Mother Mudge is quick to tell Briar if there is another family in need, but Briar is concerned that she might be too proud to tell her if she and Jack were actually hungry.

Briar smiles at Jack and flashes the sign of the Giant Killers' club. "At the thicket," she says in a loud whisper, as that has become the meeting place for the village contingent of the club.

"As soon as I've finished weeding this row," he says.

Briar moves on and finds Arley and Bridget next door. Arley too has grown, and Bridget, at thirteen, is a rosy-cheeked young tomboy. Arley and Bridget are also working, but they promise to meet at the thicket when they are done. All through the village Briar goes, flashing the secret signal and receiving the signal back from the interested Giant Killers. As she walks along, she can hardly help but notice how much poorer the villagers are growing. With every passing year they become shabbier, their homes more broken-down, their streets more squalid, the children paler and thinner. Once again she renews her vow to rid them of the rapacious giant.

She goes on into the castle proper to find Lan, who joined the Giant Killers three years earlier at Rose's invitation and has been a loyal member ever since.

Half an hour later, Briar and Jack and Lan and most of the village members have gathered in the thicket. Briar and Jack have taken a position on a low tree branch in order to be seen by everyone.

"Is everybody here?" Briar asks, scanning the group of familiar faces. "Yes? Good." She pauses, then says, "Well, here's the thing. We all know how the giant has gotten worse every year. When he came for last year's harvest, he killed four people and injured a whole lot more. Not to mention how much food he's taken out of your mouths and how the Giant Tax is bleeding your families dry. Things are getting really desperate, and we've got to do something soon—or die trying! Now, we've been practicing using our slings, and I think you've all gotten pretty good at it. I'd say we're almost ready to try an attack on the giant! Today we'll have the usual target practice just to see that everybody's keeping it up."

"Arley," Jack says, "will you set the targets along that branch up there? We'll have to aim high."

Arley, with a bag hung over his shoulder, climbs carefully to a large horizontal branch about twenty feet from the ground. Shinnying out on it, he sets up a row of small, shapeless pillows made of rags, with rough charcoal bull's-eyes drawn on them. Each is weighted at the bottom edge with a few small stones inside, so it will stand up. These make perfect practice targets, for an accurate shot, thrown with enough force, knocks them right off the branch. Boys and girls, younger children and adolescents, take turns with their slings—who knows who might find themselves in a position to use their skill against the man-killing giant?

Dudley, Jarrett, Bertha, and the others all line up and take their turns. Jarrett, Quentin, and Marian each succeed in knocking off a target. The rest come close, their stones hitting the branch with thuds and bouncing off it, and everyone gets a second try. Several others take their shots, and then Lan steps up to the mark, turning his left side to face the branch. Lan is a fine, strapping young man now. Master Olyver has him working on his own paintings these days. Yet, as serious as he is about his painting, he's young enough to harbor a secret longing for adventure. He daydreams about ways to show Rose that he can be a hero as well as an artist. Most of the ways involve killing the evil giant. He dreams of getting just one well-aimed shot between the giant's eyes.

Thoughtfully, he places his stone in the cradle of his sling, then stands very still for a moment, staring hard at the target. Suddenly he twirls the sling, rotating it once, then twice, and on the third circle, in a quick, coordinated motion, he thrusts every part of his body—legs, waist, shoulders, arms, elbows, and wrist —in the direction of the target with all his strength, releasing the stone at the top of its rotation, hurling it into the charcoal bull's-eye and knocking it clean off the branch. Jack nods and signals for him to take his next shot. Moving farther back, Lan repeats the performance and knocks off the next target as well, envisioning Rose's grateful smile as the giant topples over in a heap.

Another day dawns at the castle. Master Olyver and Lan are hard at work in their studio. Rose sits, posing for her sixth portrait in three years. Master Olyver is so smitten with her beauty that he paints her again every six months. Rose suffers this because the bargain includes her continued studying under him. In the past few years she has shown herself to be a talented beginner, and her fondest wish is to continue under his tutelage and one day become a master artist herself. It seems a nearly hopeless ambition for a princess, whose all-consuming destiny it is to run a castle, or a whole kingdom, as well as raise a family. But she refuses to think about that. She muses instead on what particular hues Master Olyver is using now for the highlights and shadows of her emerald green dress—cobalt green? viridian?—and what she might choose to use if she were painting it.

Master Olyver feels a rapture that is almost holy as he puts the finishing touches on Rose's latest portrait. Never has he seen the likes of her flashing blue eyes, her luminous skin, the silky sheen of her hair, her mysterious little half-smile. Rose at not quite sixteen has come into the full flower of her beauty, fulfilling the blue fairy's most magical wish for her. In anticipation of her sixteenth birthday, Lady Beatrice and the rest of the ladies at court are constantly speculating on which prestigious suitors will be arriving from what kingdoms and what rich gifts they may bear with them to vie for her approval, but Rose is not interested. She is too busy seeing the world through Master Olyver's eyes—a world of form and color, of light and tone and shadow—and learning his techniques for making figures and landscapes spring to life on a plain wooden panel.

And then there is Lan, who alone shares her artistic aspirations, her need to create. She does not guess that he also pictures himself as a knight, roaming the countryside performing good deeds in her honor or riding off to do battle with whole armies and coming home covered in glory. She has never told him that she already loves him exactly as he is. It is only the knowledge that nothing can come of it that prevents her from giving him the slightest encouragement. Her father, the king, and her mother, the queen, have warned her against forming any attachments. And so her love has coiled in on itself in mute sorrow, which only makes her all the more beautiful.

Rose has put off thinking about the subject of her marriage for as long as she can, but her time is running out. Her sixteenth birthday is fast approaching, and she is afraid that what is supposed to be a birthday celebration will probably be more like a cattle fair, with herself as the prize. King Warrick will look the suitors over and choose from among them the richest and most powerful, and on the day following her birthday, the last day of her freedom, he will decree who her husband is to be, a husband who he thinks will stand against the giant, refill the royal coffers, and change the dismal fortunes of their miserable kingdom. Princess Rose knows it is her duty to accede to her father's wishes, no matter whom he chooses.

Inwardly she rails against her fate. Why couldn't Lan have been born rich and powerful? But then, she wonders, would he still be the same sensitive, caring Lan? During the past three years she and the artist's apprentice have become more than friends, though they know they can never be together. By unspoken agreement they seldom meet outside of her sessions with Master Olyver, afraid as they are of becoming even closer.

However, when she invited him to join the Giant Killers in their secret meetings, he had immediately embraced their cause and become one of them. Lord Henry was not pleased to have another member of a lower class in the club, but at least Lan was an artisan rather than a common laborer, like Jack. Even so, the castle meetings had become few and far between as the former playmates grew older and more cynical. Their goal had seemed more and more like make-believe as they grew up and faced the grim realities of the situation.

All this goes through Rose's mind as she sits and waits for Master Olyver to finish painting. Lan works on another painting nearby, his eyes narrowly focused on some detail. She watches the concentration on his face as he carefully wields his brushes, and she feels her heart contract painfully.

"Rose! Rose!" cries Master Olyver. "Where is that piquant little smile of yours? I can't paint you with this look of tragedy on your lovely face—although that is lovely too, in its own way. Actually, yes. Hold that pose!" he says. He has long seen the hope-less love growing between the two young people, and he is not unsympathetic. "I'll start a new portrait and capture that look of beauteous sorrow."

Rose does not need to pose. She merely looks at Lan and her face reflects her grief, for soon she must say goodbye to him forever.

Briar, having been sent to summon Rose for a fitting of her royal trousseau, knows that the girl will not be pleased to miss her art lesson. Looking at the scene, she contemplates the fact that her life and Rose's have become so different. The exquisite Rose is surrounded by admirers. Even those who don't know her, love her for her beauty. If she receives more attention than she really wants, it seems to Briar that that's not such a terrible problem to have. Princess Rose is accorded the best of everything, yet Briar knows that Rose faces the eventual certainty of an arranged and possibly loveless marriage with whomever her father chooses for her. Briar wonders whether this is better or worse than her own likely prospect of remaining unloved for the rest of her life.

She calls out to Rose, relaying the message that she is wanted in the solar, and Rose responds with a frown, as Briar knew she would. The two young women are on their way up the stairs when they suddenly hear the giant's bell ringing, and they stop in their tracks.

"Oh! I've got to go!" Briar exclaims, taking her sling out of her pocket.

"Go where?" Rose asks.

"Up on the wall walk! I have to see how close I can get to the giant."

"The guards won't let you up there. Besides, it's too dangerous!"

"Who cares?" comes Briar's reply. She turns back toward the stairs just as they hear distant voices shouting. "Princess Rose! Princess Rose!"

"Quick," Rose whispers, "I've got to get out of here. If anyone finds me, they'll force me to stay down in the cellars."

"Where will you go?" asks Briar, impatient to be gone herself.

"Up in the bell tower," she responds. "I'll be safe enough there."

"Hurry, then!" responds Briar, lifting her skirts to go quickly back down the stairs, Rose right behind her. At the door to the courtyard they part, each making her way in a different direction through crowds of frightened people. Rose pushes through the crush of humanity in the courtyard, trying to reach the door to the tower rising up on the opposite side of the keep. Meanwhile, Briar follows the castle guard and attempts to mount the stairs to the wall walk.

"Get, back, girl!" shouts a burly soldier, blocking her way. "Are ye daft?"

Briar is forced to retreat, and she decides instead to go outside the castle and look for another vantage point from which to use her sling. She is determined to get out, despite the mass of villagers and their livestock now streaming in through the gatehouse. She squeezes through the horde, pushing against moving bodies, darting under people's arms and around sheep and cattle. She calculates that she still has time before the giant arrives, but she has no real plan for what to do once she's free of the crowd, only to get as close as she can to the giant and take her best shot. She knows that outside in the village the company of Giant Killers will do the same. This time, she thinks, the giant will not have everything his own way.

Lan too hears the giant's bell, and his one thought is that this may finally be his chance to prove himself. He pulls out his sling and starts to make his own way through the mob in the courtyard.

Beyond the far field, the giant comes stomping through the forest, avarice in his eye, mayhem in his heart. He is in a foul temper. His house is not grand enough, and he's decided that he doesn't have nearly enough gold. He is convinced that the king is holding out on him, and he is in a rage. Suddenly he stops to pull a tree twice his size up by the roots. Stripping the smaller branches off it, he drags it along with him until he reaches the castle wall. Without further ado, he lifts the tree trunk and, using it as a club, bashes down the castle wall, blow after blow after blow, until it's open all the way to the ground.

"Ha! Ha!" the giant laughs. "Now I feel better!"

Inside the broken castle, people are screaming and scrambling to escape the turmoil. The king, miraculously unscathed, stands trembling behind the battlements, heartbeats slamming in his chest, trying to gather his courage to attempt to somehow placate the giant. Putting a horn to his lips in order to be heard, he tries to make a noise, but the words won't come. Finally, he spouts, "Giant! Please, Giant. What have we done to displease you, Your Honor, sir?"

The giant, feeling a sudden pain on his ankle, like a bee sting, says, *"Ow!"* Bending down to clasp his hand over it, he sees a trickle of blood and finds himself being "stung" again and again all about his face. The Giant Killers are fighting back! From behind every cottage, bush, and tree, they sling their stones at the terrible giant. Jack draws blood from the giant's ear. Young Bridget strikes him in the neck, and Briar, who has just joined them, fires a shot to his forehead. Dudley and Jarrett, Bertha and Quentin, Maddox and Emma and Marian, and all the others hurl their best shots until the giant roars with fury. He catches only glimpses of them, but begins to stomp indiscriminately all around him as they strategically retreat.

Meanwhile, Lan has worked his way free of the panic-stricken crowds. He stands on a pile of fallen stones, squarely in front of the hole in the castle wall, watching the giant on his rampage. At last, the Giant Killers are forced to flee, and the giant, having bashed in several cottages, turns his attention to the castle again.

"Bring me food!" he bellows. "Bring me treasure! Twice as much! Do it now, before I knock this whole castle down!"

Rose, halfway up the tower stairs, hears the giant's yell and stops to look out one of the narrow windows. She can see the giant and, through the hole he has made in the castle wall, the piles of rubble and the soldiers trying to help the injured. Then she makes out a lone figure standing straight and unbowed on a pile of broken stones. There is something about him that captures her attention. She sees him turn sideways, his left arm facing the giant, his right hand holding a sling. She sees his face in profile as he puts something in the sling. Even at this distance she can tell: it's Lan! Lan, facing the giant, all alone! She starts to call out his name but chokes it back for fear of distracting him.

Lan stands very still for a moment, staring into the giant's face. Suddenly he twirls the sling, rotating it once. Twice. On the third circle, in a quick motion, he thrusts every part of his body—legs, waist, shoulders, arms, elbows, and wrist—in the direction of the target with all his strength, releasing the stone at the top of its rotation, hurling it straight into the giant's eye.

"Aaarrrgghhh!" shrieks the giant, clapping his hand over his eye and bending over double. *"You! I'll get you!"* he screams, blindly making a swipe for Lan with his free hand. Lan tries to jump out of the way, but the giant's huge hand closes around his middle, pinning his arms to his sides, and he is caught! He kicks furiously, to no avail.

The giant goes on bellowing with pain as he shakes Lan back and forth, nearly snapping his neck. A different scream comes from the tower window. *"Lan!"* For a moment Rose is frozen in helpless despair. Then she runs, panic-stricken, back down the stairs and out across the courtyard, where several of the villagers grab her arms and keep her from going closer. "No, Princess! You mustn't go any farther!" they say. Rose struggles against them, dissolving into tears and calling out Lan's name again and again.

The giant shakes Lan some more. The titan curses and moans, still covering his eye. "A special, slow death for you!" he bellows, and he turns, kicks down every cottage within easy reach, and lumbers unsteadily away, taking Lan with him.

A new day dawns, full of sorrow: sorrow for the fallen, sorrow for the ruined castle and the caved-in cottages, and sorrow for young Lan, who risked his life to fight the giant. About this last, there is great controversy. Some call him brave and laud him for injuring the giant and driving him away without stealing any of their harvest or treasure. Others call him foolhardy, and worse. They say that he only angered the giant, who had kicked in six cottages and would surely be back to vent even greater rage on them. Whichever side they were on, all were living in dread of the giant's return. None within the castle had witnessed the assault by the brave Giant Killers, who had inflicted their "bee stings" from various hiding places. Now they have put their slings away, going about their business with lips sealed.

Meanwhile, Bishop Simon offers no comfort to the giant's victims. Rather he roars from his pulpit that the villagers had brought on the tragedies themselves through their own wickedness, that they deserved this suffering. Though they dare not voice their objections, the afflicted chafe under this cold, unjust condemnation.

At the edge of the village, there is tragedy too: there is nothing left to eat at Jack's house, and to make matters worse, their last remaining cow can give no more milk. No milk means nothing to take to market and sell. They had sold the chickens' eggs until the chickens stopped laying; then they had eaten the chickens. Now no milk and nothing to sell means nothing to eat for Jack or his mother that day or the days to come. Mother Mudge hands Jack the cow's reins, wiping her brow and closing her eyes weakly.

"I feel so poorly, Jack. Here. You take her to the marketplace and make a good bargain, son! She's all we've got!"

Jack nods, patting his mother gently on the back, for in his mind is forming a desperate plan. He has long thought of going back to the giant's house, if he could find a way that was faster than the arduous route he previously traversed up the great mountain and across the clouds. He's been thinking of a nearly toothless little old man who hangs around the marketplace every autumn, always peddling some fantastic magical article. This year

Jack has seen him there, hawking magic beans, beans that would grow a beanstalk up to the sky, the old man said. The villagers ignored him. What would anyone do with a beanstalk so enormous anyway? You couldn't eat beans that big. And the old man wanted three pieces of gold for the beans! Jack would never have three pieces of gold, but he has a cow, and he sees an opportunity . . .

The whole castle is in an uproar, working in a frenzy to repair the damage done by the giant before the guests start to arrive for Rose's sixteenth birthday celebration. The king has commanded that preparations must still go on according to schedule. Turning a deaf ear to his counselors' cautions, the king is resolute that despite the giant's attack, this is to be the grandest ball their utmost efforts can produce. Amid the chaos, the lords and ladies of the court are making ready their best finery and polishing what jewelry is left to them, determined to put on a decent display for the visiting royalty, and the royals are arriving despite the widespread tales of the dreadful giant. In spite of him, all the bravest kings and princes from near and far are coming to court the stunning Princess Rose, willing to risk just about anything to be chosen as her husband.

As the preparations go forth, all but the young people are remembering that calamitous day, not quite sixteen years ago, when the infant Rose was cursed by the gray fairy. Even the elderly have not forgotten, and their hearts are breaking for their young princess and her fate. For sixteen years they have kept their fear hidden, forbidden to speak of it, so that the child could grow up without the threat of it hanging over her. And yet no one even knew about the firstborn twin, caught somewhere in mid-switch with Rose in the royal cradle. Could she have been cursed too? No one knows to ask. No one has ever questioned the story that Briar is the orphan of the Duke and Duchess of Wentmoor, and no one could possibly imagine that *she,* with her malformed face, is the firstborn princess. But Hilde has carried the secret all these years, and on the eve of the twins' birthday, she has sent for Briar, to warn her.

"You did what?" Briar asks in total bewilderment. "Switched me? With Rose? But why?"

"You must try to understand, dear. When you were orphaned and came to us, I felt an immediate kinship with you. I knew how difficult your life would be, and it seemed so unfair. I did it for you, dear, to get you some of the blessings of the fairies."

"But they were supposed to be for Rose? What were they?"

"Ah, well, you needn't concern yourself with that," Hilde says, swatting away the imp, who is, as usual, fluttering about her head in an obnoxious manner. "The important thing for you to know is that you may have been affected by the gray fairy's curse as well. She decreed that on Rose's sixteenth birthday she would touch the spindle of a spinning wheel and die—"

"Die? No! I won't let her!"

"Hush, child. It won't be that terrible, after all. The gold fairy altered the curse, so that she would only fall asleep. But just at that moment, I was switching you. So maybe *you* will fall asleep instead. Or you both will. Or possibly you both escaped the curse altogether. But even if one of you does fall into a magical sleep, the gold fairy decreed that you may be awakened by true love's kiss."

"True love's kiss? But who would ever kiss me? If I fall asleep, I'll never wake up. I'll be as good as dead!"

"Only heaven knows about that, my dear. But that's why I'm warning you. Stay away from spinning wheels! The king commanded that every spinning wheel in the kingdom should be destroyed, and that's why you've never seen one. It's like a drop spindle, but it's part of a machine. Imagine a big wheel that goes around while thread is fed onto a little spindle that's sharp on top. This is what you mustn't touch."

"But who will warn Rose? She must be told too!"

"No doubt the queen will tell her, now that the time has come."

"Maybe I should tell her, just to be sure."

"And how will you tell her that you know? No one is to speak of it, on pain of death!"

"Then you just risked your life for me!"

"That is because I value your life more than my own."

Briar puts her arms around Hilde's neck and embraces her

with tears in her eyes. "Thank you, dear godmother!" Drawing away, she says, "But if I tell Rose, I won't tell her how I know. I'll just warn her about the spinning wheel. She'll have to trust me. If she will. We don't always get along."

"You are a young woman now and must use your own judgment. It is your life you'll be risking! You must do what you think is best."

Briar is thoughtful on her way down from Hilde's tower. Another secret, she thinks, and now it is up to her to decide what to do with it. Halfway down the stairs, she is aware that the imp is following her. She swats it away from her head, but it stays with her, now flying just ahead of her, as if leading her. It precedes her all the way down the stairs, across the courtyard, and through the great hall to the stairway which ascends to her attic room. There, in a dark corner, part of the way up the stairs, the imp halts, hovering over what looks like a slight crack in the wall.

Briar recognizes this place as the entrance to the old secret passageway. In recent years the girls have mostly ignored it; after daring each other to go back in and find the bones of the mythical builder of the passageway, they had returned several times. But there was never anything important to listen in on. Not like that one time when Briar had overheard the king's counselors discussing Rose not being the true heir. All these years, Briar has tried not to remember it herself, but thinking of the passageway reminds her. What would the king's counselors have to say about it now

—with Rose about to turn sixteen and be married off as the heir to the kingdom?

The imp, perhaps with its unerring instinct for trouble, scratches and worries at the crack in the wall, tempting Briar to see if she can still open the hidden door. Despite her caution, she feels drawn toward the imp. It occurs to her that she is tall enough to reach the peepholes by herself now. She could go and listen, and none would be the wiser. What was the worst that could happen? She could overhear some other secret or have to carry some other burden to add to what she already knows? But she might hear something good, something reassuring. Or she might not hear anything at all. She listens for the sound of anyone coming, but there is nothing. Reaching out her hand, she pushes against the wall, here, there, and finally it gives, opening into a cavern of darkness. She borrows a candle from a wall sconce and enters, the imp fluttering on before her, the door closing behind her.

The passageway is even more dreadful than she recalls, the smell of damp mold permeating the air, the walls slimy to the touch, and cobwebs everywhere. But now that she has begun, the imp seems to lure her onward. She pushes through the cobwebs and tries not to think too much about the creatures who made them. Soon she comes to the flight of uneven stairs that she remembers from before. She climbs them cautiously, relying on the dim light from her candle, and keeps going. Surely the peephole is still there! She lifts the candle and begins to look for it, just a little hole in the wall. Her search is soon rewarded. She lowers the candle and puts her eye to the hole. The room she sees is empty. Disgusted that she has come through the dark and filth for nothing, she is distracted by the imp, who has gone on farther down the passage and seems to be waiting for her. *Why not?* she thinks. *I've come this far.*

She goes on, turns a corner, and follows the passage for a long way, until she comes to another flight of stairs. Trailing after the imp, she climbs them, and at the top she dimly hears voices. Cautiously, she searches to see where the voices are coming from and locates the other hole in the wall. She peers through it and finds herself looking at the king and queen in their own room. She feels a thrill of fear. This is not her business. Surely if she were caught spying on the king and queen, she would be in terrible trouble. She is about to turn and go back when she overhears the queen saying, "So you're thinking of marrying our Rose off to King Udolf? He's nearly as old as you are, and he's crass and ruthless!"

"These are not bad qualities in a king!" King Warrick replies. "Would you have him be mincing and ineffectual?"

"No, I would have him be civil and just."

Briar's attention is riveted, and she cannot turn away. She puts her ear to the hole and listens.

"Well, we must take him as we find him," the king insists, "for without him we are lost. The giant is never satisfied! And now he'll be back—and worse than ever! I've sold another hundred acres of land to the goblins just to keep the treasury going. If we keep on at this rate, *they* will be sitting on the throne!"

"And what if the fairies' spells come true and Rose is put to sleep on her birthday? Who can break the spell with true love's kiss? Not Udolf! I've heard tell of his proclivities. He's incapable of feeling anything but lust! We'll lose her. What will happen to all your plans then? She must be warned!"

"I've had every spinning wheel in the kingdom burned. How is she going to prick her finger on one? If that's not enough to calm you, we'll put her under guard! But believe me, we need only ensure that our daughter knows her royal duty. I've already told Udolf that he is—so far—my favorite. And he has hinted that if he's dazzled enough by her beauty, he'll pay a rich bride price. At any rate, you must swallow your fears and be nice to him. He has an army ten times the size of our castle guard, an army big enough to take on the giant! Surely he would defend his new bride's kingdom from the giant's depredations, and then we could finally be free of the monster, start a whole new chapter, and regain our good fortunes! Udolf will be arriving at any time with his whole retinue. Then let the feasting begin!"

"And we're hosting this great feast for Udolf and all the rest of them? I suppose you will provide for it in the usual way?"

"Oh, leave that to me, wife. Believe me, we will never go

hungry. Our secret stockpile of food and treasure will be more than adequate. As long as we have the Giant Tax, you should have no fear of it running out."

After a pause, Queen Merewyn speaks. "You run a terrible risk, husband. Beware of the news getting out, or you will have a very unhappy populace on your hands. What would they think of your double-dealing, when their own families are going hungry?"

"You needn't worry that the rabble — or the giant — will ever hear tell of it! You may be sure that only a handful of our most trusted servants know of it, and they value their lives too much to spill the secret. And there's much more to be considered than the unhappy populace. My counselors insist on being maintained in a certain style. In fact, they've forced me to raise their pay! Why, the bishop's demands alone could bankrupt me! If I didn't look out for myself, they'd bleed me dry! And what the villagers don't know won't hurt them. They'll be grateful for the leftovers."

Briar can bear to hear no more. She turns and retraces her steps through the moldy passageway, trying to come to terms with what she has heard. A secret stockpile of food for the king? While Jack and his mother, and Arley and Bridget, and Dudley and Jarrett, Bertha, Quentin, and Maddox, and all the rest of them go to bed hungry? She can hardly believe it. And Rose to be married off to some "crass and ruthless" old brute to save the kingdom from ruin? Tears prick at the corners of Briar's eyes as she castigates herself for listening in on the conversation.

"I wish I didn't know!" she speaks aloud. "I wish I didn't know." But now that she has the knowledge, what can she do about it? Would it help Rose to be warned of the fate that awaits her? Was there any alternative for her? What would Briar wish for her to do? Refuse Udolf's proposal? Run away and save herself? Let the king and the kingdom go to ruin? In a moment of sudden clarity she knows that Rose will do what she sees as her duty, no matter what the cost, and Briar grieves for her.

And the secret stockpile of food and treasure? Briar burns fiercely with the injustice of it. What should she do with such knowledge? Whom could she tell? What would happen if the peasants learned the truth? She shies away from the thought. First she must find Rose and warn her of the spinning wheel.

Rose stands despondent in the center of a group of bustling women, all of them seemingly oblivious to the expression of tragedy on her lovely face. She has barely come out of her room for days. The queen thinks she is upset because of the giant's brutal attack, but she does not know that Rose's heart is broken, or why. Since Rose can put it off no longer, the women are doing the final fittings on her ball dress—a confection in white, embellished with pale blue and gold embroidery. Twenty seamstresses with twenty needles have worked for twenty days to make this gown worthy of the most beautiful princess anyone could imagine. But the princess does not smile. She is hurting, and the strain and resentment of holding her feelings in is too much to bear. She is ready to lash out at the first person to cross her.

Briar enters the room and tries to get close to Rose, which seems at first impossible. Only after half an hour of being pushed and shoved unceremoniously out of the way does she get a chance to flash the Giant Killers' sign at her. Rose, upon seeing this, tells the women she has had enough and orders them out of the room.

"Well? What is it?" Rose asks.

Briar, suddenly unsure of herself, hesitates. "It's . . . There's something I have to tell you, and it's terribly important."

"I'm listening."

"It's about your birthday. I've just found out something. Something terrible."

"Perhaps you shouldn't repeat it if it's so terrible."

"But you must be warned!"

"Warned about what?"

Briar searches for the right words and finally blurts out, "The gray fairy put a curse on you when you were just a baby! She said that on your sixteenth birthday you'd prick your finger on a spinning wheel and die!"

An expression of distaste and dismay crosses Rose's lovely features. All her pent-up feelings of grief and resentment come rushing to the surface, and she finally lets loose. "What a horrid thing to say! Did you think I *needed* some more bad news?"

"I'm sorry. I can imagine how upset you must be about Lan."

"No, I don't think you can!"

"But—"

"I don't want to hear any more. You're just listening to a lot of jealous busybodies. If this were true, my mother would have told me!"

"Well, maybe she will. There's still time. You should know that the gold fairy softened the curse so you would just be put to sleep. But I had to be sure you were warned, so I'm telling you myself —just don't touch the spindle of a spinning wheel!"

"A spinning wheel? I never heard of such a thing. Are you trying to scare me?"

"Is *that* what you really think I'm doing?"

Rose, unable to bear any more calamities, rejects Briar's words utterly. She counters with the first denunciation she can think of. "What else are you trying to do but upset me? You're just jealous! You've always been jealous, and you can't stand it that this whole ball is going to be for me."

Briar is stung by this accusation, and anger swells in her heart. She thinks of what she has risked to warn Rose, only to be so unjustly accused. Suddenly, this very minute, she is past caring whether Rose believes her. She only wants to hurt her back. "If I really wanted to scare you, I'd tell you who your father is going to choose for your husband!"

"How would you know? Nobody will know until he announces it tomorrow!"

"I won't tell you how I know, but I do! He's already chosen King Udolf! I know that he's three times your age, and I know that he's coarse and ruthless. He's the richest and most powerful of all your suitors, and that's why he was chosen. So there you go. Sweet dreams!"

"You're so jealous, you're just about turning green! That's because not one of my suitors would even so much as *look* at you!"

In all their arguments, this is the first time Rose has ever made reference to Briar's appearance, and the volley hits home. Briar responds in kind. "So what? The only reason they look at you is because they don't care if you haven't got a brain in your head!"

"Just stop talking and go away!"

"I will!" Briar retorts as she turns on her heel to depart. The young women separate, each of them sick with anger and remorse, but both far too stubborn to admit to the remorse.

"OH, JACK. JACK! WHAT HAVE YOU DONE?" groans Mother Mudge. She shakes her head in despair. "Now we will surely starve!" she wails. "How could you be so heedless?"

Jack places the magic beans back in his pouch and puts his arm around her. "Mother, you must trust me. I'm going off to plant these beans. Stop your crying now. If I'm quick and lucky, it will all come right in the end."

With that, he grabs a shovel and sets off to search for a place beyond the far fields, where the beanstalk can grow without destroying any of the crops. After much looking about and figuring, he settles on a spot due east from the mountain, directly beneath the outer edge of the enormous cloud that always surrounds its top. He begins to dig. Hoping that he has chosen well, he makes five holes in a wide circle, ten feet apart. Then he kneels down and carefully plants each bean in its hole, tucking it in with a blanket of loose dirt and a wish. For a moment, his confidence is shaken as he realizes that he has staked everything on these five beans. A giant beanstalk was the only way he could imagine to get back up to the giant's house without a horse, and it would have to be closer to the giant's house than the mountain if he were to have a chance at escaping quickly. Would it turn out that he had been a gullible fool who had traded his cow for starvation? He refuses to believe it. Straightening up, he claps the dirt off his hands, and, looking up to the cloud, he shakes one fist in the air and cries, "I'm coming for you!"

After much agonized thought, Briar has made a decision. Shaking her head as she walks along, she mutters to herself, "It isn't fair! It isn't right!" She will tell Mother Mudge the truth about the king's secret stockpile of food and treasure, and let her decide what to do with the information. She knocks at the door to Jack's cottage.

"Go away!" comes a muffled cry from within.

Briar, realizing that something is very wrong, knocks again and calls, "Mother Mudge? It's me, Briar. Can I come in?"

Finally, the door opens, and there stands Mother Mudge, who leans against the doorframe, moaning to herself over and over again, "Oh Jack, what have you done?"

"Dear Mother Mudge, what is the matter?" Briar asks.

Mother Mudge clutches Briar's shoulder. "It's Jack. He's off on some fool's errand. He traded our only cow for a handful of *beans,* and now we're going to starve." A tear makes its way down her sunken cheek.

"Oh, Mother Mudge! You know I won't let that happen. I'll bring you food!" Before she says any more, Briar gives a moment's thought to the king and the trouble she is about to cause him; then she thinks of all her hungry friends — and she continues.

"That's what I came to tell you, Mother Mudge. There's plenty of food to be had! The king has a secret store of food and treasure! He's using the Giant Tax to hoard a stockpile for himself — even though his people are starving!"

Mother Mudge holds Briar's shoulders in an iron grip, looks into the girl's eyes, and cries, "King Warrick taxes his hungry people while he rolls in plenty?" She shakes Briar in helpless fury. Suddenly, with a visible effort, she takes several deep breaths, then calms herself and lets go, patting the girl's shoulders gently.

"You're a good girl, Briar," she says, "but are you sure? This could lead to a world of trouble."

"I heard the king himself say it to the queen! She was trying to warn him against it. They didn't know I was listening."

"And you're sure that's what he meant? Think carefully now."

"It couldn't have been any clearer! He said, 'What the villagers don't know won't hurt them.' He said, 'They'll be grateful for the leftovers.'"

"Oh, he did, did he?" Mother Mudge dries her tears and assumes a look of deadly resolve. "People ought to know! We've got to get the word out! Come along with me. We'll spread this all over the village, and you can give everyone a firsthand account." Mother Mudge puts on her shawl, and the two of them hurry out the door.

All the way up the street they go, stopping at each house, staying only long enough to deliver the message. Mother Mudge, who is known to everyone, says to them, "This must not stand!" and the villagers shake their fists and agree. Then neighbor calls on neighbor, spreading the story like fire in dry tinder. Many a voice is raised in pain, betrayal, and outrage, and a conspiracy is born.

Beyond the far field, five magic beans have sprouted, erupting from the earth like massive trees. They twist and twine into one giant beanstalk, bigger around than Jack's cottage. It grows and grows, curling and stretching, sprouting huge leaves and enormous green beans. Now it reaches clear up to the sky — just as the old man said it would — and there, halfway up, is Jack, looking down and holding on for dear life.

He sees the cultivated fields below, all in patches like a quilt. He sees the whole village and the castle, as tiny as toys. He thinks that if he falls from this height he will surely die, and he pauses, trying to summon the nerve to keep climbing. Then he realizes that falling from an even greater height can still only kill him once, and he forces himself to reach for the next branch and continue upward. The air grows cooler and cooler as he ascends, and the wind whips all around him. The knapsack of supplies he packed for the trip weighs heavily on his shoulders, and his fears and doubts weigh even more. He climbs for another hour, sweat cold upon his brow, muscles aching from the strain, until at last, gasping for breath, he reaches the edge of the cloud.

It looks so soft and hazy that he hesitates to set foot on it, even though he knows how strong it is. Finally, he leaps down and lands on the spongy surface. A pervasive mist swirls around him, concealing him up to his chest, and he takes a moment to look around. Far in the west, he sees the mountaintop rising above the clouds, just as he surmised. And there, not too far away, lies the giant's grand, tall house. Summoning his energy, he makes a mad dash across a field's width of cloud. He wears no skunk scent this time, remembering that it nearly gave him away on his first trip up the mountain years ago. He will just have to trust to luck. So far, his luck has held; he's made it up the beanstalk safely, and his calculations have proved correct. The location of the beanstalk couldn't be more perfect for a quick getaway.

Now he pauses, reconnoitering. As he decides to try his luck at the back door, he nearly stumbles upon a low window casement in the mist, and suddenly he recalls the barred window he had discovered on his last trip. Bending down, he peers between the bars into the dim room and lets his eyes adjust. There, in a corner, he sees a huddled human-size figure sitting with his knees drawn up, leaning his arms and his head upon them.

"Psst!" Jack hisses. "Hey, you in there. Who are you?"

The head comes up, and though Jack can scarcely make out its features, the figure struggles to his feet and a voice cries, "Jack! It's me, Lan! Lanford Cole! How did you get here?"

"I climbed up a magic—well never mind that. Lan—you're still alive! Are you all right?"

"I'm perishing, Jack. The giant wants to starve me slowly before he kills me, but his woman takes pity on me and slips in some food every now and then. The giant comes to my cell every day and tells me some new way he's thought of to finish me off, just to torment me. I'm half out of my mind! I can't believe you've come."

"God's teeth, I wish I had some food to give you. I've had nothing to eat myself since yesterday. Is there any way to get you out of there? I have some rope in my pack. You could climb up to the window, but it wouldn't do you any good. These bars are too close together for you to fit between them." Jack grips the bars in his hands and tries to rattle them for all he's worth, but they don't budge. "I can't help you this way. You say the giant woman has taken pity on you?"

"Yes. Do you have something in mind?"

"I'm thinking I should find her and see if *she'll* let you out."

"Best beware, Jack. She's greatly afraid of the giant. There's no telling how far she can be pushed."

"I've got to try! I'm off to test my luck. If I don't come back, say a prayer for me."

"I will, brother. I'll start now!"

Jack hauls his pack over one shoulder and trudges on for several minutes toward the rear of the house and around the corner to the enormous back door. Once there, he watches and waits for a chance to sneak in. He observes what looks to be a clothesline strung between two posts not far from the door, and he hides behind one of the posts. From an open window, he hears the sound of a hoarse voice singing a cheerless dirge of drudgery and woe. A minute later, the door opens and out comes the female giant. Not so large as the giant, she has a gnarled and withered face, a face that has seen too much. She hauls along a big basket of laundry and begins to drape the clothes over the clothesline. Jack screws up his courage and calls up to her, softly at first, and then just loud enough so that she can hear him.

She peers over the clothesline and looks directly at Jack. "What do you think you're doing here, boy? Are you crazy? Don't you know a giant lives here—a giant who *eats* ones such as you? Begone with you before he wakes up and gets a whiff of you!"

"Good lady," Jack shouts up to her, "you have a friend of mine locked up in a cell, half starved. Only let him go and we'll both be gone. Have pity on us, good woman." Jack waits for her reply, every nerve on edge.

"I couldn't let him free if I wanted to," comes the answer. "He's locked up fast, and the giant keeps the key on a chain around his neck. I just sneak the lad food through the bars on his door, but I fear the giant will soon kill him horribly. He's surpassing cruel. I work and slave for him from before dawn until after dark, yet he's mistreated me so that I'm an old woman before my time. I hate and fear him, but there's little I can do for you."

"Tell me his weaknesses, then, and let me in so I can defeat him."

The tall woman laughs derisively. "You've got nerve to spare, young man, if you hope to defeat such as him. He's half blinded now, but that won't save you. Better to get out of here quickly, before he wakes up from his nap. But wait—" she says, disappearing into the house. A minute later she opens the door and says, "Take some of this filthy gold back with you. Stolen money can bring nothing but bad luck! Here, take this bag—and good riddance!" The giantess holds what is to her a very small bag of gold, and she bends down to give it to Jack. Jack stands, staring wide-eyed at the bag. So much gold! Then he takes off his knapsack and, pulling a coil of rope out of it, stuffs the bag of gold in. Putting it back over his shoulders, he is dismayed by the weight of it, but he straightens up and thanks the good woman.

"Tell me, when does he sleep?" asks Jack, determined to glean some information before he leaves.

"He stays up counting his treasure till the moon is overhead each night. In the morning he sleeps until well after sunrise. Then he has to have his breakfast in bed, and he makes that screeching harp play for him. That's his habit, for all the good it will do you."

Jack thanks her again. He picks up the coil of rope and turns to go back the way he came, his mind already working furiously to come up with some plan for his next trip up the beanstalk. He trudges all the way back around the house to the barred window where Lan is imprisoned, and he tells Lan about the key to his cell being around the giant's neck.

"I'm going back down to get some tools and maybe some help. So hold on. I'll be back as soon as I can. Maybe tonight."

"All right. And Jack? If I don't make it . . . tell Princess Rose that I loved her."

Jack's face lights up. "Really? That's something! Does she know?"

"I think she knows, but I've never told her. It wouldn't matter anyway. She's too far above me. I just want her to hear it, for once, if I die."

"Well, don't give up hope, Lan. I'll be back!" Jack swallows hard, fighting tears, and, adjusting the heavy load on his shoulders, he leaves the rope next to the window, where it is obscured by the mist, and heads for the beanstalk. The return trip to earth is arduous and fraught with danger. Twice he misses his step and finds himself hanging by his hands, his burden of gold dragging him down as he feels desperately with his toes for a secure foothold. Once, he slips his foot into a tightly twined vine and is caught there, unable to free himself until he gives up his shoe. Tired to the bone, he carefully lowers himself, one hand or foot at a time, minute by minute inching closer to the ground. Two hours later, totally exhausted, he collapses at the foot of the beanstalk, and there he rests, almost unable to move. His growling stomach relentlessly reminds him that he needs food, and so, with great difficulty, he gets to his feet and picks up the heavy knapsack. He lurches toward home, hoping that his mother will have found something to eat. When at last he does arrive, Mother Mudge throws her arms around him and cries, "Jack! Oh, Jack! Where have you been?"

Jack takes off the heavy knapsack and drops it, then flops down on the floor by the peat fire, which burns feebly in the center of the room. "Have you found anything at all to eat, Mother? For I'm about to perish with hunger."

"Lady Briar brought us a basket of food. I've saved out some cold meat and cheese and bread for you, and a flask of mead. Now tell me, Jack, where you've been all day, and what you've got in your knapsack."

Between bites, Jack tells her of his adventure, all about climbing the magic beanstalk, finding Lan, finding a friend in the giant woman. Then he tells her about the bag of gold that nearly pulled him down to his doom. At first she can hardly believe him, never having dreamed that her son was the heroic type, but then Jack opens the knapsack and she sees the gold, and her eyes widen.

"What shall we do with it, Mother? It's money the giant stole from the treasury. Should we return it to the king? He does nothing for the people!"

Mother Mudge shakes her head. "The king has been playin' us false. He has his own hoard of food and treasure aplenty, while we pay the Giant Tax and go hungry. We can't trust it to him. And we surely can't keep it all for ourselves."

Jack opens the bag of gold and runs his fingers through it. "There's enough here to give some to every person in the village, Mother."

"Yes, I think that would be best," Mother Mudge says thoughtfully, "but this is not the time. There is great unrest among the villagers just now, and things seem to be coming to a head. Best to let them, I think. This treasure should stay buried until we see what the king will do for all of us. Bury it right here, I say, until the time is right, then spread it among everyone."

Jack finishes eating and gets to work digging a deep hole in the corner of their dirt floor. He buries the gold, laying his straw mattress over it when he is done. Then, done in, he falls on top of it and goes instantly to sleep. His mother stands over him, staring at the contours of his sleeping face, noticing how he has grown lately and the strong line of his jaw. She admires his tranquil, intelligent brow, marveling at all that her Jack has done this day, sorry now that she did not trust him about the beans.

It is the evening of Rose's sixteenth birthday. In the solar, the queen and her retinue and the young women of the castle are caught up in a whirlwind of preparations for the ball. Rose stands in the center of it all in her chemise, patiently putting up with the attention, occasionally forcing a vacant smile. She seems, in fact, to be off somewhere else, in another time and place. And so she is, back in the artist's studio, bent over some project with Lan, imagining herself finally telling him how she really feels about him. Then she remembers that it is too late. She closes her eyes and, giving herself a mental shake, straightens her spine and stands taller. She is the princess, and she must play the role. She signals that she is ready for the ladies in waiting to robe her. They lift her resplendent dress over her head and settle it around her perfect figure. Lady Arabella and Elizabeth and Jane, each proudly wearing her own new gown, gasp and exclaim over the beauty of Princess Rose and her glorious dress.

Queen Merewyn approaches her daughter with a servant by her side who bears a gold coronet on a velvet pillow. "Here is the finishing touch," the queen says, picking up the coronet with both hands and placing it on Rose's head. "The symbol of a royal princess of the realm and a token of your parents' esteem." Princess Rose is engulfed by the ladies of the court, all of them complimenting her at once and wishing her happy birthday. Everyone is lost in admiration for the princess, and everyone wants to be close to her.

Indeed, by order of the queen, she has not been left alone once the whole day, and all but the young silently understand why. Who can forget the gray fairy's curse? But there were gifts given to the infant Rose as well, and in the tizzy of excitement over the princess's sixteenth birthday, they are all but forgotten.

If anyone does think of the boons the fairies bestowed on her, no one wonders what has become of them. Beauty she has in full, and that outshines all the rest. If her voice is less than a nightingale's, her dancing less than mesmerizing, her wit less than rapier sharp, or her strength less than Herculean, no one notices or cares.

Only Briar, the possessor of those four gifts, stands ignored on the sidelines, looking on. She too is lost in her thoughts. This is one of those things, she tells herself — one of those things that Hilde has taught her about, that cannot be changed and must be lived with. This happy flurry and commotion is for other girls, pretty girls. Not for her. No one would even notice if she were not at the ball. She would far rather go to Hilde's room, where she knows she will always receive a loving welcome.

She turns to leave, when Lady Arabella puts a hand on her shoulder and says, "Where are you going, Lady Briar? You must get ready for the ball!"

Briar, trying to get over her surprise, is temporarily speechless. She looks into Lady Arabella's face, struggling to tell whether she is serious. Lady Arabella smiles warmly, and Briar wonders if perhaps the young woman is growing up, genuinely trying to make amends for her past slights. While Briar is trying to decide how she feels about it, Elizabeth and Jane show up and echo Lady Arabella's coaxing tone, urging Briar to turn herself over to their tender ministrations to prepare her for the ball. They link arms with her in a friendly way, but Briar realizes that she can't disentangle herself without making a scene.

"I don't think this is such a good idea," she objects. "Besides, I don't have a dress." She says this without self-pity, but the fact remains that no one thought to make her a new dress for the ball.

"Well, that doesn't matter," Elizabeth says. "My last year's green dress should just about fit you. I'll go get it, and you can have a look." Before Briar can object, Elizabeth disappears into the fray, and Lady Arabella and Jane enthusiastically tell her how good Elizabeth's green dress will look on her. She is torn, reluctant to go along but wanting to believe they are offering friendship. Before she knows it, the two girls are helping her off with her dress and unbraiding her dark hair. "I think you should wear it loose," Lady Arabella says, "with maybe a wreath of flowers on your head. Don't you think so, Jane?"

Jane agrees, and soon Elizabeth is back with the green dress. The girls slide the dress over Briar's head and down over her chemise. The sleeves are a bit short, but Lady Arabella assures her that no one will notice.

By this time, Rose is ready for the ball, the blue and gold embroidery on white silk making a perfect foil for her blue eyes and golden hair. Every woman in the room stops to admire her, but she is used to that and pays no attention. She looks around and, spotting Briar amid the other girls, makes her way over to them.

She looks at Briar in the green dress and says, "So, you're coming to the ball, then?"

"I don't know. I don't think it's such a great idea."

"Of *course* you're coming!" say the other girls in chorus, and Briar sighs deeply.

"I think you should come," Rose says a bit stiffly, and Briar wonders if that means that their fight is over, that all is forgiven. It occurs to her that Rose may have asked the other girls to be nice to her. She decides that it would be churlish of her to refuse to go to the ball now. She tries to arrange her hair so that it falls down over her heavy brow, and she allows herself to be led down the stairs to the great hall.

Hilde stands at the window of her tower room, gazing out beyond the castle wall to the far fields, golden in the waning sun. *This is the day,* she thinks. *The twins' sixteenth birthday.* But only one of them will be honored and acclaimed. Only Rose will be admired and adored.

What of Briar, the firstborn? Because of the face she was born with, she is denied her birthright. She will be passed over and brushed aside like so much dust. In a few weeks, if Hilde reminds everyone, maybe they will celebrate the false birthday the king and queen assigned to Briar as an infant. There might be leftover dessert from the kitchen and a few forced congratulations.

Or, like Hilde's own sixteenth birthday, no one would notice at all. Her eyes grow moist. Her hands tighten into fists. She has known from the time of Briar's birth what to expect, yet she still burns with the injustice of it. Briar couldn't be more dear to her if she were her own child.

And now either of the young women might succumb to the gray fairy's curse and fall into a deathlike sleep. Hilde thinks it would serve the king and queen right if their cherished daughter fell down, insensible, in the middle of their party. What of their celebrations then? As for Rose, surely one among all her admirers would be able to waken her anyway. Hilde shakes her head and turns from the window, pacing agitatedly in circles around her cluttered worktable. She idly sprinkles some dried mustard powder into a mixture she has been working on. She stirs it with a wooden spoon and mutters a brief incantation over it, but it does not turn into gold.

The imp, who has been bouncing around the ceiling, flutters down to buzz above her head, but she waves it off, lost in contemplation. She knows she is expected at the ball; the king and queen will want her there in case the worst happens, though what they think she can accomplish with her feeble powers against the gray fairy's magic is a puzzlement. She is far more concerned about Briar, knowing that no one else will be looking out for her. She had hoped that the girl would come to her to spend the evening, but she must have found some other haven. Hilde stops her pacing and says out loud, "I should go down," but she shakes her head again and continues her pacing, unable to get past her own wall of resentment.

That evening, Jack wakes up from his nap with a sense of a heavy weight bearing down on him, though there is nothing there, and then he remembers that he promised Lan he would return. He must go back up the beanstalk tonight, with only his wits to keep him alive. Upon rising, he sees that his mother is nowhere around. Knowing that he needs some quiet time to think, he climbs to the loft and makes himself invisible in the hay. Then he closes his eyes and replays the morning's adventure in his mind. He needs a plan. He tries to imagine how things will go tonight, and in what way he could finally destroy the giant. Imagining the difficulty and danger of escaping down the beanstalk, he realizes how much more difficult it would be for one as big and heavy as the giant to trust his weight to the precarious vine. Jack sees a possibility. It comes to him in a flash. With a new sense of purpose, he gets up and walks all through the village, giving the Giant Killers' sign wherever he goes. Before long, every young person who is free to do so is quietly heading toward the thicket. Jack meets them there, and after waiting to see that most everyone has arrived, he tells them that Lady Briar is probably at the ball and they must proceed without her. They all murmur in agreement, and Jack, assuming leadership, reveals his desperate scheme.

"Everything depends on you. If I can get the giant to chase me down the beanstalk, our only hope is to chop it down while he's still quite high in the sky, and that's going to take all of you. Arm yourselves with axes and wait at the foot of the stalk until you hear my signal. Arley, your father is a shepherd. Can you borrow his horn for me? I wouldn't ask, but it's dreadfully important that you all hear me from some distance away. By the time I'm within shouting distance, it may be too late. You're to chop the beanstalk down on my signal, even if it means that I fall too, understand?"

There is dead silence. A few of them say, "I couldn't do it, Jack," and he pats them on the back and sends them home. The rest nod quietly, their expressions grief-stricken but determined, and they quietly disperse.

Chapter Three

MOTHER MUDGE IS IN THE TOWN SQUARE, surrounded by angry villagers. They are wielding rakes and hoes and shovels, and they mutter and grumble as they listen to her impassioned speech and shout their furious responses at each pause.

Mother Mudge raises both hands to quiet the crowd. "We've worked all our lives on the king's land, haven't we?" she cries.

"Yes!" exclaim the villagers, shaking their fists.

"Clearing the land, tilling and sowing, weeding and harvesting! It's backbreaking work!"

"Yes!"

"We've harvested the king's crops while our own lay rotting in the fields! We've raised him crop after crop of good, wholesome food, and yet *we go hungry!* Why?"

There are calls from the crowd: "The Giant Tax! The Giant Tax!"

"All these years, years of sweat and toil, the king has ordered us to pay his Giant Tax!"

"Yes! Yes!"

"Unfair!"

"Unfair!"

"Then the giant comes and steals the fruit of our labor—while the bishop tells us it's our own fault! So the giant robs us blind, *but he's not the only one!* Who else is robbing us blind? Eh? Who else?"

The crowd erupts with shouts of "The king! The king!"

"Our own king!"

"*Our own king,*" shouts Mother Mudge. "And who is using innocent Princess Rose's sixteenth birthday as an excuse for gorging this night? Feasting with all the other kings and nobles *while our babes are going to bed hungry?*"

"The king! Our own king!" comes the clamor.

Mother Mudge pauses, gathering her strength, her purpose, her outrage. Then she screams her challenge: *"What are we going to do about it?"*

"Revolt!" comes the cry.

"Revolt!"

"REVOLT!"

Briar finds herself descending to the great hall with one arm held firmly by Lady Arabella. She is already making plans for how to evade the other girls and leave the party early, but Lady Arabella does not let go, and now Jane has her other arm and they are guiding her to a spot where the young people of the castle are clustered together and they can all stand and watch the proceedings.

The hall is lined with dozens of richly clad strangers. They have come from afar, all breathlessly awaiting Princess Rose's arrival, hoping for a chance to dance with her. The king and queen sit on a raised dais at one end of the room and smile benignly on their guests.

Suddenly the horns sound, and though darkness has not yet fallen, all the torches are lit in order to illuminate the much-anticipated arrival of the princess. The king stands up, grandiosely extending one arm toward the staircase, and says, "Your Highnesses, lords and ladies of the court, I present my daughter, the incomparable Princess Rose." Rose steps lightly down the stairs, her mind in turmoil. She knows that she is about to face a great room full of suitors, but she can think only of Lan, of the sparkle in his eyes and the way his hair fell down over his forehead. The way his strong, gentle hands maneuvered the most delicate brush. Lan, who was so brave, and by now had surely paid for it with his life. She swiftly closes her mind against the thought before any telltale tears can start. Summoning all her willpower, she puts on a dazzling smile and enters the hall. There are gasps of admiration, and the assembled guests all bow and curtsy to her. Then they crowd in closer to get a good look, until the king takes her by the hand and leads her to the head of the table, where a chair has been placed for her next to the queen.

By order of Queen Merewyn, a heavy guard has been posted on Princess Rose to ensure that the gray fairy's curse has no chance to come true, and so a soldier takes his place on each side of the princess, and three more behind. Rose notes this with some irritation, already looking for an opportunity to dismiss them.

Briar, meanwhile, suffering pangs of acute self-consciousness, is grateful that everyone's attention is focused on Rose. She keeps her own head down so that her hair drapes over the side of her face.

Soon it is time for the many foreign suitors to be presented to Princess Rose. Though the king has already secretly chosen a favorite, the others must be given their opportunity to change his mind. Perhaps an even better candidate will present himself. This goes on for quite a while, as names and titles are announced one by one, and Rose greets each of them properly while the rest of the crowd stand at attention or murmur their own commentary on the proceedings. Briar steals glances around her to see who is nearby and notices that most of the boys from school are present, including Lord Henry, all of them dressed in their finest doublets and hose, many wearing hats with turned-up brims or decorative feathers. Everyone, in fact, is looking their finest, and after a while she dares to hope that with her borrowed dress and her face half hidden, she looks as if she belongs in such company.

After all the introductions are over, music begins to play and couples form lines to dance. As those around her pair off, Lord

Henry comes up and whispers in Lady Arabella's ear. She grins and turns to Briar. "Lord Henry says that someone wants to dance with you!" she says. "Over here, come see!"

Briar is torn. She wants to believe that there is someone here to be a partner for her, but she is nearly choked by shyness, and she fights a strong feeling that she wants no part of this. Elizabeth and Jane hustle her forward, giggling. In front of her stand Lord Henry and a small crowd of other young men of the castle. Everyone seems to be delightedly waiting for something. Finally, Lady Arabella says, "Yes, we've found the perfect partner for you! Just look!"

She gives Lord Henry a nod, and he moves to one side as the crowd of boys parts down the middle to reveal what was hidden behind them: a dog dressed up in a fancy doublet and feathered hat. He is brought forward on a leash.

"Meet Sir Greyhound!" Henry announces with mock gravity, and every eye turns to Briar to watch her reaction. She gets it. It is all a joke—everything. The acceptance, the attention, the dress, the camaraderie, it was all to lead up to this moment, to prove how ridiculous it was to include her. Her believing that she was wanted as a guest at the ball—that was the joke. She fiercely holds back the tears that are threatening, and she keeps her face carefully blank as the laughter rings out all around her.

"Well, you said you preferred dogs to people!" Lady Arabella cries, smothering her laughter.

"Yes," says Briar calmly. "Yes, I most certainly do." And she steps forward, and taking the dog's leash, she turns to leave. The crowd parts before her, still laughing as she controls herself with what dignity she can.

Suddenly she turns back to Lady Arabella and asks her quietly, "Did Rose know about this?"

Lady Arabella barely hesitates before she replies, "Of course! It was her idea!"

The last of Briar's iron control fails her. She feels her chin begin to tremble and her eyes sting with tears. She tries to focus all her concentration on getting to the door. But there, in front of her, Bishop Simon steps forward. He is the only one not laughing. Instead he says with all seriousness, "Get you gone, girl! Go back to the kennels where you belong!"

Briar gasps at his cruelty. This, from one who was supposed to be a man of God! He may as well have declared her the castle freak. Suddenly she pulls her emotions up short. She will not cry before this man. She steps deliberately around him and continues on. The walk seems like the longest she has ever taken, with the laughter still ringing behind her. But not everyone laughs. Some there frown at the cruel joke, especially at the clergyman's additional cruelty.

Briar, however, does not see them. Finally free of the place, she bends down and pets the long-suffering dog, speaking soothingly to it as she tries to remove the ridiculous clothes. There are footsteps behind her and then a warm voice saying, "Here, let me help."

She turns to find Zane, the jester, but he isn't laughing. He bends down and eases off the dog's makeshift doublet as Briar removes the feathered hat. She opens her mouth to thank him, but the lump in her throat at first makes speech impossible. Then she chokes out, "I only want to get away—from *everyone!*"

"Of course, poppet. You go on. I'll take care of the dog."

"Thank you," Briar whispers. She hurries on her way, breaking into a run, feeling like a dam about to burst.

She flees through the village with her head down, sobbing now. She is barely aware of the distant crowd in the town square and wants to avoid everyone. As she nears the edge of town, however, members of the Giant Killers' club are dispersing from the thicket, and seeing her grief, several gather round her to offer comfort. Jack comes up to the little gathering and asks her what's wrong. She only shakes her head and says, "I can't tell you here!"

Jack takes her by the hand back to the thicket to talk privately.

"Come on, Briar. What is it?" he asks, looking into her eyes. At first she covers her face with her hands and only sobs, but slowly, bit by bit, the story comes out: the way Lady Arabella and the others cajoled her into dressing up and then hustled her down to the ball, only to make her the butt of their elaborate joke in front of everyone. Worst of all, Arabella said it had all been Rose's idea! Rose, who had once been her closest friend!

"Are you sure she was telling the truth?" Jack asks. "Seems like Lady Arabella would say anything hurtful she could think of. And Princess Rose—could she really have done such a thing?"

Briar pauses. Was Arabella's claim true, or had it been a lie just to hurt her? "Maybe," she says. "But you don't know about the terrible fight Rose and I had before the ball. I've never seen her so angry! Oh, she could have done it after that!" Briar sobs quietly for a bit while Jack struggles to find something soothing to say.

"You've still got all of us in the village," he offers hopefully. "I know we're just peasants and you're a lady an' all, but aren't we your friends?"

"Yes," she says as she slowly reins in her emotions. "You are, and that's a comfort." They sit in thoughtful silence for a bit until Briar is down to the occasional sniffle.

"Jack?" she says.

"What is it?"

"There's something else I need to tell you. It's about a curse that may have been cast on me when I was only a baby. I just found out about it, but it might come true at any moment now—before the day is over."

Jack's interest is immediately claimed, but he is conscious that time is passing and that Lan must be waiting for him—if he's still alive. "Tell me about it fast," he says. "It's urgent."

So she does.

"You see," she finishes, "I may fall asleep today, or Rose may.

Or both of us. And if I do, I'll never wake up. I would need a blind man who was in love with me, and there just isn't anybody like that. Promise me, if I go to sleep, you'll put me someplace beautiful, like maybe back by the waterfall."

"I'll take care of you," Jack says, "if I'm still alive. But now it's time for me to go back up the beanstalk."

"What? What beanstalk?"

"Follow me."

Jack leads her out of the thicket and takes her toward the far field. When she first perceives it, the beanstalk looks like a rope in the distance, but as they get closer, the last rays of daylight illuminate its silhouette. She looks up at it and is properly amazed.

"Where does it lead?"

"Up to the giant's house, in the clouds."

"Oh, Jack, you mustn't go back again! You might not be so lucky this time."

"I have to go. Lan is up there. He's locked in a cell, with bars on the window, an' the giant keeps the key around his neck. I'm not sure how I'll get the key, but maybe I'll wait until he's asleep an' try to get it then."

Briar clutches his shoulder. "Lan is still alive?"

"Yes, but I don't know for how long. He told me to tell Rose that he loves her, just in case."

"But that's wonderful! Do you see what that means? If Rose falls asleep—"

"He could wake her up! If only I can rescue him."

"Tell me about the bars on his window," Briar says. "Could I reach them?"

"Yes, but what good would that do?"

"I'm very strong. You wouldn't believe how strong! Look. Watch this!" She roots around looking for something suitable to demonstrate with and finally grabs a large branch, more than twice as thick as her arm, and tears it from a huge tree. Then she breaks it in two pieces over her knee.

Jack stands dumbfounded, then finally finds his voice. "How long have you been able to do that?"

"Oh, a long time. I just didn't want everyone making a fuss over it. But you see what I'm getting at? Maybe I could bend the bars on the cell window! Let me come with you and at least try."

"But it's so dangerous! And what if you fell asleep while you were climbin'? You'd fall to your death!"

"I'm willing to risk it. My life wouldn't be worth much then anyway."

"Yes, it would! Don't say that! There's always hope!"

Back and forth Jack and Briar go, neither giving way. Finally, Briar reminds him of the oath they took as Giant Killers so long ago, to defend each other to the death, and the code of honor, which began with valor. Briar says she must fulfill her role as a Giant Killer or lose all honor, and sighing deeply, Jack has to agree.

• • •

Princess Rose has met every suitor in the great hall and danced with each of them, her armed guard never far from her even while she's dancing. She maintains her frozen smile though her heart is breaking, and she does whatever is expected of her, but now she is dancing with King Udolf. He is the one Briar had named as her future husband. He is bragging unceasingly about his own greatness and wealth, but despite the costly appearance of his magnificent apparel, he smells bad and has dribbled food all down his front. He is, as Briar said, easily three times her age, and he looks at her as if she is some especially tasty dessert. Her revulsion for him is physical. She quails at his very touch. She feels as if she's suffocating from his overbearing attention, and the guards behind her, hounding her every step, are enough to make her scream. Mercifully, there is a lull in the music, and excusing herself politely, she turns on the closest guard and says, "Leave me, for God's sake. You make me insane with your vigilance!"

The guard, slightly taken aback, mumbles, "It's by the queen's orders, Your Highness. I can't go against the queen's orders."

Rose, flushed with anger now, makes her way to the queen's side and demands to know why she is under such close guard. "Please, Mother," Rose says tightly, "get rid of them!"

"They are here to protect you, my dear."

"Protect me from what? I demand that you tell me. I won't dance with another suitor unless you tell me!"

The queen seems to deflate, and she says, "I had hoped to

spare you this on your birthday. It should be a happy occasion. But if you must know, today is the day for you to find out. Come with me." She dismisses the guard and leads Rose into a small anteroom, ordering everyone else out. Overcoming years of reserve, she begins to tell a story, the story of Rose's birth. Even now, she carefully omits any mention of her older twin sister. She tells Rose only of her father's pride and of the great party held in celebration of her arrival. And then she tells of the gray fairy and the terrible curse she cast that day on the royal infant, and Rose turns white.

"So, it's true!" she gasps.

The queen looks at her, her mouth open in surprise. "Someone told you?"

"Someone, yes, but I didn't believe it! Oh, what have I done?"

"No need to be so upset, dear. Your father had every spinning wheel in the kingdom burned when you were still an infant. We didn't want to ruin your birthday with thoughts of such a dreadful curse, but now that you know, you'll know better than to touch a spindle if you see one. No one can force you to touch it. You're safe!"

Rose, overcome with dismay, is recalling that other thing Briar had told her. Just out of spite, she'd thought at the time. But what if it wasn't? What if that was true too?

"Mother, you must tell me the truth. I realize that Father won't announce it until tomorrow, but I have to know. Is he going to marry me to King Udolf?"

The queen does not meet her gaze. She wrings her hands and says, "You must see how much he can do for the kingdom, my dear. He's really—"

"Oh! Oh no!" cries Rose, and she turns and runs away, desperate to find a place to be alone. She hastens back into the great hall, pushes past the ladies in waiting, and, lifting her skirts, runs up the stairs, up past the chapel, up past the solar, all the way up to the tower room where she sleeps. She throws herself on her bed, her face buried in her arms, and wishes for the old days when Briar was there to share her burdens. She thinks of the repulsive King Udolf and tries to imagine that there's a way out. Only there isn't. She is the princess—the heir—and she must do what she can to save her people. But can she bear to do this? She sobs into her sleeve. Can she? If only she *could* go to sleep and not wake up until her true love woke her with a kiss. But her true love is dead, and she'd be happy now to sleep forever.

"Come and get me, Gray Fairy!" she cries out in desperation. "I'm ready! Come and get me now!"

A soft, whirring sound comes from the corner of the room. Astonished, Princess Rose looks through wet lashes at the unfamiliar machine that has suddenly appeared and the strange, intense woman, dressed in gray, who sits there working it. It has a large turning wheel on one end, and the woman feeds wool onto a twirling spindle on the other.

"Here I am, Princess," she says. "I've been watching and listening for you to call on me. I was only waiting for your invitation. And here I am! Here is my spinning wheel. And here is the spindle. Just what you wanted, eh? *Now do as you will!*"

Rose is suddenly sobered. She looks over the strange woman and her machine and sees that they are quite real. All she has to do now is get up and walk over to it and touch the spindle. And then oblivion. For a moment she is afraid. Though the woman sits unmoving, she radiates a black, simmering rage, the likes of which Rose has never experienced. It seems to turn the very air dark and evil. *But what does it matter now?* Rose thinks. *What does anything matter?* She stands up and takes a step toward the spinning wheel.

"Oh yes, dearie. There's nothing left for you here. I've watched it all unfolding in my crystal ball. Ahahaha! Think of it! Your own parents have betrayed you for greed! Sold you like a prize cow! But you can escape. *One touch,* and all your problems will go away."

Rose listens to the rant, repulsed by the woman's words. Betrayed! A prize cow indeed! She backs away, looking at the woman with doubt and loathing, but a minute's contemplation forces her to see the truth of it and she moves toward her again. Yes. The spindle.

The strange woman croons to her. "That's right, poppet. Come. Touch it. You'll just sleep. Ah, yes. Sleep peacefully."

Closer, closer Rose goes. Then she reaches out and pricks her finger on the spindle. The next moment, she lies crumpled on the floor, deeply asleep. The gray fairy, fired up by an exultant fury, lets out a bloodcurdling cackle.

"At last! At last! The fools actually thought they had beaten me! As if my magnificent magic couldn't overcome their puny efforts to thwart me! Ahhhahahaha! Now they'll see. They'll see what it costs to go against me! They'll see what pure, unbridled *hate* can do!" Then the fairy looks down on the sleeping princess, a smile of deep satisfaction on her face. "Look what I've done. Look at her sleeping there, so beautiful. So serene. *So deathlike.*

"Sleep on, sweet princess. I shall never let any man *near* enough to kiss you! Not while I live! Oh fairest, lovely, *beauteous* princess, *you're as good as dead!*"

Night has fallen. Jack and Briar stand ready at the bottom of the beanstalk, Jack issuing final instructions to the village contingent of the Giant Killers. Young people from eight to eighteen have assembled in the moonlight, armed with axes and anything else that can cut. They are ready for an all-night vigil.

Briar has changed into men's clothing and is braiding her hair to keep it out of her way. Her fingers work nimbly as she tries to mentally prepare herself for whatever awaits them at the top of the beanstalk. Jack hands her an empty knapsack, saying, "Here, we might need this—"

Briar reaches out her hand to take it, and in the very next instant she falls to the ground, as if dead.

"Briar!" cries Jack. He kneels next to her and, moaning, cradles her head in his arm. The young people gather around her, gasping with shock and dismay. Then Jack looks up at them with a tormented expression. "It's a curse," he says, and the others stand back, making the sign against evil.

"What do I do?" Jack asks. "She told me the spell can only be broken by true love's kiss." Smoothing Briar's hair with one hand as he looks at her unconscious face, he shakes his head and says, "I love her truly. I've always loved her. But how could I tell her when she wakes up that it was me who kissed her? A peasant?"

"Just kiss her anyway, Jack!" several of the villagers say. "If you love her, you'd better kiss her. It's the only way!"

Jack stares into Briar's face, stroking her cheek with one grimy finger. Then he leans down and kisses her, a long, tender kiss. Her eyes flutter open, and she looks squarely into Jack's worried countenance.

"Jack? What are you doing?"

Jack pulls back, as if stung. "Oh, nothing," he replies lamely.

"Yes, you were. You were kissing me!"

"I had to, Your Ladyship. I had to wake you up."

"So, I've been asleep? So it was all true, then. But—wait! Only true love's kiss could wake me up!"

"Yes, Your Ladyship."

"Stop calling me that! Does this mean that you . . . love me? Truly?"

"Yes, your — Lady Briar."

"Just Briar!"

"All right, Briar."

Briar is quiet for a minute, considering. It has never occurred to her that anyone would ever truly love her. Or that she could love him back. Memories of their first childhood encounter playing by the stream, that first night he came after her in the forest and brought her home to his mother, his earnest face calling for valor at the formation of the Giant Killers' club, the time he had taken her hand with such humble courage, volunteering to follow the giant up the great mountain, and said, "I can do it," the way he had always treated her with kindness and respect — all these things well up in her mind. And yet she has never had the temerity to think of him as anything more than a friend. She blinks at him, then feels suddenly shy.

She sits up and covers her deformed face with a heavy lock of hair, but Jack reaches over and brushes it aside, smiling. "Don't. It's a part of you, and I love you just as you are," he says, and some frozen, injured corner of Briar's heart melts and heals. It is exquisitely painful and sweet. Still, she can barely believe it. Glancing at the villagers, who are greatly interested in the proceedings, Briar wonders if she hadn't better have this talk with Jack privately.

But looking around, she recognizes them as friends, and so she doesn't worry about sharing this personal conversation.

"But when did this happen?" she asks Jack.

"It's been happening since we were children, since the first time I watched you dance an' heard you sing by the waterfall. I've watched you often since then. Whenever you took the path to the waterfall, I followed. An' I've watched your kindness with all the village people, an' your courage in the Giant Killers' club, and—"

"All right! That's enough. I believe you," Briar interrupts, embarrassed.

"So you're not mad that I kissed you?"

"I'm not mad," she says, blushing furiously. "In fact, I really should thank you for waking me." She wants to add that it was a *wonderful* kiss, but for this she is not bold enough. She dusts herself off, then suddenly cries, "Rose! What about Rose? Did she fall asleep too?"

Jack springs up and answers, "We'll have to go to the castle an' see."

"But that will take time, and Lan is in danger every minute. Even if Rose *is* asleep under the curse, the best thing we could do for her is bring Lan back. He could wake her if anybody can. Either way, we should go now and try to free Lan first and bring him home."

"Yes, that makes sense," Jack agrees. For a moment he looks into her eyes; then, looking away, he says, "I hate to cut this short, but if we're goin' to save him, we'd better hurry."

Briar quickly finishes braiding her hair, then dons the knapsack and steps to the mighty beanstalk.

"Quentin, your father's a woodsman," calls out Jack. "You direct the choppin' so the beanstalk falls away from the village, toward the mountain. Can you do that?"

"Yes, Jack," Quentin replies. "I've helped my pa cut down lots of trees. We'll cut out a wedge on the side facing the mountain; then, when you give the signal, we'll chop the other side until the whole thing gives way. It'll go down nice as you please."

"Good. You're in charge then. *Everybody listen to Quentin!*"

Jack too dons a knapsack, and Arley hands him his father's horn, which Jack wears on a leather thong around his neck. He steps to Briar's side. "You go first. I'll be right behind you," he assures her, "so I can catch you if you slip."

"Maybe you should go first," Briar replies. "I'm stronger."

Jack laughs. "Oh, yes. I forgot. I'll go first then." The twining beanstalk gleams blue-green in the bright moonlight, and Jack and Briar say a solemn farewell to the others and begin their climb.

The handful of guards at the gatehouse stand at attention, doing their duty, which seems to be to look impressive for all the guests. No one anticipates any trouble on this festive occasion, so the castle is only lightly guarded. The drawbridge remains down, and the portcullis up, to leave the way open for any late carriages arriving at the ball, but there is nothing much happening, and the guards are half asleep at their stations.

A large hay wagon rumbles across the drawbridge and comes to a stop at the gatehouse. Durwin, the porter, not even curious, waves it on through, and a few minutes later does the same with another hay wagon, both of which continue on in the direction of the stables.

Suddenly the first wagon pulls around a corner and stops. The second wagon does the same. Then something curious happens: the hay begins to erupt into dark shapes—shapes in the form of men and women. They are villagers, and they have come to secure the drawbridge and the portcullis, to keep the way open for the rioters to follow. They brush themselves off and quietly jump down, holding clubs and ropes and shovels and whispering to one another. They quickly split up, one group heading toward the stairs to the wall walk, the other turning back toward the gatehouse.

Cloaked by the night, their attack comes as a complete surprise. They silently overpower guards one at a time, sneaking up from behind and choking them so they cannot cry out, then tying and gagging them. What the villagers lack in weapons and armor, they make up for in stealth and determination. Confiscating the guards' weapons as they go along, they add them to their own arsenal. They take their time, careful not to make any noise or be observed, and without too much mayhem, the drawbridge and the portcullis are finally secured. The guards are held prisoner in the room above the gatehouse, and before any more of them can arrive, Arley's father calls out across the moat, confirming that the castle is only lightly guarded and summoning his compatriots in the village.

From behind every house, bush, and tree erupt scores of villagers, as angry as a hive of disturbed hornets, until a great, buzzing crowd has assembled in the moonlight.

In front of them, a small, bent figure with eyes flashing and a surprising air of grandeur, Mother Mudge, holds aloft a burning torch. "Tonight the king and all the other nobles are feasting while our families go hungry! But he is about to face a villageful of uninvited guests! Tonight we eat!" Waving her torch, she steps toward the drawbridge. "For justice!" she shouts, her voice clear and passionate. "For your hungry children! For your self-respect! Tonight we march!"

Countless others gather around her and light their torches from hers and then from one another's, until a sea of flaming brands is moving, flowing across the drawbridge and on into the castle. The rebels cry out, "Food! Food! Food!" as they swarm toward the castle keep and the great hall. They encounter a few more guards along the way but quickly overcome them with sheer numbers. Blood flows on both sides, but the rebels march relentlessly on.

In the great hall, the noise is barely heard. The king looks around to see what is making it; then the music grows louder and he decides it is nothing. The queen, who has returned to the ball, exchanges glances with him.

"Our daughter knows now about the gray fairy's curse. I had to tell her, but at least she's prepared. That's the best protection. She's rather upset."

"She had better get over it quickly. We have guests!"

"She'll be down shortly. I've sent Lady Beatrice to fetch her. I just thought I should give her a little time. Have the fairies arrived yet? I'll feel better with them here."

"I believe that's them," the king says, pointing to the chandelier, where what looks like a cluster of colorful hummingbirds seems to be drawn to the light.

"Oh, splendid. If you order the feast to begin, I'll give directions for the fairies to be seated on our right and your counselors on the left."

The king stands up and announces that the dancing is over and the feasting will soon commence. There is a murmur of excitement as the many guests clear the floor and an army of servants begins setting up trestle tables and covering them with white tablecloths. Meanwhile, the king hears noise that's too loud to be ignored. He calls for the captain of the guard and charges him with the task of seeing what is going on outside. Several of the guests, including his own counselors, are beginning to look around questioningly for the source of the disturbance. When the noise gets closer and the captain of the guard does not return, many of the brave suitors think to form a group to go out after him. But alas, they have left their weapons outside the door, it being bad manners to come armed to a social gathering. Before they can reclaim them, the noise becomes a roar. Enraged villagers pour in through every doorway, having confiscated the collection of discarded weapons for themselves. At the head of the rioters stands Mother Mudge, torch held high, crying, "Food! We want our fair share of food—and we want it now!"

The villagers push in behind her, wielding their torches, until the great hall is packed and seems to be in danger of catching fire. The king, who has faced the evil giant up close, is not easily cowed. He stands, holds up his hands, and calls for quiet. Mother Mudge also calls for quiet. It takes several minutes, but finally the clamor dies down and an uneasy hush falls over the room.

In that instant, a scream is heard, and there are footsteps running down the stairs into the hall. It is Lady Beatrice, and she cries out, "The Princess! She's dead asleep! I can't wake her! Somebody help!"

There are cries of woe from villagers and nobles alike—"Oh, no! Not the princess!"—and there are calls of "The curse! It's the curse!" from those who remember the gray fairy's malediction at the princess's birth. For sixteen years they have felt protective of her, watching her grow in beauty and grace toward her own doom, and now their hearts are breaking.

Amid the din, the eight fairies fly up the stairs to Rose's room. Assuming their human size, they gather around her fallen form.

"Oh, the poor dear," bemoans the gold fairy, wiping a tear from her eye.

"But isn't she even more beautiful in sleep?" sighs the blue fairy.

"Of course not, nitwit," replies the pink fairy. "What could be more lovely than when she's awake and her beautiful personality shines through?"

"Well, I merely said—"

"Both of you quiet down!" commands the gold fairy, who is the oldest among them. "Let us arrange her in an appropriate way. Four of us on each side now, and we'll conjure her over to the bed." This accomplished, they drape her gown prettily and dress her hair until she looks like a living sculpture carved by some passionate genius.

"But supposing someone can wake her, what will she awaken *to?*" asks the fairy in white sparkles. "What if a hundred years pass before her true love finds her? Everyone she knows will be dead! Or what if nothing stops that mob downstairs? Anything might happen! They could set fire to the place while Rose sleeps!"

"Then we'll put them all to sleep too. Perhaps a nice, relaxing rest will calm them down. We'll put everyone to sleep. That way it will all stay safe for her while we look for her true love. We will make it so. Adjust your wands. We shall freeze everything just as it is until she wakes up. First to the great hall, then spread out."

With that, the gold fairy pops back to her hummingbird size, and the others follow suit as she flies back down the stairs to the great hall. There they come upon a scene of chaos. The rioting villagers are still pushing their way into the room, shouting out their rage, while the unarmed nobles back into one corner, trying to blend in with the wall. The king attempts to make himself heard over the uproar, but no one is listening. The gold fairy puts the king to sleep first, carefully, so that he slumps to the floor unharmed, then the queen. Their crowns fall off and roll away. Next, the king's counselors are put to sleep one by one, Bishop Simon falling clumsily on his head. Before Mother Mudge can react, her torch is put out and she too is asleep. The fairies go quickly about, snuffing torches, spreading their magic over villagers and nobles, musicians and mummers and servants, until everyone in the hall is asleep, the weapons lying harmlessly on the floor. Then the fairies go into every room and tower in the castle.

Hilde has finally argued herself into putting in a polite appearance at the ball, and she is just starting down the stairs, with the imp obnoxiously poking her in the back, when the pink fairy buzzes up the stairway so fast that she ricochets off the wall and does three backward somersaults.

"What in the name of heaven are you doing?" Hilde demands after the tiny pink fairy has righted herself.

"The gray fairy's curse has come true! Princess Rose is dead asleep," she says. "So the gold fairy said we must put everyone else to sleep too!" The pink fairy pulls back her wand-holding arm as if preparing to hurl a mighty blast.

"Not me, you foo—" The fairy's magic hits Hilde squarely on the heart, and she slumps down awkwardly on the stairs. The imp squeaks in panic, dodging the pink fairy's next three blasts of magic until, with one more blast, it too is sleeping soundly on the stairs.

"There!" says the pink fairy, blowing the excess fairy dust off the tip of her wand, then buzzing downstairs again to join the others. The eight of them continue all through the courtyard, scattering enchantment everywhere. The crowds of rioters are suddenly at peace, their rage extinguished, their heads resting on each other's limp bodies. Some of them begin to snore. The fairies put every bird and beast in the castle to sleep too, even the dogs in the kennels, the horses in the stables, and the sparrows on the rooftops.

At last the fairies are done. They arrive together at the gatehouse, greeting one another with grim satisfaction.

"What else can we do?" the blue fairy asks.

"Maybe some spell to protect them all while they sleep?" suggests the pink fairy.

A sickly yellow cloud suddenly explodes on the drawbridge, and a deep voice snarls, "Protect them? Why, I have the perfect thing!" It is the gray fairy, and she seems to be in some kind of fit. Her bloodshot eyes are open too wide and her skin looks like old chalk. "*This* will protect them!" she howls, striding through the gatehouse and into the castle courtyard as the other fairies back out of her way. With a hissed incantation and a few twitches of her wand, a repulsive gray-green spot appears on the ground. It looks and smells like rot, and it spreads like oil. Everywhere it touches, things begin to grow—great foul black vines with sharp thorns, some of them as big as a man's arm. They spread with astonishing speed, enveloping everything within the castle walls, coiling over and around the multitude of sleeping bodies, shooting up so high and dense and tangled that they obliterate the moonlight. The castle is shrouded in darkness, and the smell is overpowering.

"Ahhahahahaha!" gloats the gray fairy. "What do you think of my protective spell, eh? No one can interfere with them now! *Not even you!*" The gray fairy opens her mouth in a gruesome grin and, laughing maniacally, twirls her wand in a swift spiral and vanishes, leaving her putrid yellow smoke behind.

The other fairies pop into their human size and all start talking at once. "How can she be so cruel?" asks one.

"She can't get away with that!"

"She's twisted in the head!"

"Just plain evil is what she is!"

"Someday she's going to get what's coming to her!"

"She gives me a pain right in the—"

"Oh, I would just like to get her alone without that wand—"

"All right," interrupts the gold fairy, "that's enough. Now we've got to think. What's needed is someone who truly loves Rose, loves her for herself. So how do we find him? Do you suppose any of those suitors that we just put to sleep in the great hall actually loved her? We could wake them up—"

"Pshaw! We were watching her while she danced. She didn't seem too happy with any of them when she was awake. I doubt if she'd want the whole lot of them taking turns kissing her when she's asleep!" says the green fairy.

"It does seem kind of . . . unwholesome," comments the white sparkly fairy.

"Well, I don't think we should let just anybody kiss her. She wouldn't like it. It will have to be someone special," mused the gold fairy.

"Anyone who can cut through this forest of thorns will have to be special!" remarks the purple fairy, "but it could be *years* before anyone manages that. We must go out and spread the story, far and wide."

"Yes," agrees the gold fairy. "Each of us in a different direction. I'd better stay on guard here and alert the rest of you if a likely candidate shows up to try his luck. I'll turn your wands red to summon you, so keep watch. Quick! Off you go! Be sure to emphasize how very lovely she is—and that she's as good as she is beautiful. There must be a prince for her out there somewhere."

Chapter Four

JACK IS TIRED OF CLIMBING. So tired. It is the second time today he has climbed the beanstalk clear up to the sky, and he doesn't know how much longer he can keep it up. All his muscles ache and tremble with the strain. He calls down to Briar to wait a minute as he pauses to catch his breath in the cold, thin atmosphere, and she halts as well.

"It looks to me like we're almost there," she says encouragingly. "It's starting to get misty."

"Yes, and that's making the vines slippery. It's getting hard to hold on. Briar, if I don't make it, you'll have to rescue Lan—"

"Of course you're going to make it! I am not going to lose you now! Can't you do just ten more feet? Just ten."

"All right . . . ten." Jack forces himself to reach higher, to hold tight and pull himself up while he gropes for one foothold, then another, and counts, "One . . ." Laboriously he repeats the process. "Two . . . three . . . four . . . five," more and more slowly until at last he cries, *"Ten!"*

"Good! Now rest for a minute. You're doing just fine," says Briar. "When you're ready, do it again. Just ten more."

"I don't think I'm going to make it to ten."

"Then do five. Just five. You can do that."

"All right. Five." Jack sighs. And so, a few feet at a time, they make the slow final leg of their journey together, Jack pushing himself beyond his limits and Briar cheering him on, until they reach a place just above the clouds. Then, with a last heroic effort, they leap off the beanstalk onto the cloud. Jack collapses, spent, on the spongy surface. They can see the giant's house in the bright moonlight, but they must pause for a considerable rest before going any farther. The house looks huge and menacing, and Briar asks Jack uncertainly, "Do you think the giant will smell us when we get close to his house?"

"The moon's waning. He should be sound asleep. You'll be long gone by the time he wakes up, and I'll be following you shortly."

"Wait—you're not thinking of sending me back down without you, are you? Because I'm not leaving you here."

Jack takes her by the hand and looks into her eyes. "I have a plan, but it's something I have to do alone. It's a matter of honor as a Giant Killer. You can understand that."

Briar bites her lip, but having just used the same argument on him, she can only nod wordlessly.

When strength finally returns to Jack's limbs, they set off toward the giant's house, Jack aiming toward the spot where he previously discovered the dungeon window. With a little looking, he finds it again and also finds the rope he left there on his last trip. Crouching down to put his face to the bars, he calls out, "Lan! Lan, are you in there?"

There is no answer. Jack is appalled at the silence, fearing that he has come too late. Straining to see into the inky void, he repeats, "Lan! Are you sleeping? Wake up!"

This time there is an answering moan, a welcome sound to Jack's ears, and finally Lan's voice answers, "Jack! You're still alive! You came back! Did you get the key to get me out of here?"

"No. We're going to try something else. I brought Lady Briar instead."

"Oh," Lan says. There is a long pause. "Well, it's been nice knowing you, Jack. I'm sure you did the best you could."

"You don't understand. Watch this," Jack says, and moves over to allow Briar room.

"I don't know if I can do this," she says, "but here I go." She squats down, grasps a bar in each fist, and pulls them in opposite directions for all she is worth. Bit by bit, the bars begin to bend. She strains and groans, and she can feel her face flushing red as the sinews in her arms and back tighten. She lets go of one bar and uses both hands to bend the other. Jack and Lan watch as the bar slowly yields to her efforts. Then she uses both hands on the other bar and pulls it wide aside until there is an open space between the bars that looks as if it could admit a man. Lan is jubilant, but then he says, "I can't reach the window. Do you still have that rope?"

"It's right here," Jack responds, tying one end of it firmly to a bar, then throwing the other end down to Lan. Lan is so weakened by hunger that he can't climb up unaided. Instead he ties the rope around himself, and Briar and Jack pull him up.

When he finally maneuvers through the bars, he gets to his feet unsteadily and envelops Jack and Briar in a great hug. Then he sits down, his legs too wobbly to stand.

"Here, I've brought you something," says Jack, opening his knapsack. He hands Lan a flask full of water and watches while Lan greedily gulps it down. Then Jack gets out some bread and cheese. While Lan eats, Briar tells him all about the curse that Rose is under and warns him that she may be in an enchanted sleep.

"Only true love's kiss can awaken her," Briar says, sharing a secret smile with Jack.

"I hope I do get the chance to kiss her, even if I should be thrashed for daring to kiss a princess!"

"Can you walk now?" Jack asks. "I'm goin' around to the back door and see if the giant woman is up yet. She said she starts work before dawn. If she's in a good temper, we can fill up our bags with treasure to take back. An' if our luck holds, maybe she can help me lure the giant to his doom!"

"I'm feeling much better," Lan assures him, finishing off the last of the bread. "I think I'm strong enough now. Let's go."

The trio heads off toward the back of the house, staying close to the base of the wall. They maneuver around the corner and into a position near the giant-size back door. Jack can make out a light in an open window next to the door, and with a courage born of desperation, he shouts, "Hello!"

There is a tense pause as they wait to hear a response; then the large face of the giant's woman appears at the window, a face with a blackened eye. In a loud whisper she says, "Who's that?" Then, making out Jack and the others in the moonlight, she adds, "You again! Are you looking to get killed? Get away from this place while you still can!"

"Let us in!" answers Jack. "I need to talk to you!"

The face disappears from the window. For a minute they wait anxiously to see what she will do, but the door opens a crack and the three squeeze through. They see that her hands are covered with flour and there are lumps of bread dough rising on the table.

"I see you've freed the prisoner," the giantess says, picking up several pieces of firewood and adding them to the oven. "You'd better be gone before Himself wakes up. He'll be enraged when he finds him gone! He'll hunt you down, even with one eye, and I'll be cooking you all with onions for his supper tomorrow. Or worse, he'll blame me, and I hate to think what he'll do to me. He gave me this black eye when he found that gold missing. He's merciless!"

"How would you like to be free of him forever?" asks Jack boldly.

The giantess looks taken aback, then says, "You mean . . ."

"I mean forever."

A grin spreads slowly over her face, as if she has just discovered it is her birthday, and she rubs her hands together. "I told him! I told him no good would come of all his thievin' and rampagin'! I warned him it would catch up with him, but NO! He wouldn't listen . . . but still," she says, suddenly very solemn, "you've got a mighty high opinion of yourself if you think you can win out over the giant."

"It's not just me, Mistress. There's a whole society of us dedicated to the giant's downfall, and we've got a plan. If you could just help a little bit."

The giantess puts her finger to her lips and says, "Shh!" Then, turning to look cautiously over each shoulder, she bends down toward Jack and whispers, "What do you want me to do?"

"You've seen that beanstalk growing over yonder?"

"Yes? Where does it come from? It's an oddity!"

"Well, that's the way we got up here. An' that's the way we'll go back down. I'm sendin' my friends down now, and then I'll wait for the giant."

"No, Jack, we're not going without you!" exclaims Lan.

"Please, Jack, come with us now!" cries Briar.

"Remember what I said before, Lady—I mean Briar. It's a matter of honor. I've come this far, an' I've got to see it through. Lan, when I come down, I'll need to come down fast. I need you both to be out of the way. Just trust me."

Turning to the giantess, he says, "All you have to do is wait a while after sunup an' tell him about me, tell him that I've taken his prisoner. Make sure he's good an' mad, then tell him I've gone down the beanstalk, so he'll come after me. We'll do the rest."

"Just as you say. Lucky for you, I was already up making the bread. The sun will rise soon. I can take my time serving him breakfast. When he's done eating, he makes that silly harp sing for him. I'll send him after you then, if that's what you really want. It's your skin. But I'd say the giant has more sense than to climb onto that flimsy beanstalk!"

"That's why I have to lure him down after me."

"If he's enraged enough, that might just work, but you're crazy to try it!"

"If my luck holds, I'll be all right. An', Mistress, if you please, if there's any more of that stolen treasure you'd like to get rid of, we'd be happy to take it off your hands."

"Yes, take it! Take it all! I don't care if he does beat me! That will surely send him down the beanstalk after you! Take away that hen that lays the golden eggs. That'll make him boiling mad! And that loudmouthed singing harp, be sure and take that! I'd better gag her for you first. The brainless thing has had no more sense than to bond to her new master, evil as he is. She might raise a ruckus. I'll go and get them."

"Briar? Lan? What can you carry? We've got my knapsack and your knapsack, Briar, and we have the rope. You'd better not try to carry much, Lan. You're still weak, and it's a long climb down."

"We can put the hen in my knapsack," suggests Briar. "She might not like it, but she'll be safe there."

"Then let me take the knapsack with the hen," Lan insists. "She can't be very heavy."

"I can take the gold in the other knapsack," Briar offers. "I don't mind the weight."

They discuss just how Jack can carry the harp while the giantess goes off on her mission. She returns, tiptoeing, the hen gently cradled in one arm. Petting the bird soothingly with her big fingers, she sets her down in front of the three adventurers. Briar immediately crouches low and takes over the petting, clucking softly to the hen. "I think we'd better wait until we're back at the beanstalk to stuff her in the knapsack," she warns them. "She might put up a fuss."

The giantess disappears twice more, bringing back two bags of treasure and then the singing harp, bound and gagged as the giantess had promised. The harp is about as tall as Jack's arm is long, and it takes some doing to tie her firmly to Jack's back. He makes sure that he can reach the harp's head over one shoulder. Fortunately, there's a lot of rope and the harp is not too heavy.

The treasures all secured, Jack has one last word for the giantess. "Remember, wait awhile after sunup—"

"Yes. He'll be finishing his breakfast by then, and demanding his harp. When he sees it's missing, he'll just about explode, and then I'll tell him you've got it, and where you've gone! Good luck to you, is all I can say." Briar notices that the giantess's chin quivers a bit and her eyes look suspiciously moist. "Goodbye. You're a brave lot, and if your plan doesn't succeed, well, I'll never forget that you tried." She turns away and makes herself busy, bending over the laundry so her face won't show. Briar and Lan don the knapsacks, Jack adjusts the horn hanging around his neck, and Briar hugs the hen close to her as they quietly step out the door into the predawn gloom and make their way back to the beanstalk.

Once there, Jack turns to Lan and says, "I'll say goodbye to you now, friend. I'll be waiting here until sunrise, an' then I'll start down. That should give me a head start on the giant. I'll stay near enough for him to see and hear me, so I can taunt him into coming down the beanstalk after me. The rest of the Giant Killers are at the foot of the beanstalk, waiting for my signal to chop the thing down, but I want you and Briar to go straight on to the castle and see about Rose. Don't wait for me!"

"If that's what you want," Lan replies, offering Jack his hand. Jack clasps it firmly, and the two shake in silent comradeship.

"Don't do anything I wouldn't do," Lan says, smiling bravely and clapping Jack on the back.

"Aren't you the one who faced the giant single-handed and put a rock in his eye?"

"Well, now that you mention it . . ."

Jack and Lan share an ironic laugh; then Lan grabs on to the twining beanstalk and, looking down to the earth far below, exclaims, "Whoa!" He pulls back, summoning his nerve to try again.

Briar turns to Jack. "I can't just leave you now! I'm staying with you!"

"You'd only be making it harder for me. Once the giant starts after me, I'll have to get down the beanstalk as fast as I can. Having another person with me would make it much more difficult. I don't know how I'll find the will to do it anyway unless I know you're safe. Besides, you don't know what the gray fairy may have in store for you back at the castle. Lan's still very weak. He may need your help. Promise me you'll go directly to the castle."

Briar bows her head and squeezes her eyes tightly shut, trying not to cry, but she says softly, "I promise."

Lan, inspired by Jack's words, takes a deep breath and cautiously begins his descent.

Briar immediately wants to take back her promise, but she can't disappoint Jack. He expects her to be brave. Jack gently lifts her chin. "Remember the Giant Killers' code of honor. Hold on to your hope. My luck has held so far. With a little more of it I'll be back down to earth while the giant's still far above me. Then we'll chop down the beanstalk, and that will be the end of him. That's worth taking a risk for, isn't it?"

Briar only looks at him, a tear making its way down her cheek. Jack, not quite as tall as she is, tilts his head up to her and expresses all his love for her in one galvanizing kiss. Briar, new to this, quickly learns to kiss him back. Sparks seem to fly, birds seem to sing, bells seem to ring. For a brief but glorious time they make their own magic, and then finally they part.

"Go now," Jack says, his voice cracking. Briar nods, and with tears blurring her vision, she climbs onto the beanstalk and slowly begins her descent.

It is a long trip down, and it has grown more treacherous. As the massive plant matures, hundreds of curling tendrils have sprouted here and there from the immense vines. The smallest are the length of a hand or foot, but some have grown into great coils, several feet long, as tough as wood, with pointed tips like spikes. They catch in the clothing and hair and sometimes even grip a carelessly placed shoe. Briar and Lan make their way down haltingly, helping each other get free of the snags. By the time they are halfway down, there is a pale pastel pink glowing above the horizon. Briar pauses and looks back up at the edge of the cloud where Jack waits. For a moment she remembers their kiss and wonders, with a stabbing pain through her heart, if she will ever see him again.

Shivering with cold in the whipping wind, Jack watches the eastern sky, his nerves poised for action like a racehorse held at the starting line. At last a sliver of sun peers over the mountain, its first simmering rays warming his face. Taking several deep breaths, he whispers to himself, "Now," and the racehorse is off.

Jack grabs tightly to the beanstalk and maneuvers down it with alacrity, concentrating only on the movement of one arm, the other, one leg, the other, until he achieves a kind of rhythm. He concentrates so fiercely that there is no room in his thoughts for fear or doubts, no room for reflections on his newfound love and how much he has to lose. The curling tendrils reach out to catch and scratch him, but he disentangles himself and pushes past them. On and on he toils, looking up at intervals to calculate the distance he has put between himself and the edge of the cloud. How far should he go? Can he lure the giant to his doom from here? Would the giant still be able to see him and hear him? Feeling uncertain, he stops. Better to make sure the distance is not too great, even if it doesn't give him much of a head start. He sits himself on an enormous leaf and settles in to wait.

Now thoughts crowd in on him. Can he really get down from here before the giant catches up with him, or before they both go crashing to the earth? He looks down at the ground, where a patchwork in shades of green shimmers in the morning light, and he thinks . . . probably not. For a moment, he closes his eyes and considers all that has been good in his life. It is a short list, but now, at the top of it, there is Briar, returning his love, and he feels that his life has been complete.

There is a noise from above, like the howling of a great dog, and a jolt of fear tears through Jack's body. This is it. He climbs off the leaf and grabs onto the beanstalk, his palms already growing sweaty. Staring up into the cloud, he can make out the giant's head peering over the edge of it, can hear him shouting down, "Thief! Blackguard! Canker blossom!"

Jack pulls himself together. Summoning his loudest and most audacious tone, he shouts, "That's me! Catch me if you can, you big oaf!"

Outraged, the giant screams as he grabs the top of the beanstalk and shakes it.

Jack is too far along the stalk for this to affect him, but he is desperate now to lure the giant to climb down after him. Feeling the weight of the harp he carries on his back, he suddenly gets an idea. Wedging himself securely between an enormous leaf and the beanstalk, he uses both hands to reach behind his left shoulder, where the harp's head sticks up, and he fumbles with the gag that is tied around her mouth. By touch alone, he manages to pull the cloth away from her face. The second he does, she lets out a bloodcurdling screech.

"Master! Help! *Help me!*"

"Nyah-nyah!" Jack hollers to the giant. "I'm making off with your harp!"

"Prepare to be dismembered, fool!" comes the reply.

Jack sees the giant grab hold of the top of the beanstalk and wrap first one leg around it, then the other. As his full weight settles on the stalk, the slender tip of it that he clings to curves sideways in a great arc, away from the cloud, finally bending over to form an inverted *U*. The giant lets out a yell as he finds himself clinging upside down to one end of the *U,* bobbing back and forth in the wind. Farther down, where the beanstalk is thicker and stronger, Jack smiles. Maybe he has a chance after all. He begins his descent with quick, precise movements, ignoring the caterwauling of the harp in his ear. The curling tendrils poke and catch at him, but he deftly evades them as he makes his way farther and farther down.

The giant is reduced to an upside-down, backward crawl, trying to make his way up to the top curve of the inverted *U*. His hot rage has turned to cold panic. His dull brain provoked into action, he finally perceives that there is no way now to get back up to the cloud. He realizes too late that the beanstalk can barely hold his weight—indeed the bent-over stalk might snap at any moment and send him plummeting to his death. His only hope is to catch up to the little fiend on the vine below who caused all this. Then, when he gets close enough, he can dispatch him with a mighty kick. This is the single thought that keeps him going: with his enormous bulk hanging and swaying on the end of the beanstalk, though every muscle and ligament screams with the strain of holding on, he *must live long enough to kill that thief!*

Jack makes the most of his advantage, stopping only to blow a mighty blast on his horn to signal the Giant Killers waiting for him below that the time has come to start chopping. But he is still so far away! Can they hear him? Everything depends on timing.

How fast can he get down to the ground? How soon can the giant catch up with him? How high up will the giant be when the beanstalk comes crashing down? Will the fall be enough to kill him? Will Jack go down with him to his doom? He allows himself one last, sweet thought of Briar before focusing all his attention on his descent. The way is treacherous, and the race is on.

Above him, the giant is making progress. But his size, which might have closed the distance between him and Jack with ease, has instead become his greatest weakness. Barely able to move his own weight, he has managed to establish a certain way of inching backwards, up toward the top of the U, sliding first his legs, then his hands, along the twisted stalk without releasing his grasp. He is making discernible progress. Though the larger pointed tendrils pierce his flesh, he seems oblivious to anything that might hinder him in his goal. In his mind there is room for only two things: the vine he clings to and the thieving devil he seeks to catch.

Jack is in a dash for his life. Down he goes, while the sun ascends in the sky and the giant seems to be making progress back up the U. Jack's nimble movements stop only long enough for him to give a few more desperate blasts on his horn. Do his friends hear him? Will they chop down the beanstalk in time? Or will the giant live to take out his wrath on the people of Wildwick? What then might the rampaging giant destroy? How many more might be killed? It is unthinkable. Jack cannot hope for a reprieve, yet he can't give up.

He looks down and observes the beanstalk receding into the distance below. Is that the base of the stalk he sees? Is that small dark smudge a crowd of people? But he is still so high! Too high. Higher than the birds! Looking back, he sees that the struggling giant has managed to close the gap between them considerably. Jack renews his efforts with a will, moving even faster than before. Suddenly one foot slides out from under him. He grasps the beanstalk tightly with both hands and saves himself, but his foot has rammed into a coiled vine all the way up to his knee. He is stuck fast.

He can't believe it at first. Surely he can free himself! It can't be over! He tries to yank and twist his leg, but that seems, if anything, to tighten the coils around it. Breaking into a cold sweat, he tries to bend over, but the harp tied to his body makes this difficult. Still, he manages to withdraw his knife from its sheath and reach down to hack at the vine. With the first swipe of his knife, he loses his balance and falls from his perch on the beanstalk, dropping the knife in the process. A moment later, surprised to find himself still alive, he realizes that he is hanging upside down by one leg, still held fast by the coiling vine. He sees his situation clearly. It is only a matter of time now, he knows, as the giant works his way along the bent beanstalk, ever closer to him. Which will it be? Death by falling or death by giant? *Let it be by falling,* he thinks. *Then, at least for a few joyous instants . . . I can fly.*

• • •

Lan and Briar have reached the bottom of the beanstalk to find that the Giant Killers are hard at work. They have heard Jack's signal and are zealously chipping away at the base of the mammoth beanstalk. They have already cut a wedge out of the side facing the mountain, and now, from the opposite side, they will hack and hew until the great stalk gives way and falls to the earth. While Lan wobbles with exhaustion, Briar finds Arley and Quentin looking up, staring hard as far as they can see for any sign of Jack.

"Can you see him yet?" she asks.

"No," Arley responds, "but we heard his horn. He can't be too far away."

Despite her promise to Jack, Briar feels she cannot move from this place until she sees him get safely down. She stands rooted to the spot, looking up, while the village young people change shifts so that a fresh team of workers can resume the job with renewed vigor. Lan looks at the castle in the distance and, with a gasp, points out the black fog hovering over it. "What terrible trouble is this?" he cries. "Something must be horribly wrong. Come, Lady Briar, we have to hurry!" Taking her arm, he reminds her that it was Jack's parting wish that she go to the castle with him and help him. Lan hangs on to Briar's arm and entreats her strongly, warning her that the gray fairy might still be working her wickedness. "The whole castle may be in danger!" he urges. Still she hesitates. Finally, Lan looks into her face and enunciates,

"This is the way Jack wanted it. This may have been his last wish. You have to honor it."

Briar breaks down in tears briefly, then nods and pulls herself away, but only with a promise from Arley that he will come and find her with news of any development. She and Lan divest themselves of their backpacks and put the giant's bag of treasure and the hen into Arley's care. Then, with Lan's arm over her shoulders, Briar helps to support his weight as they hobble back to the village. She is surprised to find Mother Mudge not at home and the whole village frighteningly empty and quiet. They make their way up the street toward the castle, knocking on doors as they go, but no one answers. At last they hear a baby crying and follow the sound to a large cottage where there are two small, scrawny children in the doorway, staring at them wide-eyed, looking sad and scared.

"Well, hello," says Briar gently. "Are you here all alone?" This gets a silent shake of the head from one and a finger pointing inside from the other.

Briar puts her head in the door and says "Hello?" while her eyes adjust to the relative darkness. Inside, she sees several old women, most of whom she knows. Granny Beasely is hushing a crying baby, and Agatha, the baker's wife, holds a little one on each knee while a dozen children of various sizes are milling about. The old women look up at her and ask, "Have you seen them?"

"Do they still live?"

"Are they coming back?"

Briar is at a loss. She can only answer with questions of her own. "Who do you mean? Where is everyone?"

"Is this some terrible curse?" asks Lan.

The women all talk at once, but between them they manage to inform Briar and Lan about Mother Mudge leading the rebellion—how the great crowd of villagers had marched into the castle the night before, leaving the oldest ones to care for the youngest ones at home. They hadn't come back or sent any word since. Several of the old men had ventured out some time ago to see what they could find, and they had not yet returned either.

Briar and Lan exchange glances. "We should go at once!" Lan urges. "Anything might have happened!"

Briar agrees, and they quickly take their leave. As they hasten up the street, they catch sight of a trio of elderly men hobbling toward them carrying swords and shields, and they rush to meet them.

"What news?" Lan calls out.

One old codger shakes his sword in excitement, saying, "The way is blocked! Inside the castle it's all grown over with great thornbushes! There's no way in!"

"Can't even see anything!" quavers another, using his sword as a walking stick. "It's evil, is what it is!"

"It even smells evil!" adds the third. "What on earth can we do?"

"You can give us your swords!" Lan declares.

The old men confer with one another; then one of them says, "They're old and dull, but you can have them, for all the good they'll do you."

"Thank you!" says Briar. "And can we have your shields as well?"

"Yes, yes, and good luck to you," comes the reply, and they are handed over.

Briar and Lan accept the gifts gratefully and take their leave of the old men.

Once again they head for the castle. All is eerily quiet as they cross the drawbridge. Only a crow's rough call pierces the ominous stillness. All at once, the stench hits them, a wave of putrescence that makes them gag, and now they can see in through the gatehouse to the impossible tangle of black vines and deadly thorns within the castle.

"Can anybody be alive in there?" Briar wonders aloud, then swallows hard.

"Rose! She's got to be; she's just got to be!" Lan pauses, trying to calculate how many hundreds of blows it will take to open a pathway to the castle keep. "There's only one way to find out!" he says, and after backing away from the smell to take a few deep breaths, he charges in through the gatehouse and strikes a blow with his sword on the first foul vine he encounters, rending it from its roots. "Ha!" he exclaims as Briar circumvents a three-foot thorn and strikes her first blow.

"At least it can be cut!" Lan says, noticing that a brown sap is oozing from the chopped ends of the vine, and the horrid smell grows suddenly stronger, strong enough to sting his nostrils. A drop of the sap falls onto his arm, where it sizzles and smokes, burning right through his sleeve and into the skin beneath it.

"Aaagghh!" he cries, and shouts out to Briar, "Watch out for the sap! It burns!"

Briar draws back, avoiding a dripping globule of sap from the vine she has just cut. She hesitates, then realizes that she must risk getting burned in order to proceed. "I'll try to go faster," she says, hoping to forge ahead before the sap can ooze out.

"I'll keep chopping as long as my arm and my sword hold up!" Lan responds. Sheltering himself somewhat with his shield, he lifts his sword again and again, a surge of extraordinary strength coursing through him now at the thought of saving his loved one. Suddenly his sword breaks, yet even so, he hacks away at the forest of thorns with half a sword. But his days of confinement and near starvation have left him with little endurance, and he begins to falter. The sword and shield seem to become heavier, until his arms can barely lift them. Faintness threatens to overtake him. Finally, he calls out to Briar, "I'm done in! You go ahead. I'll try to follow."

Briar nods; then her eyes widen in a look of horror as she discerns two inert bodies lying among the tangle of vines and thorns. "Look! I think they're dead!" she cries, pointing at the fallen men. She turns and carefully carves a path over to them. Kneeling to listen to their chests, she still can hear faint heartbeats. She tries to rouse them, but there is no response. "It's some kind of deathlike sleep, like the one I was in. It must be an enchantment!"

"I dread what lies ahead of us," Lan replies, "but we must go on." Lan smothers another cry as the foul sap burns into his back. "Hurry, or we'll be burned alive! Hurry!"

Briar tries to quell her fear and anguish. Holding her shield above her head, she cleaves even broader strokes with her sword, slashing away at the snarl of monstrous plants as though her own life depends on it. She tries to go faster, for with Lan forced to follow behind her, he is in greater danger from the caustic sap. Though he covers his head and shoulders with his shield, she hears him cry out with pain as the sap falls, sizzling, on his foot. She turns to him, cringing at the sight of his smoking burns. "Oh no!" she exclaims. "I'm sorry!"

"Go on!" cries Lan. "I'll be all right! Go quickly!"

Briar turns back to the seemingly impossible task with renewed vigor. She decides to make for the great hall in the castle keep, thinking that would be the most likely place to find anyone. She can barely judge her direction in the thick forest of thorns, but through it she dimly perceives the large double doors of the stables on her right and more bodies scattered at the foot of them. She tries to look away, but it seems there are human figures lying limply everywhere, and she and Lan find it necessary to step over or around them. Looking more closely, Briar recognizes many of them from the village. When they finally can make out the door to the great hall ahead on the left, they have to pick their way more slowly and carefully over the bodies, now crowded closely together, while the accursed sap drips on them. Briar is appalled to be causing such harm to these innocent people, but it is impossible to turn back. It's only a short distance now to the doorway, but even Briar's great strength is flagging. Two strokes. Three strokes. How many more can she manage? She takes a deep breath and, with all her strength, severs the last gnarled vine before her. Then, climbing gingerly over a heap of human forms jammed in a doorway, she collapses into the great hall, Lan following after her.

"No more thorns!" Briar cries with great relief as she and Lan look around, taking in their surroundings.

It is a scene they never could have imagined, and it tells a story. Tables covered with white linen fill the center of the room, as if in preparation for a great feast, but where are the guests? Peering into the diminished light, they discern groups of bodies crowded into each corner of the hall and around the tables in the center. Here, near the main door, are peasants' bodies, many of them lying on top of their weapons. Briar puts her head down and listens to several of them breathe. "Still alive. These must be the rebels," she speculates. "And look! There! It's Mother Mudge! She looks so peaceful. But why are they all sleeping? It is an unnatural sleep."

Massed at the farthest corner of the room are bodies with no weapons but decked out in silks and sparkling jewelry. "Look there," says Lan, pointing. "It's the royals and the nobles, all backed up as far as they could get. I bet they were cowering in their boots! And over there!" He indicates the raised dais with the two thrones on it, two bodies lying prone before them. "It's King Warrick! And the queen too! *Everyone* has been put to sleep!"

Just then a small, buzzing voice above them calls, "Not everyone! We fairies put all the people to sleep, but *we* are quite awake." A fluttering motion draws their attention upward, where they observe what looks like a tiny golden bird hovering around their heads. "I stayed here to guard Princess Rose while the other fairies are off looking for her true love."

"*I'm* her true love!" cries Lan. "I may not be a prince, but my love is pure and strong, and I've come to awaken her!"

"Oh, splendid! This is good news indeed!" the gold fairy exclaims. "I'll summon the others. They'll be *so relieved!* It really is too difficult to find true love these days!" She shakes her wand vigorously, and it turns red. "There! They'll be here directly. Now, you'll find Princess Rose in her room at the top of the stairs. Go quickly, before the gray fairy—"

There is a noise like a thunderclap. "Before I what?" comes

a voice dripping with venom. "Before I ruin your little birthday party? Before I make you wish you had never been born? Before I curse you all into oblivion?"

The three turn, choked with apprehension, and see the gray fairy standing in the middle of the floor, the tables tumbled all around her, burning into cinders.

Chapter Five

JACK KNOWS THAT HIS FATE WILL catch up with him soon. It has been some time now, and still he dangles by his leg, half a mile above the earth, held in the grip of a coiled tendril of the beanstalk. He can feel the blood rushing to his head, making it throb and ache. Meanwhile, he observes that the giant's struggle to get to the top of the upside-down *U* formed by the bent stalk has merely resulted in bending even more of the beanstalk down to the giant's own side. He is hanging lower than when he started, getting ever nearer to Jack's level. Jack, on the other side of the *U*, has a vague hope that the tip of the stalk will break off and send the giant plummeting to his death, leaving Jack unharmed. So far, though, the beanstalk has proved too flexible to even crack.

Helpless to do anything but wait, Jack grows calmer as he observes the giant's frantic efforts to get within grabbing distance. Even now, Jack knows, the Giant Killers must be working away to ensure the giant's doom. He knows he will not die for nothing. And Briar must be safely on the ground by now. He ponders gratefully the brief wellspring of love that they found, knowing it would have been brief anyway. She is a lady and he is a peasant, and they never would have been allowed to be together. He hopes with all his heart that she will not pine away for him, that she and his mother will be a comfort to each other.

The giant is nearly level with him now, roaring with frustration. An idea lighting up in his evil brain, he swings one enormous arm to set himself swaying, back and forth, back and forth, just a little at first, then farther, wider, closer and closer to Jack. His huge hand is stretched out, reaching, reaching to catch hold of the lad. Once . . . twice . . . three times, and the giant nearly has him. Jack closes his eyes and prepares himself to meet his fate. Four . . . five . . . six more swings, and the giant's hand just misses him.

Then a sharp crack from below tells Jack that the Giant Killers are through! They have won. A smile spreads across his face as the giant's sweaty hand closes tightly around his head and body, yanking him away from the beanstalk seconds before the whole thing begins to collapse in a mighty avalanche of green. The giant's obscene glee instantly changes to shock and terror, the last things he will ever feel as he finds himself falling, and falling, and falling.

The gray fairy stands leering evilly amid the flames, in a haze of swirling yellow smoke.

"You . . . you . . . *witch!*" buzzes the gold fairy.

"Oh, no," sneers the gray fairy. "Nothing so prosaic as a witch! I'm far more exotic, more stupendous, more unique, more *extraordinary!* I've been planning my revenge for *sixteen years,* and I've always known you would do your utmost to interfere! I've got a whole new repertoire of tricks to try, so go ahead! Exercise your feeble powers! Just see what I will do!"

There is a small *pop* and a flash of light as the hummingbird-size pink fairy appears above their heads, and another *pop, pop, pop* as the green, blue, and white sparkly fairies arrive in small flashes of light. The gray fairy, startled, throws her arm up to protect her face, staggering backwards. Her eyes grow dilated, the whites showing all around the irises, but she quickly recovers her nerve. "You're no match for me!" she howls. "No matter how many of you there are!" and she begins hurling bolts of sizzling magic at the other fairies. With their tiny size and quick, darting motions, they make difficult targets. Suddenly there is another *pop,* and another, and another, with three more flashes of light. The purple fairy, the yellow fairy, and the red fairy appear, but before the others can warn them to scatter, the gray fairy's bolts of magic strike the three and turn them instantly into rats. They fall to the floor with little ratlike cries and skitter away into the shadows.

"*That* was uncalled for!" responds the gold fairy furiously.

"Oh?" drawls the gray fairy archly. "You're all against me. You've always been against me! Now see how it feels when *I* am against *you!*" With a flash from her wand she summons forth a flock of hungry sparrow hawks, and the great hall becomes a flurry of bloodthirsty hawks, flying feathers, and fleeing fairies.

The gold fairy pops into her full human size. "Shame on you!" she declares severely, flapping away two surprised sparrow hawks with one arm. The other fairies quickly follow suit, popping into their full size well away from the gray fairy, who laughs maniacally at her own cleverness. While she is thus distracted, the gold fairy puts one hand behind her back, waving Briar and Lan toward the stairway, and the two creep quietly in that direction, hiding behind their shields. With the painstaking concentration of tightrope walkers, they step carefully over the sleeping bodies, hoping to escape the gray fairy's notice.

Suddenly the gray fairy whips to attention, as if sensing something amiss. She bats away the frustrated sparrow hawks darting about her head and, with a swift motion of her hand, makes them all go up in smoke. "Who wants to be next?" she snarls, a line of spittle trailing from her mouth. "You!" she cries, pointing at the gold fairy. "You and I have come to a day of reckoning! You really think you can thwart me? Ahhahahaha! Fabulous! You have no idea what I am about to unleash!"

Briar and Lan are now only a few steps away from the archway at the bottom of the staircase, but fluffy feathers are still scattered in the air, and they waft about, tickling and teasing at the tip of Briar's nose. Briar feels a sneeze coming on. She holds her breath and contorts her face for several seconds until the urge passes.

Lan, whose larger feet make the going more difficult, stops

several yards behind her and, rubbing his own nose, whispers, "Are you all right?"

She turns and nods, then takes a few more steps, but the sneeze is not done with her. With a sudden, uncontrollable "Ah-*choo!*" she is given away. She makes a run for it. Dropping her shield and sword, she clambers over bodies, dashes under the archway, and leaps for the stairs.

"*Ha!*" bellows the gray fairy, sending a powerful blast of magic after her, collapsing the archway into a wall of rubble just before Lan reaches it.

He turns to face her, and in a burst of fury and daring, he hurls his broken sword straight for her head. In half a heartbeat, the gray fairy stops it in midair, turning it to ice. It drops to the floor and shatters. All about her, the other fairies gasp as they see that Lan, too, has been turned into ice.

Briar, having narrowly escaped the gray fairy's destructive blast, finds herself on her hands and knees on the stairway. She turns and calls Lan's name, but there is no reply. Was he buried somewhere underneath it or had he somehow escaped? And if he had, would the gray fairy let him live? Her shoulders slump, and tears spring to her eyes. Lan is probably dead, and it has all been for nothing. And here she is, trapped in the castle keep, when all she wants is to be back at the beanstalk, waiting for Jack to come to her. Could he be there now, looking for her?

"Jack?" she cries aloud. "Jack? Where are you?" She closes her eyes and is still, listening for some sort of inner response, but none comes. She gives in to bitter tears. Finally, her mind is overcome with questions. What should she do now? Where should she go? What would Jack want her to do? What would Hilde say to her? Briar supposes she should go find Rose. Rose, who had betrayed her. Rose, who was once her friend. And with that last thought, she kicks free of the heavy rubble and begins to climb the stairs.

In the great hall below, the gray fairy cackles with glee. "Did you *really* think I would let him pass?" she gloats.

"What I think," says the gold fairy, "is that it is not too late to change your course before your hatred consumes you. You still have a choice. Let the young man live. Let him awaken the princess. Then go back to your tower and find another way to live."

The gray fairy is incensed by the gold fairy's words. "Bah! Don't try your perverse tricks on me! Spare me your goody-goody hypocrisy! I know what you want. You want me to lower my guard so you can undo my powers! It's what you've always wanted! But I am too powerful for you! Too powerful!"

"I am a hundred years older than you are, and I've gained a certain amount of wisdom in that time. You would do well to listen to me. There is more than one kind of power. There is the quiet power of love. It may yet win out in the end."

"You can't possibly win against me! I am unassailable!" The gray fairy shimmers and fades, and in her place a hissing dragon fills the center of the room, smoke streaming from its nostrils. "See me now!" roars the dragon. "Behold my greatness! You think to tame me? One breath, and I will melt your frozen hero into a puddle!"

And she unleashes a blast of flame directly at the statue of ice that is Lan.

Briar drags herself up the stairs one by one, dispirited and drained. She knows what she will find at the top, but she hardly cares. When at last she sets foot in the room where Rose lies, she is almost taken aback by her beauty, so ethereal and exquisite. *Yes,* Briar thinks, *but it is only skin-deep.* She sits on the edge of the bed and sighs profoundly, sorrowfully. Whatever happened, she wonders, to the unspoiled girl who had played with her by the stream, splattered with water and mud and wreathed in smiles? Briar smiles to herself briefly, and then the smile disappears. What had happened to their untroubled devotion to each other?

Suddenly the floor seems to tremble, and she hears a muffled roar from below. *The gray fairy has won,* she thinks. It will be over soon. Would there ever be another brave hero who could truly love Rose for herself? But that self was far away now in the land of perpetual sleep. All that was left of Rose to love was her beauty. Alone, it was nothing.

Briar sits and ponders while the castle trembles. She can't think what to do next, so she stays at the bedside for a while, lost in sad and fearful thoughts. And then, from somewhere, it occurs to her . . . that maybe . . . just maybe . . . it doesn't have to be a hero that kisses Rose awake. True love . . . maybe it could come from anyone.

"But not from me!" she says vehemently. A scene flashes into her head with lifelike clarity: she is at the ball, wearing a fancy dress and flowers in her hair, when Lord Henry and the others stand back to make an aisle. And there, at the end of the aisle, is her proposed escort, the dog dressed up in finery to be her dance partner. Faces split with laughter leer at her on every side. And then Lady Arabella's face, smug and cruel, assures her triumphantly that it had all been Rose's idea. All Rose's idea!

"No!" Briar cries as she leaps up and backs away. "I won't kiss *her!* I won't even try it! I don't love her!" Just to prove it, she comes back and, bending over Rose's sleeping form, reaches out and messes up her hair. "There!" she says, satisfied with the effect. "You don't look so pretty now!"

She sits down again on the edge of the bed, and more memories rise to the surface. She recalls a whole gallery of perceived wrongs and injustices, from the first beating she got after they had played in the water together as girls to the many unjustified beatings she received over the years at the hands of Bishop Simon —Bishop Simon, who never disciplined Rose for a thing. She loathed the way Lady Beatrice and the ladies in waiting always thought that she, Briar, was guilty of everything—and that Rose was always innocent—and the way Lady Arabella and the other girls had frozen her out, and the way Rose had defended them. And now there was this whole extravagant ball for Rose's birthday: dancing, music, feasting. Who would give a second thought to Briar? All they would remember was that she was the butt of that cruel joke, a dog's dance partner. All these things fill Briar's troubled mind, and she folds her arms over her chest and says, "Why should *I* help *her?*"

The gold fairy counters the dragon's fiery blast with a wall of water. The flame sizzles out and turns to steam and foul, dark smoke, which fills the room. The frozen statue of Lan remains untouched, but there is a steady drip now. He is starting to melt.

The gold fairy waves her wand, and the air around her is suddenly bright and clear and filled with silver light. The dragon backs away, hissing.

"I'm warning you," says the gold fairy. "I too have been preparing for the last sixteen years. I have my own crystal ball, and I've watched you digging your pit of hatred, pursuing the dark arts. You can still renounce it all and start over. Again I say, *leave your hatred behind—now—*or you will be destroyed by it."

"The hate only makes me stronger, and I will never renounce

324

my powers! Never!" howls the frenzied dragon. "Your wheedling words *madden me!*" The dragon grows even larger, its arched neck touching the ceiling of the great hall as it seems to be gathering its strength for a fresh onslaught.

"There's still time. It's not too late to change your mind," the gold fairy says quietly.

Briar stands, hands on hips, staring down at the sleeping princess. "I don't love you!" she declares. "In fact, I think I hate you!" Her expression is stern and unfeeling, yet tears are welling up in her eyes. "You can sleep for all eternity for all I care!" She bends over to wipe some dirt from the floor, then smears it on the end of Rose's nose. "There! Not so perfect now!"

Once again she hears the jeering laughter at the ball. She sees Lady Arabella's triumphant face saying it was all Rose's idea. But was it? Would Rose have thought of something so cruel, even if she was angry? It wasn't like her. It was more like Lady Arabella! Briar paces about the room as the whole castle seems to shake, thoughts and memories churning through her head. Almost against her will, she remembers a crisp fall day several years earlier, and the two of them sitting in the gnarled old oak tree in the thicket where they had always played. That day they had become suddenly serious, lounging on a low branch of the tree, inhaling the sweet smell of fall leaves as they discussed the more practical points of good and evil.

Rose's words drift back to her. *What if there's no reward for good-ness? . . . What if everybody else was evil?*

And what had she replied? *I'd go off by myself and just be normal.*

The whole conversation was coming back to her now.

So it wouldn't matter if you were evil by yourself? Rose had asked.

No, because nobody would be affected by it.

But what about you? Would you be affected?

Who would care? Briar had asked, shrugging.

I would care, came Rose's clear reply.

But you wouldn't be there . . .

. . . I would be with you in spirit, and I would care.

Well then, Briar had said, *I'd try harder to be good.*

So here she was, all alone. If she didn't try kissing Rose, there was no one to blame her. No one would ever know. No one would care . . .

I would be with you in spirit, and I would care.

Briar covers her face with her hands and moans.

"Enough of this!" cries the dragon. "You cannot destroy me with your tricks! I am all-powerful! Behold while I open the bowels of the earth!"

"Don't do it!" the gold fairy warns her. "Such magic is beyond anyone's power to control!"

But the gray fairy has lost all caution. "Beyond *your* powers,

326

maybe, but not beyond mine!" she crows. "I am powerful beyond your wildest dreams! I am the most stupendous, extraordinary, stunning—"

"Extraordinary, stunning. Yes, yes," says the gold fairy. "But I fear you do not have the power to stop yourself."

"Aha!" the gray fairy cries. "I feed upon your fear! Fear this: all eight of you shall be swallowed up by my rage! Never again will you interfere with me! You shall be consumed! *Fear me!*" The floor in front of the dragon glows red and swells into a boil, an ominous rumbling still shaking the castle. The dragon cackles as the glowing boil burns into a hole. Black smoke and brimstone fumes spurt out, and the fairies choke and gasp as they look on in horror. The terrible hole widens. Tongues of flame flicker upward out of it. A horrendous noise, a sound like screaming and groaning and a dreadful metallic clanging, emanates from deep inside the hole, and even the dragon backs away from the chasm.

Quickly the gold fairy pronounces a spell, surrounding each of the other fairies, including the three rats, with a protective blue glow. Then she spreads the glow to cover Lan and all the sleeping bodies around the edges of the room.

A deep chasm has opened in the middle of the floor, and it grows so large that the flames leap at the dragon's feet and belly. She shrieks. There is no room for her to retreat! In a desperate gesture, she shrivels back into the gray fairy and attempts to fly away, but the intense heat singes her wings and the edges of her gown, and they start to curl and blacken and smolder. The whole room is darkening again with dense, foul smoke, and the gold fairy can no longer see the gray fairy, but she shouts, *"Your time is up!"*

Amid the noise and the conflagration, the gold fairy finally hears hissing and a diminishing whine. "Aaaaaiiiiiieeeeeeeeee . . ." And then silence.

Briar sits back on the edge of the bed, crying freely now, and stares at Rose, with her mussed-up hair and the smudge of dirt on her nose. She has to admit that it doesn't make a bit of difference. Rose is still heartbreakingly lovely. With the dirt and the tumbled hair, Briar sees in her the guileless companion who once sat by her side in the tree and assured her that she would always be with her in spirit, that she would always care. What if she was wrong about Rose being responsible for the cruel joke at the ball? What if she was accusing her unjustly? What if . . .

Briar, lacking a handkerchief, sniffs loudly and wipes her nose on her sleeve. "Maybe I do love you . . . just a little bit. Maybe enough," she whispers. For a long moment, she hesitates, then bends down and kisses Rose softly on the cheek.

Nothing.

Briar sits back and watches Rose closely for any sign of wakefulness. Is there a slight flush on her cheeks? Did her brow twitch? Briar pokes her on the shoulder and says, "Wake up, lazybones!"

Nothing.

Briar pokes her again. "Come on! You're supposed to wake up! Open your eyes!"

The great hall is suddenly silent. The gold fairy peers into the blackness, straining to see something, to find out what has happened. The flames have disappeared, as has the chasm, and all is dark. "Fairies?" she calls tenuously. "Pink? Blue? Green? White? Are you here? Are you all right?" She dimly hears them respond. Then, out of the gloom, she hears the other fairies, the ones that had been turned into rats: "We're here too!"

"Help me clear this smoke away!" the gold fairy directs, and the fairies all wave their wands back and forth until the murk has cleared; then they relight the candles on the great chandelier. There is no sign left of the gray fairy's rage. She is gone as surely as if she had never been. Only the still forms of the villagers and nobles remain, having slept their enchanted sleep through clamor and cataclysm.

The other seven fairies gather around the gold fairy, asking what happened.

"Ah," says the gold fairy. "The gray fairy was consumed by her own evil. Let us hope all her evil spells are gone as well."

Rose's eyelids flicker and open. "What?" she demands in sleepy irritation. "I was just having the most wonderful dream. I was painting a picture, but it was real, and you were in it, and Lan was in it—"

Briar's heart contracts painfully. Should she tell Rose that she and Jack had rescued Lan from the giant—only to have him taken down by the gray fairy, and that they still might suffer her wrath themselves? Then she notices that the castle is no longer shaking, although she can't tell whether this is a good sign or a bad one.

"What am I doing here?" Rose wants to know, sitting up. "What has happened? I don't remember . . ." Suddenly light dawns in her eyes. "The spindle! I touched it. I wanted to get away—from everyone!" She takes Briar's hand. "You were right! You were right about everything, about the curse, and about my parents planning to marry me off to King Udolf. It was all true! I never should have doubted you. But who woke me up? Didn't you say it had to be my true love?"

"Well, there wasn't any true love to do it, so I tried it."

"You? You love me truly? Is that it?"

"Don't go getting all sentimental over it. I almost didn't do it."

"But why? Was I so terrible to you? Talk to me."

"Terrible to me? I guess you thought it was a pretty good joke, giving me a dog as a dance partner. I was the only one not laughing."

"What? Did that really happen?"

"As if you didn't know!" Briar says, really hoping to be contradicted.

"I *don't* know! I would never do such a thing! You must believe me. I never played such a mean trick on you! May I be struck dead if I'm not telling the truth!"

Briar stops short, looking into Rose's eyes for any flicker of deceit. Rose responds with a steady gaze.

"You really didn't?" Briar asks. "Lady Arabella said it was all your idea."

"Then Lady Arabella *lied!* Oh, how could she? And how could you believe such a thing?"

"I . . . maybe I should have known," Briar admits. "Maybe I should have trusted you too."

"We've been foolish," Rose says, "to allow anything to get in the way of our friendship. I've missed you."

"I've missed you too."

Rose holds her arms out. Briar returns the gesture, and for a brief moment they hug each other lovingly. Then Briar, worried about what might be going on belowstairs, quickly informs Rose of the situation.

"Lan is alive? I think I could bear anything if I knew he was alive."

Briar warns her that Lan had been forced to face the gray fairy. "It's quiet now," she says. "It may mean that the gray fairy has won —or that she's been vanquished."

"I must know if Lan is still alive!"

"Then we'll have to go down and see. If the gray fairy's wall of rubble is still there at the bottom of the stairs, we'll know she won."

The two young women join hands and make their way haltingly down the staircase, Briar in the lead, both of them listening intently for any sound coming from below. As they round the last corner, Briar sees the open archway and turns to Rose. "The gray fairy must have been defeated! Her spell is undone!"

"But what about Lan?" Rose asks. "What did she do to him?"

The two enter the great hall, where light blazes from the chandelier. There, at the foot of the stairs, is the ice statue of Lan, the fine details melted and dripping, but still unmistakably Lan.

"Oh!" Rose gasps, her hand to her mouth.

Briar looks past her just as the cluster of fairies in the center of the room turn and see her with Rose.

"Princess Rose!" they exclaim, all talking together.

"Why, look! It's the princess!"

"Isn't she lovely!"

"But who woke her up?"

"Somebody must have."

"Well then, we should wake everyone else up!"

"But wait!" says the gold fairy. "Maybe she can restore that valiant young man who came to save her! That spell didn't go away when all the others did. It must need something more."

"Maybe *she* should kiss *him!*" titters the pink fairy.

"Yes! Yes!" the others chime in.

Rose barely hesitates. *So what* if her father intended her for King Udolf? She wasn't married yet! She stands on tiptoes, puts her hands on Lan's icy shoulders and her warm lips to his frozen ones, and closes her eyes. At first his lips are very cold and wet, but then there is a tingling, a definite tingling, and then a bit of warmth, then a definite warmth, and he's kissing back! She opens her eyes and beholds Lan, thawed but a little damp, smiling at her with the most delightful, charming, captivating, delectable, wonderful, spectacular smile she has ever seen.

"You're awake!" he says.

"You're safe!" she says, and they stare into each other's eyes as if no one else were even there.

Meanwhile, the gold fairy confers with the other fairies, who all agree that it is time to start waking people up. The gold fairy sends each fairy off in a different direction, and they begin the happy task of waking people and animals.

"What happened to the gray fairy?" Briar asks the gold fairy. "There was roaring, and the whole castle was shaking."

"She burned in her own fire. I tried to warn her, but she wouldn't listen."

Despite Briar's loathing for the gray fairy, she doesn't want to think about her last horrible moments. Wiping her brow, she looks down at her torn and scorched clothing and sighs heavily. "Could you maybe help me out?"

"My dear, are you all right?" asks the gold fairy.

"I think so. It's mostly my clothes and some scratches and burns."

"Well, the clothes I can help with!" says the gold fairy, and with a few swishes of her wand she has transformed Briar's outfit into an elegant purple gown.

"Oh, thank you!" Briar says. Then, looking at Rose and Lan, she adds, "Maybe you should do Lan too. He's been locked up in a dungeon for a while, and then—"

"I'll fix him!" the blue fairy squeals, and she aims a bolt of magic at Lan that leaves him looking like a young prince.

Rose, staring deeply into his eyes, barely notices.

"Perfect!" says Briar. Then she and the gold fairy look on as the other fairies flit about the hall, sprinkling magic dust over everyone. People are sitting up, yawning and stretching, and rubbing the sleep from their eyes. Briar whispers in the gold fairy's ear, "You do know that most of these people are here to stage a rebellion? They might be pretty mad when they wake up and remember what they came here for—"

The pink fairy hovers nearby, listening in. "Oh, piffle!" she interrupts, and she flits off and sprinkles some magic over the musicians. They slowly awaken and stretch, then pick up their instruments and begin to play, lending a festive air to the proceedings. "That makes it so much nicer," declares the pink fairy. "Who can be angry, listening to such beautiful music? We'll entertain them too!" She gently awakens the jugglers and acrobats and the jester, Zane, who observes the fairies sprinkling their magic on everyone and asks for some fairy dust so he can help too. The pink fairy sprinkles some liberally on the end of his baton, and he goes merrily bopping the sleeping people on their heads with it.

"Awaken! Awaken, my pretties! Open your eyes and behold your princess—all well and good!" Zane cries. The people awaken, looking peaceful but confused.

The pink fairy suddenly remembers the strange old woman she put to sleep on the tower stairs, and she flits off to find her. She flutters up several stairways before finding the right one, and then, with the air of a child expecting to be rewarded for a job well done, she shakes loose a dose of magic on Hilde's recumbent form and a dash on the small red imp.

"—ool!" Hilde's eyes pop open as she completes her long-interrupted sentence. She looks all about and then, spotting the pink fairy, demands to know what has transpired.

"Princess Rose has been awakened from her enchanted sleep! We fairies are waking everyone up again!" With that, the fairy whisks herself away, and Hilde, who knows nothing of the gray fairy's firestorm or even of the smoldering riot in the great hall below, drags her creaking bones to an upright position and, reluctantly, descends the stairs.

Slowly, riddled with confusion, the villagers are awakening. The musicians and mummers are presenting an improvised version of

St. George and the Dragon, a perennial favorite, and the visiting royals are distracted by this entertainment while the groggy villagers are trying to remember why they are here. With a sprinkle of fairy dust, the king and queen open their eyes and try to recall how and when they ended up prone on the floor. They wobble to their feet, recovering their crowns and placing them crookedly on their heads. Then they dust themselves off, embarrassed to be seen as less than regal. The king's counselors are awakening as well, Bishop Simon looking about for someone to blame for his aching head.

The queen has barely gotten to her feet when she remembers Lady Beatrice's terrible announcement: the princess in a deathly sleep! The gray fairy's curse come true! "Rose!" she cries, and abandoning any attempt at royal formality, she runs toward the staircase, needing to get to her child. But there, at the foot of the stairs, she sees her daughter, quite awake and happy, staring lovingly into the eyes of the painter's apprentice as if she never wanted to look away. The queen is overwhelmed with relief. She is so relieved, in fact, that she barely cares that Rose is obviously in love with this commoner. Never mind the planned betrothal to King Udolf. Never mind the fate of the kingdom. She wants only to hold her daughter in her arms and be reassured that she is safe and well. She envelops Rose in a hug, which Rose accepts stiffly, remembering all too clearly that her parents are preparing to marry her off to the noxious King Udolf.

"My dear daughter," says the queen, "how happy I am that you are restored to us!" She holds Rose's face in her hands and kisses her on the forehead. Then, recalling her queenly duty, she observes the crowd of dazed villagers shaking themselves and picking up their weapons. Hoping to forestall a resumption of hostilities, she takes Rose by the hand, saying, "We must spread the good news at once!"

Rose allows herself to be led, her other hand holding firmly on to Lan, as the queen quickly makes her way back to the dais. The king, busily rousing members of the palace guard, suddenly sees his daughter, and a huge smile splits his face. He briefly abandons his great dignity and enfolds her in an embrace; then he signals a bugler to blow his horn and calls out loudly for attention. Still half asleep and befuddled, the villagers look to him questioningly.

"My people," he calls out. "I have joyous news! Princess Rose has been awakened from the curse that nearly took her from us! And here she is!" The villagers have been anxiously protecting their beautiful young Princess Rose from the knowledge of the gray fairy's curse for the past sixteen years. They fill the air with cries of relief and joy. The musicians strike up a song of celebration. The years of secret dread are over! Their princess has survived the curse! Then the pink fairy appears, full size, by the king's side and whispers in his ear. If possible, his smile grows even broader. "And I have more news," he calls out to the crowd.

"The gray fairy is gone forever and can do no more harm!" There is a collective shout of exultation and cries of "Huzzah!" But the blithe spirits are short-lived. As the villagers come to full awareness, a murmur travels through the crowd. They remember what they came for, and they are not to be distracted from their purpose.

"What of the years of near starvation?" a voice yells out, and the music dies down.

"What of the hidden stores of food?" bellows another, more loudly.

"What of the king's duplicity?" cries another.

More voices are raised. The murmur becomes a rumble.

"Will our children go hungry while we do nothing?" wails a tormented father.

"Will we roll over and die like sheep?" howls an enraged mother. This last is picked up and repeated, spreading like wildfire until the rumble becomes a roar. A host of villagers, hardened by the lethal combination of deprivation and vengeance, rend the air with their rage. They will not be put off!

Mother Mudge tries to make herself heard, but the crowd is no longer listening to her. They are brandishing their weapons in fury! She soon sees that her rebellion has gotten out of hand, as rebellions will. A contingent of angry villagers has surrounded the dais and are doing battle with the king's guards, the most skilled and well-trained warriors in the kingdom. At first the villagers are turned back by them, yet they so greatly outnumber the guards that the battle rages fiercely on. The guards begin to fall back, one by one, until the mob surges forward. Lan shields Princess Rose with his body, keeping her separate from the fray.

Briar looks on, horrified, as everyone around her gets caught up in the chaos. What will the king do now? she wonders. What will *she* do now? Once again, the weight of anguished worry descends on her heart. Where is Jack? Does he yet live? She has done as he asked, helped Lan to make his way to Princess Rose. The threat of the curse is past. Now she is free to return to the foot of the giant beanstalk and face the truth, whatever it may be. But what of this rebellion? She knows she helped to cause it, spreading the news about the king's secret hoard. But it has grown into something terrible, with a life of its own. The mob is dangerously out of control, and Briar realizes with growing despair that there is nothing she can do to quell it.

All she can think of is finding Jack. But how can she leave now? She closes her eyes, bracing herself against the sea of impervious bodies, frozen by indecision, until she hears, above the clamor, a voice crying out her name. She spots Arley in the crowd, and more of the Giant Killers coming up behind him. She waves frantically. Suddenly she is terrified by the thought that he has come to bring her bad news.

Arley pushes through to Briar's side and tries to say something, but she cannot hear him above the din. He tries again, blasting in her ear, *"The giant is dead! The giant is dead!"* Briar drops her head in her hands and begins to sob with relief. At last, at long last, everything that every child in the village has hoped for, planned for, fought for, for the past seven years of their lives has come to pass. The giant is dead. Never again will they suffer his depredations. Never again will he steal and kill and maim. Never again will they have to give up their crops and rebuild the castle wall and bury their dead. The long night is over, and Jack ended it. But at what price?

Chapter Six

BRIAR PULLS HERSELF TOGETHER and faces Arley and the other Giant Killers, and she calls out one question, "What about Jack?" Arley looks away, then shouts next to her ear. "We don't know! He must have fallen when the beanstalk came down. Everyone is out scouring the countryside, looking for him!" Briar nods. At least it is not the worst news. Not yet. As the crowd grows wilder, she realizes that she now has the one thing that will distract them, if only she can get their attention.

"Help me get to the dais!" she calls to Arley and the Giant Killers, and they form a circle around her, pushing and shoving people out of their way. Finally, they reach the dais, where the villagers have surrounded the king. They hold him at attention while Mother Mudge shouts out their demands to him.

"You must do away with the Giant Tax! We cannot bear it! And the sick must be taken care of!" she yells. "And the widows and the orphans too! And you must open up your secret stores of food and treasure and distribute them among your people!"

The king is panic-stricken. All his greedy double-dealing has caught up with him. He wants to know how she knows about his secret hoard, but he dares not ask. As to the people's demands, he looks out at the angry crowd and knows that he has no choice but to agree.

Briar, glancing around, spots the bugler shoved up against the wall, his horn by his side. She manages to inch closer to him and finally reaches out and snatches his horn away. Before he can react, she puts it to her lips and blows a mighty blast. She keeps on blowing as she approaches Mother Mudge and the cadre of villagers surrounding the king and queen. The villagers fall silent. Most of them know and trust Briar from the years she has spent assisting the sick and the most unfortunate among them, and they are willing to listen to what she has to say. Finally, she lowers the horn and shouts simply, *"The giant is dead! Jack defeated the giant!"*

This is met with a silence so stark that the people hear their own hearts beating. It lasts only a moment, and then the crowd erupts in wild jubilation. Weapons are dropped and the king is released as people embrace one another and weep with joy. The musicians start up a triumphant tune. Hats are thrown in the air. Dancing breaks out. The people cannot contain their glee. On and on goes the celebration while Briar watches, her exultation warring with her sorrow.

"If only Jack could see this," she whispers, but no one hears her amid the revelry.

Just then the crowd opens near the main door to admit a throng of children and youths. Briar can see Bridget, Dudley and Jarrett, Bertha and Quentin, Maddox and Emma and Marian, and scores of others, and they are glowing! Exultant! Some of their parents recognize them and call out to them, but the young people are oblivious, all their attention centered on the progress of one figure, borne up on the shoulders of the tallest youths, a laurel wreath around his head.

"Jack!" screams Briar, leaping off the dais and running toward him. The crowd parts to let her through, and there he is, pale but triumphant. His mates set him down gently, and he stands wobbling on a makeshift crutch, simply overcome with the joy of being alive—against all the odds—and seeing his true love coming toward him. She throws her arms around him, and a cheer goes up from all the Giant Killers as they close in around the two, shielding them while they embrace.

"Jack! My Jack!" cries Mother Mudge, turning away from the king to call out lovingly to her son, all else forgotten for the moment. Finally, Jack and Briar part, and Briar leads him up to the dais, where the king actually steps forward to meet him. Despite the king's recent humiliation, Briar gives a curtsy, and Jack bows before him, as best he can with his injured leg.

"Your Majesty." Briar speaks up so that everyone can hear. "I present Jack Mudge, who risked his life to lure the giant to his death."

Jack turns and signals several of the Giant Killers to come forward. One is carrying the singing harp, one is carrying the hen that lays golden eggs, and two are struggling to carry large, heavy bags. They set the bags down in front of the king and open them so that he can see that they are filled with glittering gold and jewels. King Warrick's eyes light up. He is flabbergasted. Wealth beyond measure has been recovered, and that speaks more loudly than any words, proving to him as nothing else could that the lad has indeed killed the giant.

He looks Jack up and down and says, "But how can this be? The giant killed by one scrawny peasant? Speak up, lad!"

"I didn't do it alone," Jack says. "It took all of us, all the village children. We formed a secret society, the Giant Killers. We've been planning for this for years."

"It was Jack's plan," Briar adds. "But all of us helped."

"That's my Jack!" says Mother Mudge to the king. "He did it! He defeated the giant!"

Jack silences her with a look that clearly says *Not now, Mother!*

"Four years ago I followed the giant up the mountain and onto the clouds to see where he lived," he tells the king. "I found the giant's house sitting on the clouds, but I barely escaped with my life. I dared not go back unless I had some means of quick escape. Four long years went by before I found the way—a magic beanstalk that climbed up to the giant's house. Then yesterday I climbed the beanstalk, and Lady Briar did too. Lady Briar rescued Lan from the dungeon, and the giant's woman gave us back some of the treasure. She said stolen treasure is bad luck. There's more there, and I'm sure she'd give it to us if we went back up the mountain."

"But *how* did you defeat the giant?" King Warrick asks, irritated —in spite of the near miracle—that this boy could accomplish what he, the king, and all the other adults could not.

"It was the beanstalk that gave me the idea," said Jack. "I had the thought that if I could make the giant chase me down the beanstalk, the Giant Killers could chop the beanstalk down and he'd fall to his death. And that's what happened."

"But where were you, if he was chasing you down? Why didn't you fall?"

"I did fall, but the giant had me in his hand. He dropped me just as he crashed, but I landed on his stomach. I bounced off and hurt my leg when I landed. But I'm alive!" Jack reports joyously.

King Warrick pauses, taking this in. "And you say there's more treasure up there? That the giant's woman doesn't want it?"

"That's right, Your Highness. Now it can be returned to the people!"

The king contemplates the bags of treasure for a moment and realizes that the giant is really dead and will never come back, stealing and demanding and destroying. There will be plenty for everyone. His kingdom has been saved! He raises his head and looks out at the crowd of his subjects, driven here by hunger and desperation. Finally, he looks into the eyes of the young Giant Killers, and moved by the bright hope on their faces, he shouts,

"The Giant Tax is no more! And the sick shall be taken care of and so will the widows and orphans!"

There is much murmuring among the villagers, and Mother Mudge cries, "You'll really care for the sick and the widows and orphans? Do you swear it? Now, in front of all your people?"

"From my own riches! On my life I swear it!" the king replies, his hand on his thawing heart.

"We'll remember this, word for word, and hold you to it!" says Mother Mudge. Suddenly it is as if a great weight has been lifted from the poor villagers. The hall is filled with a communal sigh of relief, and then cheers of victory. Their every wish has been granted, and they have become buoyant.

"And you, young lad Jack," says the king. "In recognition of your extraordinary service to a grateful kingdom, you are from this day forward Lord Jack, Earl of — well, I shall grant you some lands for you to be earl of, just as soon as I think of them." The queen chooses this moment to whisper something in his ear, and he nods a little reluctantly. "And here," the king says, picking up the hen that lays the golden eggs and holding it out to Jack, "is a token of our personal appreciation and gratitude. May it reward you amply."

It is Jack's turn to be flabbergasted. For him, his wildest dream was to defeat the giant and live to tell about it. This extraordinary change in his fortune is almost too much for him to take in. Mother Mudge is equally dazed, while Briar looks on, bursting with pride. Jack stutters a gracious, "Th-thank you, Your Majesty," and steps back.

Before anything more can develop, the pompous King Udolf, seeing the dramatic improvement in the kingdom's fortunes, shoves his way forward to address King Warrick. His deep voice demands attention as he presents himself, in all his dirty finery, insisting that King Warrick announce him to be Princess Rose's intended bridegroom, then and there—before Warrick can change his mind. "You have said as much to me, and so I will have satisfaction!" His eyes seek out Princess Rose, and he smiles unctuously at her, all the more eager as he thinks of the king-dom's new and fantastic prospects. Rose shrinks closer to Lan's side and tries to make herself invisible as several fights break out among the other nobles over who is worthier of her than Udolf.

Meanwhile, lost in the crowd, Hilde is fuming. She watched while Briar took control of the room, watched while the villagers listened to her with respect. Anyone can see that the girl was born to rule! But still, it is Rose. Beautiful Rose. All about Rose! Even now, the fools are squabbling over Rose's beauty. Even when it is painfully obvious that the girl wants none of them! Hilde has kept her silence through the rioting and then the rejoicing and now the indecent lust after the princess. Now she herself has come to the end of her tolerance. The imp, who has been hovering just above her shoulder, gives her one strong push toward the dais, and something snaps inside her.

Hilde reaches into her store of lightning powder, rubs a little on her fingertips, and pronounces the incantation:

"When circumstances grow too frightening,
   Change this powder into lightning!"

There comes the sound of a thunderclap, and everyone jumps. Hilde marches forward through the still-warring nobles, jolting them out of the way with small bolts of lightning. She reaches the dais, her purpose throbbing in her heart and making her strong, and she plants herself firmly in front of the king and queen. Turning to address King Udolf and the other suitors, she raises her hands and roars, *"Enough!"* as lightning shoots from her fingertips, illuminating the deadly serious expression on her craggy face.

The crowd quiets at once.

"You! And you! And you!" Hilde cries, pointing at the nobles. *"You've all been lied to! And you! All of you!"* she adds with a broad sweep of her arm at the villagers. *"For sixteen years, you've been lied to!"*

The king and queen grow suddenly pale, afraid of what she will say next but too frightened of the lightning bolts she wields to try to stop her. The crowd gasps.

And then it comes. *"Princess Rose is not the rightful heir to the throne!* I tell you this, though it may cost me my life!"

There are cries of dismay, disbelief, from the audience. A few shrill screams. And then voices erupt into a confused babble. Hilde flashes more lightning to silence them, and then she continues.

"I, Hilde, was *there* at the princess's birth. I tell you there were *twins!*"

There are howls of shock and surprise. The king and queen hold on to each other, paralyzed by the truth, looking as if they are barely able to stand. Princess Rose, more shocked than anyone, looks questioningly to her parents, but they do not meet her eyes. Lan takes her hand and squeezes it in support.

Hilde continues. "I delivered the firstborn babe myself and held her in my arms. It was not Princess Rose. It was . . ." Here Hilde takes a few steps closer to Briar and puts her hand on the girl's shoulder. "It was *Princess Briar!* Burn me at the stake, and I will scream it to the skies with my dying breath! *Princess Briar!*"

Briar is stunned. She looks at Hilde in astonishment and then out at the villagers, many of whom are cheering and applauding and calling out her name. Suddenly she hears some otherworldly music, music so beautiful it brings tears to her eyes. *This,* she thinks, remembering her inchoate longing at the waterfall. *This was the thing I could never grasp.* She turns to the king and queen, looking for confirmation, but her eyes well up so that she can barely see. Still, she knows it's true. *This* was the terrible secret about the heir! But to speak of it would mean death! Briar is suddenly filled with an intense fear for Hilde's safety, but Hilde surges on.

"Princess Rose was the second born," she declares, "but with a beauty so great that it changed men's hearts. What came next is a sad episode in our kingdom's history. Those in power believed that you, the people, would never accept Princess Briar as the heir to the throne. The king was told that she was defective, and evil, and incapable of rule! Her fate was cast. It was given out that she was the noble orphan of the house of Wentmoor, and Rose, the beautiful babe, was named the heir in her stead. For sixteen long years Princess Briar has remained ignorant of her own parentage, until now, the day after *her* sixteenth birthday, she is learning the truth for the first time!"

Rose, upon hearing this, runs forward and throws her arms around Briar, who hugs her tightly as the crowd virtually explodes with approval. All the resentments and disagreements that have stood between the two young women melt away as Briar and Rose realize that they are, and have always been, *sisters*. Suddenly their shared memories of happy times together take on a new meaning and a glow of benediction. They are greater than two together; they are ascendant, indomitable, shining! They part and, turning to the people, raise their clasped hands in unity.

For once, the king does not know what to do. His royal edict has been flouted, and yet he has just received the gift of the return of his firstborn daughter. Anger, relief, and, yes, even love flicker on his face. To erase all doubt, the queen comes forward. "Hilde speaks the truth!" she declares. "Princess Briar and Princess Rose are both our daughters, and Princess Briar was the firstborn child!" She puts one arm around Briar and says, "Forgive me, my dear. I did the best I could for you. I have watched your progress proudly from afar." She puts her other arm around Rose and says, "Your graciousness becomes you, my dear!"

Then the king, feeling that something official is expected, steps forward, announcing, "I hereby proclaim that Princess Briar is my firstborn child and the rightful heir to the thro—"

"Forgive me, Your Majesty, but I must object!" comes a voice from behind him. Bishop Simon steps forward, seething with malice. It was he, more than anyone, who had declared the disfigured infant unfit to be the heir, implying to the other counselors that she was a demon, a changeling, a punishment to all of them. For years he has been forced to observe her terrible imperfection with loathing and condemnation in his dried-up little heart. Now he sees her being hailed as royalty—his own pronouncements being questioned and ignored—and it is too much for the old hypocrite to bear.

"I must protest!" he declares, his double chins quivering in outrage. "I have had the sorry task of attempting to shape this girl's character and educate her for the past ten years, and I tell you, she is unfit to rule! Her outward appearance is but a sign of her inward foulness! Besides being wicked and deceitful, she is *dull in her wits!* Ignore my warning at your peril!"

Princess Rose and Princess Briar look at each other. Rose steps forward and, taking Briar's hand, speaks to her father and the entire assembly. "These accusations are untrue and unjust!" she cries. "Lady—*Princess* Briar has been the victim of this man's baseless hatred from the beginning! He deliberately misinterpreted her every word, even though she was in the right! He punished her so often for imagined infractions that we realized he was jealous of her quick wits. So she and I came up with a plan, that she would pretend to be dull in order to avoid his wrath! And it worked! His beatings became less frequent, and he was more often satisfied to merely make her wear the donkey ears as the sign of a dimwit. But she is sharp-witted and wise beyond her years. She can do calculations without the abacus, and she can translate Latin faster than he can, and she knows all about astronomy and history, and even about Hilde's herbs and cures! Test her, if you don't believe me! And she is neither foul nor deceitful—except in his eyes!"

"Preposterous!" cries Bishop Simon. "Jealous, indeed! The girl was born wicked! I myself have been forced to beat the wickedness from her for the good of her soul, but to no avail! Obviously, Lady Briar has worked her malign influence on our young Princess Rose! The demon must be banished from the kingdom before she corrupts her utterly!"

There is angry murmuring among the villagers, and someone shouts, "Innocent! Briar is innocent!" The cry is taken up by the others until the room resounds with it.

The king, quick to sense which way the crowd has turned, has listened to Bishop Simon with a show of outrage. He feels no compunction against turning the tables on the bullying bishop. No longer can the bishop claim to save them from the marauding giant, and suddenly the king is less worried about his immortal soul and more concerned about preserving his own skin. After all, how better to shift blame from himself than to rouse the throng against the unpopular bishop? "*My* firstborn a dimwit? A demon?" he cries. "*My* daughter Rose corrupted? You overstep the bounds, Bishop! Take care you do not malign the royal princesses. They are *my* progeny, after all!" he announces, as if this is all the proof needed.

Bishop Simon, much taken aback, stands with his mouth open, but no words come out. The king has never spoken to him this way. Finally he says, "But . . . but . . . but I have been your chief adviser for nearly twenty years! And I am the head of the church! How dare you oppose me? And think! Who will root out evil if I do not?"

Now the queen steps forward. "Perhaps," she says, "the evil is in your own eyes and heart! Perhaps it is time we had a new head of the church. One with compassion in his soul!"

Cheers erupt from the assembly, for many have felt the sharp edge of the bishop's invective. This is all the king needs to spur him on.

King Warrick points directly at Bishop Simon. "*You* have been the cause of all this!" he thunders. "*You* poisoned my mind against my own daughter! You have tormented and abused her ever since! I accuse you of plotting against the royal family! I will send a petition this day for a new bishop to be head of the church in this kingdom!"

Bishop Simon freezes, his eyes bulging in disbelief. He cannot accept that the king has questioned his authority and turned against him. "Your Majesty, surely you cannot mean — surely she has not worked her evil spell on you too —"

"Enough!" roars the king. "You have said more than enough!"

At this, the bishop attempts to slink away. He is grabbed by the bystanders, who hold him, pale and trembling, while the king considers what to do with him. The queen whispers in his ear, and he nods. "It is my royal wish that Bishop Simon shall depart this day on a long pilgrimage . . ."

The queen adds, "And he shall go barefoot — for the good of his soul!"

There is cheering as Bishop Simon is assisted on his way by the crowd.

Then the king puffs out his chest and loudly resumes the announcement that he acknowledges Princess Briar to be his first-born child and heir. He grasps her hand, forgetting the fears and prejudices that led him to disown her so long ago, and he proudly says, "Well, of course she's fit to rule! She's my daughter, after all!"

In a gesture that moves everyone present, Princess Rose, with a barely noticeable tear in her eye, lifts the coronet from her own head and places it on Briar's.

To Briar, King Warrick says, "I see, my daughter, that I have done you a great injustice. Allow me to offer a small gesture to make it up to you. I shall grant you three boons. Anything your heart desires that a king can obtain for you, ask and you shall receive it."

Briar is dumbfounded. As if anything can make up for the difference it might have made to her to have a sister and two parents, to be the king's daughter and the heir! She can't begin to calculate the loss. But this is a majestically generous offer! Can she think, right now, of what she most wants? As Briar considers the possibilities, the hall becomes so quiet that even a cricket chirp can be heard. Looking about her at the poor, hungry, desperate villagers, the first request takes form in her mind.

Summoning her courage, she faces the king and says steadily, "You are my father, but you are a bad and selfish king. From this day forward, I want Mother Mudge to be your chief adviser. You shall do nothing without her approval."

King Warrick nearly chokes as his eyes start from his head. "Well I didn't mean *anything*—" he begins, but an angry buzz comes from the crowd.

"We want Mother Mudge!" someone calls out, and others follow suit until the whole contingent of villagers is chanting, "Mother Mudge! Mother Mudge! Mother Mudge!"

The queen takes his arm and says, "You had best keep your promise, my dear. This mob is turning ugly again, and a much worse fate may await you!"

All eyes are on the king, who stands speechless, turning at first nearly purple with apoplexy. But as the crowd becomes even louder and more enraged, he begins to pale. At last, realizing he has no choice, he splutters, "It shall be done." Mother Mudge comes forward and takes her place next to the king, nodding and waving amid wild cheering from the audience.

When the noise finally abates, the king, looking much subdued and apprehensive, asks, "What next, daughter?"

Briar knows what she wants next, something that will give her happiness all the days of her life, but she puts that off till last. Then, imagining the one place where she has always gone to mend her broken heart and lift her spirits, she says. "There is a tract of land, deep in the Enchanted Forest, by a waterfall. Might it be set aside as my own?"

The king, relieved that it wasn't something worse, says, "It shall be yours. The royal surveyors shall be at your service to map out the land."

Her next request, the one she has saved for last, seems even more obvious than the first, though it takes her a minute to figure out how to word it. "What I'd like most of all," she finally says, "is for you to enact a law proclaiming that royal princesses in our kingdom may marry whomever and whenever they please!"

At this King Udolf cries out angrily, still hoping for the beautiful Rose as his bride. King Warrick has to swallow hard before he replies, but after a slight hesitation he says, "It is done!"

Rose, her lovely face suddenly flooded with relief and delight, throws her arms around Briar once again, saying, "Thank you! Oh, thank you! I shall thank you till the end of time!" Then she turns to find Lan, and they stand contentedly, arm in arm.

Jack smiles at Briar with a twinkle in his eye. Then Zane comes up behind them and, taking Briar's hand, puts it in Jack's hand and raises the clasped hands high above their heads.

"Blessings on you, my little dumplings," he says. The villagers respond with wild acclamation. Basking in their approval and in Jack's loving gaze, Briar suddenly feels *blissful*.

Hilde hugs herself delightedly and melts back into the crowd, her work done, the danger passed. Slowly she makes her way to her tower room, the imp following after, and begins once again with her alchemy. This time, though she's not sure how, she actually succeeds in turning a pan of unlikely ingredients into gold. She stares at it for a moment, enjoying her success. Then, quickly growing bored, she dumps it out and decides to try something new, turning a toad into a small dragon, perhaps, or changing a feather into a hummingbird.

EPILOGUE

NIGHT FALLS IN THE KINGDOM of Wildwick. The sunset has spent itself in a glorious display of color. The portcullis is up and the drawbridge is down, while the courtyard is thronged with satisfied villagers. The rebels, having won their demands, have turned into revelers, singing and dancing away the agonies of yesterday. The giant is dead, their stomachs are full, their children will not go hungry, they have Mother Mudge now to look out for them, their favorite son is a hero, and their benefactress has been crowned a princess. The king and queen have gained back a daughter, and they rejoice. Rose and Lan can look to the future, surrounded and immersed in their art, and they rejoice. Briar and Jack, given the best seats next to the thrones, are content to let the merrymaking go by. They are rather tired.

Briar sighs happily. "This was a day well spent," she says.

"Yes," Jack agrees, yawning. Yes.

Yesss . . . High above the castle and the great forest, a full moon rises in the sky, spilling its lambent light on an ocean of treetops. Some gaiety borne on the wind inspires the sea of leafy limbs to dance and sway, murmuring softly to one another of new beginnings. Massive oaks and chestnuts, a thousand years old, catch the whispers in the wind and feel their sap rise. They sigh to their neighbors, passing on the sibilant message, *Yesss.* Small silver birches, glowing white in the moonlight, slap their round leaves together in excitement, while the towering beech trees, the sentinels, watch and wait.

Yesss. All is well in the arc of blue-black sky, in the array of stars, in the music of the celestial spheres. Quiet jubilation plays at the edge of consciousness. It is there, in the hoot of the tawny owl and the churring trill of the nightjar. It disturbs the hunt of the wild creatures prowling far below the forest canopy—the wolf, the fox, and the pine marten. They pause and listen. It cools the savage temperament of the badger and the wild boar. It rouses the diminutive roe deer from their sleep, tantalizes the moths, and bestirs the crickets. Even the mice and the moles, tunneling away beneath the earth, feel it. *Yesss.* All is right with the world.